Also by Graham

Praise for other books by Graham Seal

Great Anzac Stories

'. . . allows you to feel as if you are there in the trenches with them.'—*The Weekly Times*

'They are pithy short pieces, absolutely ideal for reading when you are pushed for time, but they are stories you will remember for much longer than you would expect.'—*Ballarat Courier*

Great Australian Stories

'The pleasure of this book is in its ability to give a fair dinkum insight into the richness of Australian story telling.'—*The Weekly Times*

'. . . a treasure trove of material from our nation's historical past'—*Courier Mail*

'This book is a little island of Aussie culture—one to enjoy.'—*Sunshine Coast Sunday*

Larrikins, Bush Tales and Other Great Australian Stories

'. . . another collection of yarns, tall tales, bush legends and colourful characters . . . from one of our master storytellers'—*Queensland Times*

The Savage Shore
'A fascinating, entertainingly written, voyage on what have often been rough and murky seas'—*Daily Telegraph*

'Colourful stories about the spirit of navigation and exploration, and of courageous and miserable adventures at sea.'—*National Geographic*

'. . . a gripping account of danger at sea, dramatic shipwrecks, courageous castaways, murder, much missing gold, and terrible loss of life'—*Queensland Times*

Great Australian Journeys
'Readers familiar with Graham Seal's work will know he finds and writes ripper, fair-dinkum, true blue Aussie yarns. His books are great reads and do a lot for ensuring cultural stories are not lost. His new book, *Great Australian Journeys*, is no exception.'—*The Weekly Times*

'Epic tales of exploration, survival, tragedy, romance, mystery, discovery and loss come together in this intriguing collection of some of Australia's most dramatic journeys from the 19th and early 20th century.'—*Vacations and Travel*

Great Convict Stories
'More than just a retelling of some of the most fascinating yarns, Seal is interested in how folklore around the convicts grew from the colourful tales of transportation and what impact that had on how we see our convict heritage.'—*Daily Telegraph*

'With a cast of colourful characters from around the country— the real Artful Dodger, intrepid bushrangers [...] *Great Convict Stories* offers a fascinating insight into life in Australia's first decades.'—*Sunraysia Daily*

GREAT BUSH STORIES

Colourful yarns and
true tales from life on the land

GRAHAM SEAL

ALLEN&UNWIN
SYDNEY • MELBOURNE • AUCKLAND • LONDON

First published in 2018

Allen & Unwin
83 Alexander Street
Crows Nest NSW 2065
Australia
Phone: (61 2) 8425 0100
Email: info@allenandunwin.com
Web: www.allenandunwin.com

 A catalogue record for this
book is available from the
National Library of Australia

ISBN 978 1 76063 304 2

Set in 11.5/15pt Sabon by Midland Typesetters, Australia
Printed and bound in Australia by Griffin Press

10 9 8 7 6 5 4 3 2

For Harriett, Millicent, Miles, Owen and Hugo

Contents

CONTENTS ix

Logger in his camp putting the billy on, Victoria, circa 1900.

Introduction
The sunburnt country

Where is it and what is it? When we think of 'the bush' it is, for most of us living in cities and suburbs, somewhere else, usually far away. It starts somewhere beyond the outer suburbs and ends—well, where exactly does it end? Over the mountains? Across the plains? And then, where does the 'outback' start? Where the desert begins? And how far does it extend? These questions are hard to answer with any precision. But, somehow, everyone knows what is meant when we speak of the bush and the outback.

Australians have been calling those places outside large towns and cities 'the bush' and 'the outback' for a long time. For much of the early history of European Australia, most people lived in rural areas. That began to change from around the end of the nineteenth century and we have since become one of the most urbanised nations. But we have not forgotten the bush. Instead, we romanticised it into our national identity and now have a deep, if sometimes contradictory, relationship with the vast regions beyond settlement.

Good, bad and occasionally very ugly, the stories of bush and outback are central to the Australian experience. Encounters with fire, flood, drought, distance, flies, rabbits and the endless other plagues and blights that afflict us are sagas played out on

1

a vast continental scale. The trials of explorers, bushrangers, gold diggers, free selectors, pioneer women and bush workers of all kinds expand the story to one of epic proportions. The savage suppression of indigenous people that marred Australia's many frontiers is a constant tragic theme, accompanied by environmental degradation. From these elements, factual and fictional, we have written and told a national story. The enormous, unknown spaces of this sunburnt country have a permanent place in the national consciousness and continue to intrigue, puzzle and entertain us.

There is a distinctive way of life and worldview among rural folk. These differences stem from the undoubted hardships of pioneering and the challenges of surviving—and sometimes thriving—in an unforgiving environment. The attitudes, activities and often the aspirations of bush folk are not necessarily those of city folk, who may view 'bushies' as backward in some ways, though their resilience in the face of an endless list of environmental and practical difficulties is admired and applauded. Scratch a 'townie' and you soon discover that the qualities most often associated with being Australian—a fair go, independence, equality and resilience—are based on bush and outback life, past and present. Country ways may not be city ways, but they are celebrated more than they are knocked.

The history and legends of rural Australia revolve around people—bush folk. Characters of every imaginable, and sometimes unimaginable, type parade through our folklore and literature, entertaining and appalling us in sometimes equal measure. The endless variety of colourful identities and their antics are the basis of the yarn tradition. What they did, or didn't do, and what they might or might not have actually done, hardly matters. But their stories matter to us and we love to tell them time and time again.

We have fought locusts, termites, fleas, ants, flies, mozzies and the rest with bush remedies, pesticides, insecticides and swatters. We have built fences to stop rabbits, dingoes, foxes, emus. We have used biological warfare in the form of myxamatosis, calcivirus and a host of chemical brews like DDT and, once, we used machine guns. We have introduced foreign species in our efforts to tame the wilderness, often to discover that the cure is worse than the complaint, the case of the cane toad being only one of the more recent biological disasters. We have tried to control the spread of unwanted plants (which we introduced), like prickly pear, Paterson's curse, lantana and the funeral flower or arum lily, with axe, shovel, saw and poison. These wars have raged since European settlement. We do not seem to have won many victories. But we keep at it, even while regularly fighting fire, flood and drought. Perseverance and resilience are characteristic of bush and outback life, mainly because there is no other choice.

In between dealing with blights and natural disasters, bush folk have found many ways to entertain themselves and to be entertained. The dances at country halls and woolsheds are a fondly remembered part of the past. Occupational skills associated with horses, cattle and other aspects of bush life have long been popular, if often dangerous. Country pursuits inevitably include hunting but there are also more reflective and creative responses to the land and its beauty, as well as its demands.

There is, of course, a dark side to everything. Crime is just as much a feature of bush life as it is in the city. Some notable crimes and criminals blot the pages of the past, and still do. Well-known examples include bushrangers. Most of these figures were straightforward criminals but a few had a less cut-and-dried image and their crimes were considered to be in some ways justifiable, another aspect of the contradictions of the country. There is often something especially chilling about evil deeds committed in the bush or outback. Often it is the vast emptiness of the location and the total helplessness of the victims that makes us feel this way. Films like *Wolf Creek* and the recently revived *Wake in Fright* play on this unsettling undercurrent. Further back, but well within living memory, the still-controversial case of Azaria Chamberlain goes straight to the core of our complicated relationship with the outback.

One of the many not very complimentary terms for the outback is 'the dead heart'. This term conjures up the image of empty expanses of dry, dusty nothingness. The saying derives from an inability or unwillingness to see the land for what it is and to accept it on its own terms. If nothing is visible, then it must be empty. But indigenous people can see what is in the landscape, both physically and spiritually. Settlers have mostly understood only its grim deadliness, a place peppered with lonely graves, skeletons of those who have 'done a perish' and countless stories of those who have—sometimes—managed to survive misadventure or stupidity in the unforgiving country of scrub, desert and mountain.

The people of the bush and outback are no strangers to hard work. In the era before electricity, almost everything was done by hand, sometimes with a little help from steam. But even in these highly mechanised times, tough jobs and long hours are common. There is an almost inexhaustible fund of stories about bush working life and those who do it, a few of them are told here.

Battling on, getting by, making do. If it isn't available you either go without it or make it for yourself. Making do is one of the great traditions of bush and outback life. The inventiveness of those without options was displayed from the earliest days of settlement. Before that, Aboriginal people spent perhaps seventy thousand years learning to adapt the environment to their needs. They continued this skill by adopting aspects of European technology. Those settlers who could see through the prejudice that often blinded the newcomers to the value of indigenous knowledge, learned valuable lessons in bush medicine, tucker and many other things of value to their comfort, work and survival. And they made inventions of their own, including the Coolgardie safe, the stump-jump plough and Wolsey's machine for power-assisted shearing, among many others.

Henry Lawson famously described the bush as 'the nurse and tutor of eccentric minds, the home of the weird, and of much that is different from things in other lands'. Very real crazed swaggies, old 'hatters' and jokers of every description provide no end of eccentric entertainment in the lore of the land. But we are never far from the odd and the unexplained. The great distances between settlement, the sparse population and what were, for a long time, the largely unknown and unmapped regions of the country have generated many puzzles and mysteries.

Through all the difficulties and hardships of the bush and outback runs a strong thread of optimism. Whatever their environmental sins and crimes against indigenous peoples, settlers have been sustained by visions of fruitfulness, plenty and prosperity. Australia was, and is, seen as a land so blessed with natural resources that there are few limits to its development. As the national anthem puts it:

> We've golden soil and wealth for toil;
> Our home is girt by sea;
> Our land abounds in nature's gifts
> Of beauty rich and rare.

Perhaps there is now a growing awareness that progress is not just about exploitation of the land's bounty but about caring for its people. Rural depopulation, unemployment, lack of resources, suicide, drug and alcohol abuse, and domestic violence are firmly at the centre of political and economic policy through every level of Australian government and throughout society in health care, welfare and education. Progress that leaves many behind is no longer acceptable. The hard work, inventiveness, resilience and hope that have always powered the bush and outback are still valuable assets that can link material development with community wellbeing and growth. As somebody once said—or, if not, should have—limits are only the barriers we think we see.

Through the history and folklore of the bush range a vast array of characters, exalted and ordinary and everything between. There are outstanding individuals—explorers, pioneers and entrepreneurs, as well as notorious bushrangers, con artists and wild-eyed optimists. There are recognisable types—the swaggie, the new chum, the battler and the cocky farmer among them. These and many others usually struggle though epic adventures, fatal 'perishes', goldrushes, cattle droves, rescues, fires, floods, cyclones, droughts and the host of other hardships that the Australian environment throws at the arid continent and its dwellers. Some of these events are well-known. Others are known only to people in particular parts of the country or with direct involvement of some kind. But whoever, wherever or whenever, the stories of the bush are a great and inescapable dimension of our national mythology.

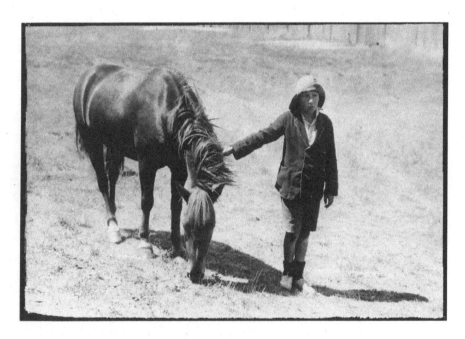

Nine-year-old farm boy Lennie Gwyther with his beloved pony, 'Ginger Mick', on his 1000-kilometre journey from his home in Leongatha, Victoria, to Sydney for the opening of the Harbour Bridge in 1932.

1

Bush ways

Happily the bush people do not yet know the claims of social superiority, and behave as if all were natural equals.

Francis Adams, *The Australians*, 1893

Across the Blue Mountains

For thousands of years, Aboriginal people crossed over or through the sprawling mountains to the west of Sydney. In the early years of European settlement, convicts tried to escape through this Great Dividing Range, often in a deluded quest to reach China. The Blue Mountains, as they soon became known, were first officially crossed by Blaxland, Wentworth and Lawson in 1813. Nine years later the first settlers made their precarious way through the dark forests and savage ravines to begin a new life on the western plains.

Retired naval officer Thomas Fitzherbert Hawkins, his wife Elizabeth and their family arrived in Sydney in January 1822. Three months later they hitched up their bullocks to wagons, drays and carts, gathered their stock, and set out westward. Elizabeth, her mother and seven of the children travelled in a 'tilted cart' or covered wagon, while her husband and eldest son rode their horses. At the Parramatta Female Factory they picked up a convict servant and at the first day's end they were being entertained at Government House in Rooty Hill. Another eight convicts would be added to the cavalcade by the time they reached their destination.

Travel on Sunday was forbidden by law, but on Monday they crossed the Nepean River to Emu Plains. When they reached Penrith, the party was forced to wait for transport to arrive on the far side of the river as their wagons had to return to Sydney. They then struggled up Lapstone Hill where they camped. The cattle strayed during the night, forcing Hawkins to return to Emu Plains while the rest of the family made for Springwood. Here they lodged in a large dwelling 'completely in a wood' and run by an ex-army man and his wife. In her journal which was later published, Elizabeth recalled the experience:

> The corporal's wife (an old woman, who had been transported 20 years previously) came forward with pleasing manners to show us in . . . The kitchen contained a long table and form, and stumps of trees to answer the purpose of chairs. Several persons were here, to rest for the night. We were shown to the small back room, which had nothing but a sofa, with slips of bark laid on it for the seat. There I felt desolate and lonely. It was nearly dark, and still Hawkins did not arrive. At length the store-keeper from Emu Plains came to tell me that he could not get in until fresh horses were sent . . . On going out I saw what appeared to be a scene of great confusion—men, tired with their day's work, swearing while releasing horses and bullocks, with the glare of the fires over all. At length I found Hawkins, and felt easy.

The landlady turned out to be a worrying hostess:

> The old woman (a most depraved character and a well-known thief), with a candle held high above her head, screamed out: 'Welcome to Springwood, sir!' Hawkins said, when he looked

round, he felt sure that his welcome would be the loss of whatever she could steal from us . . .

I spread my mattresses in the store room, the earthen floor of which was dirty, cold, and damp. We put the children to bed without undressing them. I laid down for a few minutes, but sleep was out of the question, the place being infested with vermin, and other sleep-vanishers were the noise kept up by the quarrelling of the men and the noise made by a flock of sheep camped next [sic] the wall of the room. Hawkins remained on the green in the cart all night watching, but the old woman (before mentioned) contrived to steal some spoons from our basket. It was not with any regret we next morning departed from the house at Springwood.

The family battled on through rain and bush for eleven days, nearly losing one of the drays over the precipice along the steep slope of Mt York. Finally:

Without further mishap we reached Bathurst Plains, where the sight of the open country, with 'Home' in view, put us all in good spirits. It was dark when we reached the Macquarie River, the crossing of which was a serious work. I believe everyone in the settlement came to witness the sight. We crossed in safety, and got to our 'Home,' which consisted of three rooms, with brick floors; so some difficulty was experienced in finding room for ourselves and belongings. Mr Lawson, the Commissariat Officer, came to see us next morning, and promised to do all he could for our comfort, and he started by adding two rooms to the house, which work took seven months to complete.

At this time, 'the Settlement', as Bathurst was known, consisted of no more than the Government House, the Hawkins' slightly smaller dwelling, a court house, barracks, the government stores—of which Thomas was to be the keeper—and huts for convicts, as well as 'a good garden, from which we were well supplied'. The 220-kilometre journey took eighteen days.

The Hawkins family later 'secured', probably by official

grant, 2000 acres of land which they named 'Blackdown' and eventually produced the first wine to be cultivated west of the Blue Mountains. Thomas died in 1837 but his and Elizabeth's pioneer line proliferated through eleven surviving children: 'The descendants of Mr. and Mrs. Hawkins are numerous, and, like their progenitors of 1822, have done yeoman service in assisting to bring up and advance the best interests of Australia.

In 1822 Elizabeth Hawkins, only recently landed from the old country, had no other words than 'a wood' to describe the vast and threatening forests through which she and her family trekked to a new frontier. They even survived an exciting night at a rude hostelry in a settlement called 'Springwood', an inescapably English way of naming the wilderness. By the time Elizabeth died at the great age of ninety-two in 1875, everyone spoke of the country beyond the towns as 'the bush'.

Send 'er down, Huey

Nobody is quite sure how the rain god came to be called 'Huey'. But farmers have long called upon him to ease drought and surfers may call upon his assistance to catch a good wave. The name is sometimes said to derive from a St Hugh who was traditionally associated with rainy weather, though there are at least half a dozen St Hughs. There is also said to have been an amateur meteorologist called Mr Huia who could be the origin of the term. Others have patriotically suggested it derives from Billy Hughes the politician, though what his connection with rain might be remains mysterious. Another theory is that it is of Maori origin.

Wherever Huey hails from, his blessing is essential in this arid continent and farmers have a range of signs to work out when it might fall upon their crops. These vary from place to place but they commonly depend on observations of bush birds, animals, plants and insects.

Certain birds turn up frequently in folk weather forecasting. Depending on where and when, their manner of flight or other activities are said to predict rain. Black cockatoos seem to be a favourite indicator in many parts of the country. If they are winging their way from the hills to the coast, or flying east, rain is due. Flocks of galahs or corellas circling, crows flying high or swallows flying low over water are also good indications of rain, while the warbling of currawongs heralds a southerly change.

Birds behaving unusually may indicator a downpour. Kookaburras laughing more frequently or in the middle of the day, mallee fowls cleaning their nests at odd times or plovers arriving earlier than normal are apparently infallible signs.

Other animals can give clues that rain's on the way, including lizards, cows, cats and horses. Roosters are said to be reliable in these matters. If one should crow at evening, then it will certainly rain the next day. But if it crows during rain, the weather will improve that night. If the ewes are irritable during shearing, it will rain; as it will when the hair of a draught horse's tail fans out.

Insects can also be helpful rain forecasters. Large numbers of March flies hatching early or an abundance of wood moths in the evening are sure signs, as are ants building up their nests or moving their eggs up walls or posts. If bees are very active in autumn, there will be poor spring rains. Conversely, if they are not active, there will be good spring rains. Rain is also likely when spider webs are seen floating in the air and catching onto grass and plants.

Gum trees are the most popular sources of arboreal weather prediction. A heavy flowering of new growth is a certain sign, as are bark falling heavily or leaves having a glossy sheen. It will also rain if there's prolific flowering of mallee trees or they drop oil in late summer or autumn.

Out in the bush, the sky is the most reliable indicator of rain, with the size, shape, colour, position of clouds, moon and stars being the most usual ways to forecast. Other natural signs include the amount of dust hanging in the air and the direction of willie-willies or dust devils. If they are turning clockwise, it means rain is coming; counter-clockwise means you will keep dry.

These, and the almost endless variations on the ability of natural phenomena to forecast rain or other aspects of the weather, may also vary from season to season, as well as region to region. In South Australia's Murray River valley, it is said that fog in late March heralds rain; while in the mallee region, rain is forecast by lizards facing east on the top of fence posts or in trees. Winter rains will not start until four to six weeks after the last tropical cyclone in Western Australia's northern reaches. Similar local variations are known to those who live on the land, in whatever part of the country. But the colour and diversity of Australian weather lore, accurate or not, still depends on the whim of Huey, the rain god.

On foot to Appin

The Quaker missionary and naturalist, James Backhouse, visited Australia in the 1830s. He travelled widely through all the colonies, frequently on foot. In September 1832, he was journeying from Campbelltown to Wollongong, both then in the process of developing from original bush settlements. Progressive in his views of Aboriginal people, Backhouse was not immune to another strong prejudice of his period towards the Irish and Roman Catholics in general. His account of the way from Appin to Wollongong, complete with naturalist's notes, describes how most people got from place to place in those times, and for long after:

> 19th. We proceeded on foot to Appin, near which, we became the guests of a respectable widow, with a large family. The village of Appin, consists of two public-houses, a few slab huts, and a wooden lock-up house. The country between this place and Campbell Town, is undulating, and the soil strong. It is more extensively fenced, cleared, cultivated and settled, than any other part of the Colony, we have visited. There are, however, few

respectable settlers: most of them are low Irish. We felt but little liberty in distributing tracts among the benighted population; and in a few cases in which we offered them, they were received with a sort of fear, the evident result of Popish restrictions. The people are afraid to receive religious instruction, lest their priests should find fault; and though the priests visit them, with an attention that binds the people to them, many of them seem to exercise much more care, to prevent their leaving the Church of Home, than to turn them from the service of Satan.

Next day, the son of their host guided the travellers further along a complicated way:

The road for several miles lies over an elevated, sandstone country, covered with low forest, intermingled with a great variety of beautiful shrubs, and interspersed with marshy flats. The elevation above the level of the sea, is about 2,000 feet. Among the shrubs of this district were four species of Grevillea, one of which had brilliant, scarlet blossoms, also a gay Mirbellia, with bluish, purple flowers, and several species of Dillwynia, Pultenaea and Boronia. On some of the rocky ground, there was a profusion of the Gigantic Lily, Doryanthes excelsa, which bears a compound head, of dull-crimson, lily-like blossoms, among large floral-leaves of the same colour, upon a lofty stem, furnished with numerous, dagger-shaped leaves, diminishing in size toward the top. The stem rises from the centre of a large crest, of upright, sedgy leaves, about four inches wide, and as many feet long. It was not in blossom here. The vegetation is much more luxuriant on the top of the coast-range of mountains, the precipitous fronts of which, and the low ground, between their base and the sea, are covered with forests of the greatest luxuriance, and richest variety. Cedar, Sassafras, Swamp-mahogany, Cabbage-palm, large Fig trees, and numerous climbing-shrubs, with Tree-ferns, form a striking contrast to the low forest, of the sandy tract just left behind. The rich prospect, bounded by the ocean beneath, and exhibiting some bold, mountain projections, and a spot of cultivated land on the coast, affords a treat to the eye, such as is seldom enjoyed among the vast forests of Australia.

We descended by a rough track, called the Bulli Road, the sides of which were ornamented by a gay Prostanthera, Pimelia hypericifolia, Pittosporum undulatum, and another fragrant species of this genus, and a handsome, white Clematis. This road is difficult for horses, and impracticable for carts, except by the assistance of ropes, passed round conveniently situated trees, by means of which, in a few instances, they have been got down. After reaching the beach, our way, for eight miles, was along loose sand, to Wollongong, near which, our toils for the day, found an end, in the hospitable dwelling of Charles Throsby Smith, the chief proprietor of the place, which we reached when it was nearly dark, after a walk of twenty-seven miles.

Backhouse and his companions thought nothing of this marathon trek. In those days it was a matter of either walking or not going at all.

Bush generosity

The difficulties of bush life encouraged hospitality to travellers, as the upper-class new chum, Walter Spencer Stanhope Tyrwhitt, observed in the 1880s:

It is impossible to say too much in praise of the social qualities of Queensland squatters, and of the upper class in the towns. Personal jealousies may exist among neighbours, and do all over the world, but it would be hard to find a society where there is so little clique. Anybody who is travelling in the Bush may go up to a station where he is an entire stranger, and so long as he gives his name, and has the manner of a gentleman, he will be entertained as a guest. Squatters and their wives have to exercise much discrimination in this matter, and as dress and style are not distinctive marks of gentility in this country, mistakes sometimes occur. However, if a gentleman is sent to the kitchen by mistake, he cannot lay much claim to the title if he is determined to take offence where none is meant. Australian hospitality is proverbial, and justly so because no one has ever over-rated it. It is a great credit to the squatters that they continue to keep open house as they do, as their kindness is often much abused. Their system is, to receive the superior class of travellers as their own private guests, asking no questions but the names of those they are entertaining. Stockmen and men employed on neighbouring stations are sent to the kitchen. Men travelling in search of work are allowed to camp in the shearer' huts or other vacant place of shelter, and if unable to pay for their rations have tea, sugar, and flour given them free of charge.

Most squatters however, and with good reason, demand a certain amount of work in return for the rations, and set men to chopping wood and so on. Some very wisely make this an inflexible rule. There is a story of a well-known owner of many thousands of sheep and cattle. When managing one of his stations, a man came up one evening 'humping his swag,' as the expression is for carrying a bundle, and asked for rations and somewhere to camp. All the work was done for the day, there was positively nothing left for the man to do, but our squatter wasn't going to break through his rule for all that. 'Look here,' says he, 'see that gate over there? Well just you go and swing it backwards and forwards till sundown, and then come in and, I'll give you the rations.'

The man goes off and sets to work. In a few minutes up comes another and demands rations. 'Well, you must do some work first. See that man swinging the gate over there?'

'Yes.'

'Well, you go and help him.'

By this time several more have come up, and before long about a dozen men might have been seen swinging gates, an unproductive form of work, but a good example to enforce the rule.

Tyrwhitt went on to mention another group of bush wanderers:

There is a class of men in Australia called 'sundowners' from the fact that they always turn up at stations, nominally in search of work, at sundown, never coming in before for fear of having to work for their rations. They are 'mean cusses,' and a cause of some yearly loss on a station near the main road, but it is impossible to refuse them food, so many of them live in this way.

The sundowners reflected the sharper edge of the relationship between squatters and workers. A station owner who failed to meet his obligation to provide rations for these members of the 'nomad tribe' might find one or two of his sheep had been stolen or, worse, his fields set alight by 'Bryant and May', the bush term for arson, taken from the name of a brand of matches. A bush song of the period paints the picture:

You often have been told of regiments brave and bold,
But we are the bravest in the land.
We're called the Tag-rag Band and we rally in Queensland,
We are members of the Wallaby Brigade.

CHORUS:
Tramp, tramp, tramp across the borders,
The swagmen are rolling up I see,
When the shearing's at an end we'll go fishing in a bend,
Then hurrah for the Wallaby Brigade.

When you are leaving camp you must ask some brother tramp
If there are any jobs to be had,
Or what sort of a shop that station is to stop
For a member of the Wallaby Brigade.

You ask if they want men, you ask for rations then,
If they don't stump up a warning should be made:
To teach them better sense, why, 'Set fire to their fence',
Is the war cry of the Wallaby Brigade.

The squatters thought us done when they fenced in all their run,
But a prettier mistake they never made,

You've only to sport your dover [knife] and knock a monkey
    [sheep] over,
There's cheap mutton for the Wallaby Brigade.

Now when the shearing's in our harvest will begin,
Our swags for a spell down will be laid.
But when our cheques are drank we will join the Tag-rag rank,
Limeburners in the Wallaby Brigade.

The 'Wallaby Brigade' and the 'Tag-rag rank' were slang terms for swagmen. 'Limeburners' means having dry throats, a side-effect of burning lime.

Whoppers!

Liars and furphies—unsubstantiated stories—are not only found in the bush. The term 'Tom Collins', meaning someone who spreads falsehoods, derives from Collins Street in Melbourne, for some reason. But a great many tall tales are set in the bush and it is the place where an awful lot of accomplished bullshit artists like to exaggerate a little. Noted liars are celebrated in bush tradition almost as much as the whoppers they tell, their most noted tales passed on, honed and finely polished by many tongues. The topics of these tales are almost endless, but bullock team stories are constant favourites, as told by the man from Jugiong:

The man from Jugiong held the floor, and the talk veered around from politics to bullock punching.

'Struth,' he said, 'you blokes should have seen a thing that occurred our way the other day. One of Mr. Osborne's teams was crossing spewy pipe-clay ground with a load of timber when the vehicle sunk to the axles.

'The bullocks made a game effort, but gradually became wrapped in the pipe-clay until only their backs were visible. Chummy, bullocky's cattle dog, rushed to investigate, and was soon swallowed up, all but his bark.

'The driver managed to get out by climbing his whip handle, and went and got another team, which he hitched on, and out came the half-buried bullocks with Chummy hanging on to the heel of a poler. Chummy always was a good heeler.'

'What became of the waggon?' asked a Gundagai sceptic.

'Oh, it is still in the pipe-clay, and will be dug out when fine weather comes,' said 'the Jugioneer'.

Here's another from the legion of yarns about bullock teams and their drivers:

The river is running a banker. The bullocky and his team are struggling through wind and rain to deliver their load to a distant location. There's no way around it, they will have to get across the river, no matter how badly it is flooding. The bullocky wades into the water and finds that it's not as deep as he feared and so decides to attempt a crossing. He goes back to his team and speaks to each bullock, telling them what they needed to do to get across to the other side. He cracks his whip and the team moves into the water, taking the strain. The bullocky walks alongside, encouraging them to keep pulling against the weight of water. Finally, they reach the far bank and stop for a well-earned rest. The bullocky looks behind him and is amazed to see that his bullocks have done their job so well that they have pulled the river twenty metres off its original course. No word of a lie! They were a fine team of bullocks.

Dan Sheahan was part-author of the poem that eventually became Slim Dusty's famous song 'The Pub with No Beer'. He was a great bush poet and yarn spinner who could turn just about anything into a tall tale, as he did with his famous description of his battle with Bellingen fleas.

In the poem, Dan is camping in a well-appointed tent in 'A green shady gully near South Arm Creek'. Relaxing on his wooden bush bunk after finishing a cup of tea, he is suddenly assailed by hordes of giant fleas—'Seeking to plunder and tear

me asunder/Roaring like wild native dogs on a scent.' Barrels
of flea powder are of no avail and the fleas just keep coming
at him. He has his trusty shillelagh—a large, stout stick—and
lays into the pests, knocking the ringleader to its knees. But still
the fleas come at him. He tries the language he learned from
bullockies. No result. He tries the blarney. No good. Eventually he climbs into the wooden cross frame holding up the
tent, kicking down the fleas that follow him up while 'seven
battalions stood guard at the door'. His strength fading, Dan
fears he will be dead by morning and the fleas will be picking
his bones.

This dreadful tale ends with a few lines addressed to the
reader:

You're sick of my story and wish it to glory,
And think it was time that I'd taken a halt—
If you cannot swallow this verse crude and hollow
I humbly request that you take it with salt!

Getting the better of a jackaroo is also a popular topic of
whoppers:

For two solid hours me and Steve had been sinking pots in the
Carriers' Arms when in blows a jackaroo cove, an noticin' we
was lookin' dry he asks us to have one. We excused ourselves for
not refusin' and jackeroos ain't got nothin' on us, so we fills 'em
up again. The jackeroo was a good spender, but a skite, an' I had
to dig up yarns to keep pace with him. By sundown he was in his
deadliest form an' finishes up boastin' of his escapes from death
while shooting in the jungle. At last he paused and gazed around
the bar.

'You fellows have never known experiences like those, have
you?' he asked.

To my surprise old Steve staggers out of his corner an' said,
'Spare, me days—I was once slewed in a scrub on a cloudy day an'
all I had was me old 32' an' one bullet.'

'Really,' said the jackeroo, 'and how did you manage to get away with your life?'

Steve grins and says, 'While I was wonderin' whether I should starve or not, 13 ducks flew past. I fired an' the bullet passed through all their heads. In fallin' the ducks hit the branch of a tree. This came down an' hit an old man 'roo on the head, in his death struggels [sic] the 'roo kicked a wallaby and it come sailin' through the air and knocked me in to a creek. When I came up I had all me pockets full of fish and an eel in each hand, and a couple of crayfish hanging from each ear. Now me jackeroo bantam, can you beat that!'

Probably not.

Talking bush

First published in 1897, W. Goodge's brief poetic take on swearing manages to summarise the entire colourful field of Australian bad language. Although city folk swore as prolifically as those in the bush, Goodge chose to make his skilled swearer a stockman in 'The Great Australian Adjective':

The sunburnt—— stockman stood
And, in a dismal—— mood,
Apostrophized his—— cuddy;
'The—— nag's no—— good,
He couldn't earn his—— food—
A regular—— brumby,——!'
He jumped across the—— horse
And cantered off, of—— course!
The roads were bad and—— muddy;
Said he, 'Well, spare me—— days
The—— Government's—— ways
Are screamin'—— funny,——!'
He rode up hill, down—— dale,
The wind it blew a—— gale,

The creek was high and—— floody.
Said he: 'The—— horse must swim,
The same for—— me and him,
It's something—— sickenin',——!'
He plunged me into the—— creek,
The—— horse was—— weak,
The stockman's face a—— study!
And though the—— horse was drowned
The—— rider reached the ground
Ejaculating: '——?——!'

(A 'cuddy' is a small horse)

The bush has not only been implicated in the art of swearing.
Many of the colourful expressions and idioms of Australian
speech depend on a knowledge of the bush or at least some
familiarity with its characteristics. If you are 'flat to the boards
like a lizard drinking', you are far too busy to be bothered by
anything else. 'Stone the crows', 'Fair crack of the whip' and
'In a pig's arse', or simply 'pigs', are venerable and well-known
expressions.

The large stock of vernacular insults in Australian speech
include many with a bush connection:

Mad as a cut snake
Kangaroos in the top paddock (crazy)
White ants in the billy (also crazy)
Useless as piles to a boundary rider
A head like a rotating mallee root
A head like a half-sucked mango
Ugly as a box of blowflies
More arse than a paddock-full of cows (cheeky; forward;
    overconfident)
Lower than a snake's belly

Or you could simply be described as a 'drongo' or a 'galah'.

A few of the many other bush similes in the 'great Australian slanguage' include:

Fit as a mallee bull
Pissed as a parrot
Stir the possum
It's Sydney or the bush
Bald as a bandicoot
As lean as a whip
As dry as a sunstruck bone

A once-popular saying was, 'What do you think it is—bush week?' This played on the townies' belief that bushies were unsophisticated and gullible. It translates as 'Do you take me for an idiot?' For their part, the bushies had their revenge in many a joke like this one:

The smart-arsed city slicker pulls up at the farmer's gate and arrogantly calls out, 'Hey, Jack, how do I get to Burramugga?'
'How'd you know my name's Jack?' asks the farmer.
'Just guessed,' smirks the city slicker.
'Well,' replies the farmer, 'you can just guess the way to Burramugga.'

Bush names

A similar colourfulness and inventiveness can be heard in some of the place names around the country. Tasmania ('Tassie') has some especially odd examples: Bust-Me-Gall Hill and Break-Me-Neck Hill are on the road from Hobart to Orford. No one knows for sure how these two names originated, but early settlers had trouble getting heavily laden bullock drays up the two steep sections of road. Flitch of Bacon was named after the colour of a local cliff, and was not far from Queer Street, a scrubby plain where travellers were easily lost.

Historians have puzzled over the unusual name for the

settlement of Humpty Doo, 40 kilometres southeast of Darwin. A nearby—a relative concept in the Top End—cattle station boasted the same moniker for half a century before the town got going in the 1960s, but there are many other colourful origin stories. It might be an attempt to render a local Aboriginal name, or it might have something to do with Morse code, Darwin having been a telegraph town. Or it might have come from a slang phrase of the nineteenth century: to be 'humpty do' was to be, figuratively, upside down or in an unfit state—basically, stuffed. Some have linked this to the old 'Humpty Dumpty' nursery rhyme, but what it all has to do with the name of the town, known to some locally as 'the Doo', is anyone's guess.

Nicknaming and affectionate shortenings of place names seems to be an Australian specialty, according to those who study 'hypocoristics' (don't go there!). We use more than a thousand of these playful clippings to abbreviate just about anything. Pub names are a favourite for the verbal chop. Locals will be familiar with 'the Wello' in 'Brizzy' (Brisbane) and the 'Bav Tav' in Hobart, not to mention the fabled 'YJ' (Young and Jackson's) in Melbourne. The same formula is obsessively applied to celebrities and personalities in sports—'Thorpie' for Ian Thorpe the swimmer, also known as 'the Thorpedo', and 'Warnie' for Shane Warne the cricketer. And so on and on.

Bush towns are especially rich in these short, or otherwise altered, forms:

The Rock—Uluru (after its previous name of Ayer's Rock)
Silver City—Broken Hill
The Alice—Alice Springs
The Isa—Mount Isa
The Bun—Kaimkillenbun
The Curry—Cloncurry
The Dangi—Urandangi
The Gabba—Wooloongabba (not to be confused with The Gabba, a famous cricket ground)
Kal—Kalgoorlie

Toc—Tocumwal
Shep—Shepparton
Rocky—Rockhampton
Gundy—Goondawindi
Bundy—Bundaberg

Most colourful of all, perhaps, Charters Towers is known as Charlie's Trousers.

As with the names of settlements, official and unofficial, the origins of many personal nicknames are lost in time and improbable yarns, but occasionally someone records the events that bore them—allegedly, at least. Jack Fitzgerald was known as Jack Without-a-Shirt. He died at Wilcannia in 1908 after a life as a bush cook. Jack was an independent type who insisted on handing out rations as he wished:

He got his nickname in this way. A traveller came to him for rations and said he had no bags, having lost everything but what he stood up in while crossing a flooded creek. 'Never mind,' said Jack, pulling off his shirt, 'this will do.' He tore off the sleeves, and knotting them at the wrists, stuffed one with tea and the other with sugar, then filled the body of the shirt with flour. His only other shirt being at the time in the wash, for the rest of the day he went about his duties with only trousers and boots on.

Cabbage-tree Ned was a famous Cobb & Co. 'whip', or driver. These men were used to dealing with distance, rough tracks and bushrangers. Here's how Ned got his name and reputation:

From 1853 (when he was only seventeen) to 1862 Ned drove a six-in-hand between Geelong and Ballarat. During the first two years his wage was £16 a week, and his tips from lucky diggers, for whom he conveyed gold to the banks, averaged even more than that. The roads at the time were frequented by Captain Melville, Black Douglass, and other bushrangers.

Ned had many narrow escapes, and on one occasion his

coach was stuck up and his passengers robbed of £800 by the notorious Ned Jordan, afterwards hanged for the murder of Squatter Rutherford. Devine got his sobriquet from the fact that he usually sported a wide-brimmed cabbage-tree hat, made in Parramatta for the London International Exhibition held in 1851, and subsequently presented to him. It was a conspicuous part of his dress for fifty years.

The boy with the pony

He was the same age as his pony. Nine-year-old Lennie Gwyther rode his beloved 'Ginger Mick' 1000 kilometres from Leongatha in Victoria to Sydney in 1932. Then he rode all the way back again.

What was the goal of young Lennie's epic quest? 'I did want to see the biggest bridge in Australia and the greatest ocean-going liners that call at Sydney's beautiful harbour.' A (very) big bridge and big ships were especially attractive to a bush boy from southeastern Victoria in the grey trough of the Great Depression. With Ginger Mick, named after the C.J. Dennis character so beloved by World War I diggers, Lennie left home in February and started riding.

This was an extraordinary event, but Lennie was no ordinary kid. His ancestors were Gippsland pioneers and his father a decorated war hero. He was used to riding his beloved dark chestnut—a 'stylish and game pony . . . who does not mind double-dinkey'—4 miles to school and back through winter floods through which they sometimes had to swim. He did many of the chores on the family farm: 'Last Melbourne Show holidays also, when my father was in hospital I harrowed and "smodged" twenty-four acres of ground with a four-horse team.' This heroic effort saved the crop and Lennie's father was so pleased he gave in to the boy's pestering about riding to the opening of the Sydney Harbour Bridge.

Lennie had special shoes made for the pony that would last on made-up roads, though much of the journey was on bush trails. The route took them to Cann River and then to Canberra. Here, Lennie got to shake hands with Prime Minister Lyons and take tea with the Members.

Along the way there was a bushfire to contend with and an encounter with a mad swagman. But by the time the duo reached Sydney, they were national heroes, interviewed by journalists and feted by the lord mayor and shown the sights, including the zoo and Bondi Beach. On 19 March, the opening ceremony for the bridge included Lennie and Ginger Mick in the crowds walking across the structure for the first time. Even better, a couple of days later, Lennie met Don Bradman and received a signed bat from the cricketing legend.

And then it was time to go home. Lennie apparently convinced his father to allow him to return unaccompanied, just as he and his pony had come. They were received like heroes by towns along the way. At Gunning they were hosted by the Commercial Bank and Lennie gave the local school children a talk. He turned ten while he was there, receiving a one-pound note from the local council as a present. After a couple of days at Widgiewa, they were given a reception by the shire president and Lennie was a guest at the annual children's ball.

Five months after they had trotted off from Leongatha, Lennie and Ginger Mick returned home. They were 'received by an enthusiastic crowd of about 800 people, and . . . given a civic reception by members of the Woorayl Shire Council. Lennie Gwyther delivered to the President of the shire a letter from the Lord Mayor of Sydney'.

The great adventure was over. Ginger Mick lived on the family farm to the age of twenty-seven. Lennie grew up, married, had a daughter and worked for General Motors' Holden. He is remembered in the family as an adventurous man who, aged seventy at his death in 1992, was building himself a yacht to sail the southern seas.

The story of Lennie and Ginger Mick has inspired a musical and a book and, according to the Long Riders' Guild, who should know, Lennie is 'the youngest known person to make a solo equestrian journey', anywhere, ever. Now, there is a bronze statue in Leongatha to commemorate the event. Not bad for a kid and a pony.

The man from furthest out

'I own, without a doubt/ That I always see a hero in "the man from furthest out",' wrote 'Banjo' Paterson in 'An Answer to Various Bards'. Paterson was firing a poetic shot back at Henry Lawson in the famous 'city or the bush debate' between the two poets held in the pages of *The Bulletin* in the early 1890s.

As Paterson recalled many years later:

Henry Lawson was a man of remarkable insight in some things and of extraordinary simplicity in others. We were both looking for the same reef, if you get what I mean; but I had done my prospecting on horseback with my meals cooked for me, while Lawson has done his prospecting on foot and had had to cook for himself. Nobody realized this better than Lawson; and one day he suggested that we should write against each other, he putting the bush from his point of view, and I putting it from mine.

'We ought to do pretty well out of it,' he said. 'We ought to be able to get in three or four sets of verses before they stop us.'

This suited me all right, for we were working on space, and the pay was very small . . . so we slam-banged away at each other for weeks and weeks; not until they stopped us, but until we ran out of material.

Lawson opened the manufactured hostilities with 'Up the Country' (originally 'Borderland'):

Those burning wastes of barren soil and sand
With their everlasting fences stretching out across the land!
Desolation where the crow is! Desert where the eagle flies,

Paddocks where the luny bullock starts and stares with reddened
    eyes;
Where, in clouds of dust enveloped, roasted bullock-drivers creep
Slowly past the sun-dried shepherd dragged behind his crawling
    sheep.
Stunted peak of granite gleaming, glaring like a molten mass
Turned from some infernal furnace on a plain devoid of grass.

And it gets grimmer as it goes on. Other poets chimed in as the rhymesters slugged it out and who won the contest depends on whether you prefer Paterson's sunnier depiction of bush life or Lawson's much grimmer version. But both poets were celebrating the same figure in debating the relative virtues of urban and rural life. That figure was 'the man from furthest out', more generally known as 'the bushman'.

Almost as much myth as reality, the bushman is the central figure of much yarning and outback legendry. Lawson would even pen a poem titled 'The Bard of Furthest Out' in 1906:

He longed to be a Back-Blocks Bard,
And fame he wished to win—
He wrote at night and studied hard
(He read THE BULLETIN);
He sent in 'stuff' unceasingly,
But couldn't get it through;
And so, at last, he came to me
To see what I could do.

The poet's light was in his eye,
He aimed to be a man;
He bought a bluey and a fly,
A brand new Billy-can.
I showed him how to roll his swag
And 'sling it' with the best;
I gave him my old water-bag,
And pointed to the west.

'Now you can take the train as far
As Blazes if you like—
The wealthy go by motor-car
(Some travellers go by bike);
They race it through without a rest,
And find it very tame—
But if you tramp it to the west
You'll get there just the same.'

Lawson goes on to extol his version of the bush creed:

'The lonely ridge-and-gully belt—
The spirit of the whole
It must be seen; it must be felt—
Must sink into your soul!
The summer silence-creek-oaks' sigh—
The windy, rainy "woosh"—
'Tis known to other men, and I—
The Spirit of the Bush!'

That spirit revolves around one essential virtue: 'Mateship is a thing that you must take for granted there,' Lawson solemnly advises.

He then tells the aspiring bard to take the track to 'find a new Australia there' and return to the city and write about it 'for all the world to read'. The poem ends:

I've got a note from Hungerford,
'Tis written frank and fair;
The bushman's grim philosophy—
The bushman's grin are there.
And tramping on through rain and drought—
Unlooked for and unmissed—
I may have sent to furthest out
The Great Bush Novelist.

Another great, if lesser-known bush poet, Will Ogilvie, had his own take on the same theme with 'Men of the Open Spaces':

These are the men with the sun-tanned faces
and the keen far-sighted eyes—
the men of the open spaces,
and the land where the mirage lies.

However he appears in the lore and language of the bush and outback, 'the man from furthest out' is the ideal Australian. This powerful image would be the basis for the national-istic mystique surrounding the 'digger' of the Anzac tradition, though that is another story.

Bob, the Railway Dog, South Australia, 1892.

Railway crew congregated around a locomotive with Bob, the Railway Dog, perched on top of the driver's car, Port Augusta railway yard, South Australia, 1887.

2

Bush folk

He is growing old and grizzly—but we none of us grow young—
And the native wit and humour still comes tripping off his tongue

Anon, on Bundaburra Jack

Burgoo Bill

The 1850s were a time of wild optimism and dashed hopes as tens of thousands sought their fortunes on the goldfields of Victoria. As the gold petered out or was taken over by commercial interests, 'the garrulous, gaunt, grim, gnarled, yet oft-times genial old Josephs of the more sensational gold-digging days' moved on, always searching for another strike. As Duncan Campbell recalled half a century later:

> Those were the days when the individual was nearly as often known by a sobriquet as by his correct name. How the quaint old nick-names come back to one adown [sic] the visionary vista of the years: Battleaxe, Bullswool, Boomerang, Mopoke, Native Cat, Possum Jack, and Yankee Jim. Others whose made to order appellation appropriately indicated their eccentricity, their foible:

Blueshirt Tom, Concertina Charlie, Quandong Charlie, Eureka
Sam, and Eucalyptus Tim (the latter so known for his peculiar
penchant for drinking strong black tea well flavored with the
leaves of the eucalypt). And then again Bandicoot Bill, Doughboy
Dan, Cold Potato Tom, Pancake Charlie. Clear as the memories
of yesterday come back these thoughts of other times and timers.

One of these goldfields characters was known as 'Burgoo Bill',
from his habit of eating only porridge, 'burgoo' in bush slang.
He was:

> . . . a grotesque apparition of a man. Around the rim of his ancient
> battered hat dangled a line of bobbing corks, i.e. 'fly-frighteners'.
> He was almost lank as a lath. His coat was wretchedly frayed
> and torn and the sleeves flapped idly in the breeze, like the
> undeveloped wings of the emu. Similar to Joseph's garment of
> Scriptural writ, inasmuch, it was of many colors, though possibly
> not so artistically arranged. Flannel, cloth, anything, has been
> indiscriminately utilised in a laudable endeavor to preserve it from
> the ravages of time. And what a vision the pants were! Down the
> thigh to the knee was let in a large piece of hessian sugar-bag
> material on which was prominently lettered in black 'A.1. 70lb.'
> From a rear point of view he was a veritable perambulating
> advertisement. Legended patches assured the spectator of the
> superior qualities of flaked oat-meal, and also intimated 'Dis is
> wot I growed on.' Bowyangs of stringy bark adorned his knees.
> Odd boots, gaping widely to heaven, proclaimed that he wore
> 'Prince Albert's,' a bush euphemism for rags wrapped round the
> feet and so worn in lieu of socks.

Religion was something Bill considered to be a practical matter,
as one of his mates described:

> Me an' Bill . . . was workin' together on Teapot Creek, our luck
> had bin out. We'd struck only a few blessed penny weights, an'
> had bin feedin' orf possum an' dry bread for a couple, of months,

so's not to run up too high a bill at Bob Goodfellow's store. Bob had stuck to us both like treacle to a fly's leg. So one day me an' Bill got talky—talkin' things over, an' he ups an' says 'How about waftin' a prayer to the Jasper Throne, Jim?' I hadn't no faith in them round-robin appeals to the Almighty, but I says 'Right-o, Bill, jest wait till I gets below an' pans out a few more dishes. Then you switch yer suplercations on fer all y'are worth.' Down I goes, while Bill gets his prayin' plant set up an' workin' in first-class order. I hears him a-goin' full lick till he almost roared.

'O Lord,' prays he. 'I don't often turn me optics up to You a-cadgin'. You knows wot a d—— crook spin me an' old Jim has had the last few months, no tucker, an' our stomachs that sunk in that an Egyptian mummy is a fool to us. We has to pull our belts in twice round to keep us from fallin' through the seats of our pants. O Lord, all this You knows, an' as I ain't never arsked a favor of You before, please, oh please do the 'andsome thing by us this 'ere time, for Christ's sake, Amen.'

When Bill had finished takin' Jehovah into his confidence he looks over to me an' sings out, 'Hey, there below. How's she goin', Jim?' 'Not a d—— color in the dish, Bill,' says I. Then Bill cursed and swore like a bullocky a-speakin' sweet nothings to his team. He said he ain't got no time anyway for the marrer-bone bendin' act, nor for prayer-petitioning nohow.

Bill may or may not have been a Scotsman, but wherever he started from:

He had been wherever there was a field to be opened up, and, by one of fate's little ironies, he died at last under a fallen boulder at the very moment when he had unearthed the gold he had spent a lifetime seeking for. He had 'humped the bluey' and 'taken the wallaby track'.

In a small abandoned mining field, situated in the vast confines of Gippsland. With the tenaciousness of the obdurate theorist, he always stubbornly insisted to scoffing sceptics that gold was still there and in a certain run. So he stayed on for years in that lonely spot obtaining provisions once a week by a packer and working a 'hatter' (that is by himself). But his belief was verified. Simultaneously he found his fortune and his death.

Bundaburra Jack

The bush is full of characters with wonderful nicknames. The Freshwater Admiral, Death Adder and Pigweed Harry were blokes around Borroloola around the start of the twentieth century. But the Territorians have no monopoly on memorable monikers. In New South Wales, Forbes tradition includes Elastic Neville, Handkerchief Jones and the legendary Bundaburra Jack.

Jack Murray was an Aboriginal man born in 1829. He got his nickname from many years working on Bundaburra Station (also called Bundaburrah), though he seems to have travelled widely later in his long life. He was widely known and admired for his sense of humour and his skills as a drover, shearer and horse-breaker. His travels and occasional trials were reported in the regional newspapers of the day and he was even celebrated in verse:

> Did you ever hear of Bundaburrah? Bundaburrah Jack?
> If you travel down the Lachlan, on the Murrumbidgee track
> From the town of Forbes to Nap Nap, there is not another black,
> With a lovely sense of humour like old Bundaburrah Jack!
> He is growing old and grizzly—but we none of us grow young—
> And the native wit and humour still comes tripping off his tongue.

As with many bushmen, Jack was not averse to a drink, or even two. In one yarn, he is short of a 'bob' (a shilling) and asks his mate where he might pick up some change. His mate says that there's a dead dog in the back of the pub and if Jack lets the publican know, he might pay him to get rid of it.

So Jack told the publican who gave him a drink and sixpence to remove the offensive item, which Jack did. But instead of disposing of the corpse, Jack placed it in the yard of the next pub. He went in and told the landlord about the dead dog in his yard and once again received a drink and sixpence to remove it.

Jack repeated his clever trick at every pub in town until he got to the last one, now very well oiled. Here, the publican didn't believe Jack's story of the dead dog until he went out to check. But he came back and agreed that it was there and needed removing, inviting Jack in for a drink and then offering him sixpence to remove the (well-travelled) corpse.

'It'll be two bob,' Jack said. The publican refused to pay this much.

'All right, boss,' replied Jack. 'I report you longa sergeant for givin' whisky to an Aboriginal.'

The publican paid up.

Jack's relationship with the grog was like that of many bush workers, and according to one local newspaper:

> The Aboriginal 'Bundaburra Jack' who paid a short visit to Wyalong a few years ago, and amused those who had plenty of leisure by his queer sayings, and his rendition of 'Wait till the Clouds roll by,' has been so often before the Forbes Police Court that he must by this time have a record established. He was sent to gaol for drunkenness and insulting language last week, for one month and fourteen days, the P.M. [Police Magistrate] expressing regret that the law did not give him power to send him to Bathurst Gaol for a long term. Poor Jack was at one time a most reliable drover, from the start to the finish of the trip would not touch spirits, but day broke him up so far as good resolutions were concerned. He was warned off this field by the police, and returned to his native land, the Lachlan.

Many of the yarns told about Bundaburra Jack depict him as a wry humourist who, like the mythical Aboriginal Jackie Bindi-I, often used that humour to undercut the pretensions and prejudices of whitefellas.

In a certain town up West there flourishes a son of Ham by name 'Bundaburra Jack.' Now, this native is fond of beer, and his white 'step' brothers equally fond of filling him up; so much so, that the local magistrate recently gave him 'three months.' Bundaburra thought for a moment after hearing the sentence; then, with face full of dismay, said—'But, Mistah, me no tink me can spare de time to do tree monse; dey'll be shearin' at Station in a fortnight, and dey can't do wi'out me!'

Elsewhere, Jack was heard to observe that 'This the black man's country.' When a white man standing by replied, 'Yes, but the white man came and took it,' Jack responded: 'Well, and a pretty mess you've made of it!'

Among Jack's legendary feats was going two rounds with the notorious bruiser, 'Cook's River Paddy', in a bar fight. Paddy couldn't floor the then younger and nimbler Jack. When Jack found out who he was fighting, he walked over to his opponent and shook his hand, saying he was only playing and didn't want to fight the champion. Paddy shouted Jack's rum for the rest of the night.

When the fabled Jack died in Forbes Hospital in 1909, he was thought to be around eighty years of age and the oldest Aborigine in the district. Locals paid for the funeral and 'a very large crowd' turned out to see him off.

His jokes, true and tall, were retold for years after his death, and he was still well enough remembered to win a Mr T. Daley the prize for most original costume at the Burringbar Church of England Ball in 1923. Now that *is* fame.

Bundaburra Jack's antics—real or not—were still featuring in country newspapers and *Smith's Weekly* during the 1930s and even the 1940s. His legend is living yet.

Bob, the railway dog

The story of Red Dog, the wandering mutt from Western Australia, is now well-known through books and movies.

But Red Dog was not the only dog with itchy paws, nor was he the first.

Back in the 1880s a bitser pup named 'Bob' was given to the owner of the Macclesfield Hotel in South Australia. The dog, which may or may not have been an Australian koolie, immediately took a liking to the railways and began hitching rides on the trains. Lots of them. And so stories of the scruffy but lovable Bob's travels and adventures abound.

A railway guard named William Ferry saved him from life as a rabbit-trapper's hound and Bob travelled the track on all Ferry's journeys for many years. Ferry was promoted to station master in Western Australia in 1889 and from then on Bob travelled by himself, though never alone.

Bob was known in many railway towns throughout his home state. He travelled to Broken Hill, around Victoria and as far north as Brisbane. He was also seen at the opening of the railway bridge across the Hawkesbury River in New South Wales and is said to have attended a banquet for the opening of the Petersburg (now Peterborough) to Broken Hill line.

Bob's lovable character, epic wanderings and increasing celebrity status ensured that he was never without a meal and a bed. He was effectively a railways mascot, with workers taking him home at the end of a shift and returning with him for the next one, waving the paw-loose pooch off on whichever service he had selected that day.

The railways even had an engraved brass plate made for his collar, bearing the lines:

> Stop me not, but let me jog,
> For I am Bob, the railway dog.

Bob was particular about his rides, though, as a South Australian Railways worker recalled in the 1930s:

> Because of the confined space inside their cab Bob could not be
> induced to ride far on the suburban engines. Consequently, when

he wished to travel on the Port line, he would enter one of the old third-class carriages, situated in those days at either end of the train, and by vigorous barking at all stations, usually succeeded in convincing intending passengers that the coach had been reserved for his special benefit. Bob's bark was what might be described as robust, and often caused strangers to believe that he was being aggressive when he really intended to be friendly.

He was reportedly happiest aboard locomotives of the American frontier design, with the big cow-sweeper at the front and large whistle and smokestacks on top. There is a photograph of Bob sitting atop one of these steaming beasts some time in the late 1880s.

Jumping on and off trains is a dangerous habit, even for a nimble dog. Bob was lucky to survive various accidents, including one where cinders from the firebox set his fur on fire. His tail was also mangled at least once. He had to be clever, and careful, particularly on the narrow-gauge railways which had no platforms, meaning Bob had to jump aboard from the ground.

Bob eventually became an international as well as a national celebrity. He featured in an article in the English magazine, *The Spectator*, in 1895: 'He has no master, but every engine driver is his friend,' wrote the author. It was a fitting epitaph for the famous railway dog who died later that year. A poem appearing in an Adelaide newspaper the same year summed up Bob's legend:

> Home-keeping dogs have homely wits,
> Their notions tame and poor;
> I scorn the dog who humbly sits
> Before the cottage door,
> Or those who weary vigils keep,
> Or follow lovely kine;
> A dreary life midst stupid sheep
> Shall ne'er be lot of mine.

For free from thrall I travel far,
No fixed abode I own;
I leap aboard a railway car;
By every one I know;
Today I am here, tomorrow brings
Me miles and miles away;
Borne swiftly on steam's rushing wings,
I see fresh friends each day.
Each Driver from the footplate hales
My coming with delight;
I gain from all upon the rails;
A welcome ever bright;
I share the perils of the line
with mates from end to end,
Who would not for a silver mine
Have harm befall their friend
Let other dogs snarl and fight,
And round the city prowl,
Or render hideous the night
With unmelodious howl.
I have a cheery bark for all,
No ties my travels clog;
I hear the whistle, that's the call
For Bob, the driver's dog.

So famous had Bob become that the engineer-in-chief of the South Australian Railways took the trouble to write to the editor of *The Spectator*, believing his passing to be worthy of notice in that august periodical:

'Bob' very soon came to consider himself as one of the railway staff, and although civil to passengers who spoke to him, he never made friends with any but railway employees, whom he seemed instinctively to recognise. The engine-drivers and stokers were his special friends, and for many years he travelled all over the South Australian lines, and occasionally over those connected with them in the other Colonies. His favourite seat was on the tender, and his whole demeanour showed that he considered himself an important adjunct to the locomotive. He belonged to the department, not to any individual driver, and I have seen him jump off one engine and join another, apparently without any reason, when passing at small roadside stations hundreds of miles from the terminus. His license was always paid for by the men.

Bob was stuffed and exhibited at railway stations and later preserved in a glass case at the Exchange Hotel. And he is still remembered fondly. In 2009 a statue of the travelling canine was erected in the main street of Peterborough. South Australians donated for the bronze statue, which describes Bob as the 'Legendary train traveller and engine drivers' companion'. Bob is also celebrated in Terowie, where he narrowly escaped the fate of rabbit-trapping.

It seems that Bob's adventures were at least as interesting as those of the famous Red Dog, and no doubt often as folkloric—the perfect combination of fact and fiction for a movie. Filmmakers, get on board!

Bill Bowyang

Just as the Great War ended, the trade union newspaper *The Australian Worker*, ran a gossip column called 'Pars About People'. One of the people was a man who was already on his way to becoming a bush legend. He called himself 'Bill Bowyang', slang for an everyday worker from the name of the string or leather ties that labourers wore around their trousers to keep out the dust and ants—'bowyangs'.

Sergeant Frank Read [*sic*], one of the batch of Anzacs on furlough on this side, who has splashed some ink artistically on the Australian literary track, under the names of 'Bill Bowyang' and 'Camelero', is well known in Queensland Labor circles. Born in the wilds of Winton 34 years ago, he launched early into a vigorous and adventurous career, being a pearler and beachcomber on Thursday Island at 13. After two years of it he went back and finished his education before taking another dose of the same life. From Thursday Island he migrated to the pine-cutters' camps in New Guinea where he improved his muscles swinging the axe and shoving the crosscut saw. Later, [he] blew over to Sydney, then to Gallipoli, Egypt, and Palestine.

'Frank Reid' was, in fact, Alexander Vindex Vennard. Like many men, he enlisted in the Australian Imperial Force (AIF) under an assumed name, though he used 'Frank Read' as a pen name for a number of his books. He had entered journalism before the war as a printer and then moved into writing and editing, becoming well-established as a Sydney journalist. Always restless, Vennard took to the track again in 1913 and when war was declared the next year he was among the first to enlist. He fought at Gallipoli and later served in the Middle East, continuing to write. In 1918 he and the celebrated war artist, David Barker, produced *The Kia-Ora Cooee*, a soldier newspaper that enjoyed significant circulation among the troops.

Very much a man of the people, Vennard had an ear for stories and ballads that reflected bush life and also wrote more than a few himself. His journalism was published under pen names that included 'Island Exile', 'Island Trader', 'Fossicker' and 'Wirraroo', among others, though he was best known as Bill Bowyang. Using whichever of his numerous pseudonyms, he wrote and collected material for which there was an audience. He wrote about beachcombing and life along the Great Barrier Reef and Australia's northern islands, as well as World War I diggers.

Much of his prolific output was reprinted across the country in local newspapers, spreading his yarns, ballads and personal anecdotes through extensive audiences of bush readers. His most famous work was 'On the Track', a column he edited in

The North Queensland Register for nearly twenty-five years until his death in 1947. Readers also contributed their own stories to 'On the Track', making the column a collection and dissemination point for tales about the lighter side of bush life. Bill Bowyang knew his readers, their interests and characteristics, as in this anecdote from one of his early 'On the Track' columns:

The drought in this district is now a thing of the past, and the farms which have been waiting for a bath for months now wear a carpet of rich grass. One would naturally think that our farmers would be in good humor these days, for this has been no mere, cloud-drip that has come to wet our lips and then vanish like a mist of childish tears. I sit down on a large black log near the road, and try to scrape the sticky clay from my boots upon a sharp stone edge. Steam is rising into the sunshine from every crack in the log; from every post and rail in the fence; from moist rock surfaces, and the backs of cattle and horses sunning themselves in the cultivation paddock. Ah! Here comes the old man himself.

'Goodday, Jack,' I cry in salutation before he gets within a chain of me. 'Great rain, old man? Do the world of good. Must have been nearly four inches.'

The old man pulls up without replying to my rhapsodic greeting, leans down over the mare's left shoulder, looks under and rearward, and says in those slow half-cracked tones of his 'Brushin' in that orf 'ine-leg, ain't she, the cow? I got Harry Skinner to shoe 'er 'eavy on the rim specially to make her chuck that 'oof out, the cow! Thort I yered 'er clickin'.'

'Great rain,' I venture to remark again. The old man looks hurt. He pulls out his pipe, cuts a filling, and laboriously proceeds to fill it.

'Great rain great rain for me orl right' he drawls, and vainly endeavours to strike a match on the damp box. 'Bledin' matches are orl rotten we get now. No blindin' 'eads on 'arf of 'em, and wot's on won't strike—drive a cove barmy tryin' to light his pipe when thaise a puff er wind.'

'I wonder what rain they had at Proserpine?' I observe, offering him a few dry wax matches.

'You gotter taryble lot er floot about the blanky rain,' he replies, 'but I ain't goin' down in the mud sayin' prayers about it. Wot did it do for me? A bloke down the river offered to buy all the grass in that paddock. He was to be 'ere larst night. Offered a good price too. Then the lovely rain comes, and he don't turn up, acourse. I knew my cake was dough. He don't want no grass now—got grass to spare soon of his own, I s'pose. But I lose my cash, all the same. Lovely rain! beautiful rain!! glorious rain! Jus' come in the nick er time—I don't think.'

The full body of Vennard's work is an unofficial history of bush life and lore, commemorating the large, colourful and quirky characters who wandered the tracks and creeks of a mythic country. Here he is on 'Talented Swagmen':

One meets some queer characters in the bush, and occasionally they possess rare talent . . . Remember a swagman who dropped into Barwon (N.Q.) one day, just in time to hear that the local pianist, who was to officiate at the annual hospital ball, had suddenly been seized with illness. The swagman volunteered, and after being fitted with a decent suit of clothes, he played dance music such as was never heard in that town before. Heard later that in the dim past, before Dame Fortune frowned on him, he was one of the most brilliant pianists in England.

Then there was the fortunate appearance of a good medical Samaritan:

On a lonely cattle station in the Gulf district (North Queensland), in 1912, a man named Larkin, who was out mustering, was thrown against a tree, receiving a fractured leg and arm, and also serious internal injuries. It was 180 miles to the nearest doctor, and even if he had been telephoned for he would not have arrived at though station before two days. Camping in an outhouse on the station, was a swagman who had arrived the previous day. Hearing of the accident, he approached the homestead and offered to attend to the injured man. In a professional manner he placed though fractured limbs in splints and also attended to the other injuries. It was with difficulty that the owner of the station ascertained that, at one time, the swagman was a well-known Melbourne doctor.

True to life, not all of Vennard's characters came to happy havens:

Some years back, a swagman named Young Stewart travelled through North Queensland, stating that he was collecting information for a book which he intended to write, and which was to be called 'Across Australia with a Swag'. He could speak several languages and was made welcome wherever he went. He was drowned while trying to cross a flooded creek near Cloncurry. From papers found in his swag, the police discovered that in the past Stewart was a well-known London journalist, and was for a time on the literary staff of the 'Times.'

Alex Vennard's prodigious writings are scattered through the newspapers and magazines of the past, including *The Bulletin* and *Smith's Weekly*, among many other local and regional publications. These brought information and humour to the people of the bush and were avidly read throughout the country. The racism and sexism that frequently featured in these stories are no longer acceptable but reflect how most people thought, spoke and wrote at that period. They remain as testament to the prejudices that were, for a long time, the unremarkable norms of Australian society.

Jack-the-Rager

Edward Sorenson's sketch of one of the many odd characters who populate the outback, or the 'great central depression', as he called it, is a classic. Jack had two empty jam tins, one labelled 'This Week', the other 'Last Week'. On Monday morning he took a pebble from the seven lying in the 'Last Week' tin and dropped it into 'This Week'. He did the same for the next six mornings. When all seven pebbles were in the 'This Week' tin, he knew it was Sunday. He'd wash his clothes and cook himself a brownie to celebrate the Sabbath. Next morning, the process began all over again as Jack religiously moved each of the seven pebbles from one jam tin to the other.

One of the fraternity, whom I came to know in the great central depression, was known as Jack-the-Rager. Most of his life was cast in monotonous places, yet he was a very entertaining old chap when he came in from his hatterage, and spent an evening with the men in the station hut. He could tell a good yarn. He could recite, too; but his best efforts were delivered when standing alone at his camp fire. Having a strident voice and a somewhat extravagant sense of dramatic attitudes, he once in a while astonished a benighted wanderer bearing down on the inviting blaze, and caused him to sheer off with cautious and accelerated step.

He told me how the boss had ridden on to him one night when he was more than ordinarily wound up. He had not been long on the run then, and as yet was only plain Jack Smith. It was election-time, and Jack was putting up for No Man's Land. Standing beside a gidgee-stump, on which stood a quart pot of water and a pannikin, he orated with great empressement, punctuating with hand clappings and 'hear hears,' interjecting and making sarcastic remarks, and wheeling this way and that way to reply thereto. Now and again he would point a thumb at the wilga-bush on his left, and tell the mulga-tree on his right that a gentleman wanted to know what he was going to do about the deceased's wife's sister; then, having put in a general laugh, would inform the audience how he intended to dispose of that troublesome lady. He had closed a successful meeting, carried a vote of confidence in himself, and thanked the chairman, when he was suddenly semi-paralysed by hearing a real clap and a real 'hear hear' in the darkness beyond. It was the boss. After that the candidate was known as Jack-the-Rager.

Jack was a conscientious and organised man, who never deviated from his routines, whether they were for managing his horses, or where he hung his mop and tea towel. He slept in a bed of his own invention:

His bunk was simply a couple of bags with two poles, resting on forks, run through them; his safe was also a bag, suspended lengthwise from the limb of a tree, with a piece of board laid in for bottom. His washstand consisted of three stakes driven in the ground to hold a tin dish, and nailed to the tree-trunk alongside was a sardine tin, with perforated bottom, for soap. If a chance visitor happened to use it, he was told to cover it up when he had done, so that the crows could not see it. Crows and ants were two persistent items that Jack had always to keep in mind. He cooked in the open, wet and dry, his fireplace being merely a couple of forks, with a pole across them, from which dangled a few wire hooks.

To be fair, Jack was more than a touch paranoid:

Before riding away in the morning, if no one was left in charge, Jack would carefully sweep over the bare patches around the domicile with a brush broom. He departed backwards, sweeping out his own tracks as he went. On returning he dismounted several yards away and approached his door slowly, examining the ground for evidence of callers. Having entered and found everything right, he went back by a circuitous route round the camp to his horse and let him go. If someone had called during his absence, the amount of tracking he did would seem a waste of time and energy to any but a bushman. He studied closely the man's tracks, the shape and size of the horse's hoofs, and, having ascertained that he came from the direction of the stony rise, that he dismounted near the broken stump, stood at the door for a while and looked round, and finally rode away in the direction of Thompson's Tank, he worried his brain for hours trying to solve the mystery of the person's identity. And he mostly wound up with 'a good idea who he was'.

To amuse himself in the long nights, Jack would play games with his knife and have animated conversations with the slush lamp that provided the only light:

If you came quietly on to his camp at night, it was not unusual to hear a heated discussion going on between him and the fat-lamp. He spoke in one tone and voice for himself, and in another for the fat-lamp. As he tersely put it when surprised, 'Just a little argument between me an' Slushy.' Sometimes they had a row, and an imaginary fight, and Slushy was kicked out of the tent. At other times he sulked, as a result of the pigheadedness of the other fellow, and wouldn't speak to the fat-lamp for a week. He would even 'see him farther' before he would light him. Yet no one who knew this man would say that he had a mental kink in his composition. Many men, and women too, in the bush talk to themselves, and have excited arguments with people who are not present, expressing their opinions in a loud voice, and saying in return what they think the absent party would be likely to reply. I can recall one good old woman who indulged in this way every washing-day over her tubs, beginning with 'Good-day, Mrs.——,' and going at the rate of knots until the final 'Goodbye'—not forgetting the invitation to call again; and she would drop down and laugh till her face was aflame, and the tears ran down her cheeks, when surprised. Yet no one would call these people eccentric. It is the craving for conversation, for someone to talk to.

Another of Jack's pastimes was playing cards—with himself. Each hand would draw cards:

When it was right hand's deal, left passed or ordered it up. If right was weak, he turned it round and left made it. The old man was careful to hold the cards back to back, so that right wouldn't see what left had got, overlooking the fact that one head was super-intending both hands. He got awfully interested in the contest, too, which was mostly for the championship of Burton's Tank or Gidgee Creek, or probably for 'the new girl down at Barney's'.

Like many old bush hands, Jack was inventive:

He had a peculiar sundial, though what he had constructed it for I don't know, for he was seldom there when its services would be required. It consisted of stout pegs stuck in the ground, at a radius of ten feet, round a tree. There were ten of them, standing exactly one hour apart, so that the shade, lying across the first at 8 a.m. would be on the last at 5 p.m. A traveller with a watch had camped with him one Sunday, and between them they had evolved this crude timekeeper. He complained, however, that it required a lot of regulating, as it didn't accommodate itself to the changing of seasons. Once when miles away from the clock I asked him the time. Taking a small twig, he broke it into two pieces about three inches long, and, holding his left hand palm upwards, he stood one piece between the second and third fingers, and the other between the third and fourth. Then, facing due north, he held his hand straight out before him, and I noticed that the shadows of the twigs were just a trifle east of a direct north and south line. ''Bout 'alf-past twelve,' he said.

Don't mess with Jess!

She 'nearly kilt me dead', the big Irishman told the court. He was giving evidence against a remarkable woman known by various names. On this judicial occasion at Liverpool in February 1919, she was appearing as Jessie McIntyre. Already on bail regarding another offence, the evidence demonstrated her capacity to fight her way through a tough life.

John Ahern's version of events that took place one evening a month earlier was that: 'He saw defendant about 7 p.m. on an open paddock at the Cross-roads. The woman rushed him and they came into holts [*sic*]. She was waving a tomahawk over her head and said to witness: "You rotten old b——".'

Ahern dismounted from his horse, found a stick and defended himself against the irate bush woman who believed he was interfering with her cattle. She threw the tomahawk at him but, fortunately, the weapon missed its mark: 'Then she made a rush at him, ducked down, put her head between his legs, caught him by the legs and turned him over, and "Nearly Kilt Me Dead." She caught him in a tender place and badly hurt him. McIntyre in the struggle kept saying he would not be able to camp with his wife after she had done with him, and also made an unprintable remark.'

In response to questions from Jessie's defence lawyer, Ahern said:

> She came at me in a fighting attitude, and had me down before I knew where I was. She got me by the throat and another place. I struggled to get away, but she tried all she could to throttle me, and I Don't Thank Her for Not Being Dead Now! I can feel it yet. She swung the battleaxe, and then side stepped, and swung it again. I am in fear of this woman, and have complained to the police on two other occasions.

Even without Ahern's exaggeration of the altercation—what he called a 'battleaxe' was more likely a hammer—we can be sure that Jessie was a very tough customer. She stated to the court that she was merely defending herself against Ahern's attack on her. Fortunately, she had a good defence and, as in quite a few of her other court appearances, she got off and was discharged.

Who was this feisty woman?

Born in 1890 in Burraga, New South Wales, and given the name Elizabeth Jessie Hunt, she was given away to a circus troupe around the age of eight. She learned many skills of circus life, particularly handling horses and other stock. She later took up with a buckjumping show and its owner, then ran the business for a few years after his death.

In August 1913, Jessie pleaded guilty to a charge of horse stealing but not guilty to several other counts involving horses, fowls and other property: 'After having pleaded not guilty to the last charge, the girl sat down in the dock, with a smile on her face.' Her defence pointed out that Jessie was only twenty-two, and that:

> She was really married, but, for reasons of her own, she did not wish to disclose the identity of her husband. She had lost her parents when a child, and, after that, had been living with relatives. She followed a roving life, and for some time was a rider at Martini's circus. She lived a lonely life at Bankstown, and had evidently fallen the victim of temptations. He asked for clemency.

The judge agreed that her 'wild life' was the result of her environment and committed her to twelve months light labour in the Long Bay Reformatory: 'The sole object of the sentence would be the girl's own improvement. He hoped it would have the desired effect.'

Paroled, and now known as Jessie McIntyre, she worked as a housekeeper for a cattle dealer named Jack (John) Fitzgerald. She learned the dark side of the business from Fitzgerald, but he was an abusive partner. She told a policemen in 1918:

> There's more between Jack Fitzgerald and me than is worth coming out. I lived with him as his housekeeper for 18 months off and on, and he treated me well until towards the last; then someone started telling him yarns. He came home one day and threatened to cut me down with an axe. He hit me, and I set him a go, and gave him as good as he gave me.

In one version of Jessie's troubled relationship with the shady Fitzgerald, she is said to have killed him in self-defence and buried his body. If so, Jessie was an outstanding success as a murderer, as Fitzgerald's body has never been found, nor is there an extant death certificate.

Never far from trouble, Jessie was again in court in 1919, charged with 'negligently driving a vehicle', in this case a horse: 'Constable Morressey stated that defendant drove sharply round the post-office, colliding with a child on a bicycle and narrowly escaping a serious accident. He mounted the bicycle and went after defendant who did not stop when called upon. Defendant said she did her best to pull up her horse and she did not hear the constable whistle or call to her.'

Jessie was fined 20 shillings and sixpence in costs, or seven days in jail.

The following year, Jessie married returned soldier Ben Hickman. They stayed married for eight years but eventually Jessie told him 'she would sooner live under a sheet of bark in the country than live in the city'. He said she was 'very fond of animals, horses and cows' and left him to live in the bush. Jessie established herself in a cave in the rugged Kandos and Rylstone region, around what is now Wollemi National Park. Her life of rural crime and defiance of the law began to grow into legend.

Like all bushranger heroes, she continually eluded the police with her bush and equestrian skills, often riding in men's clothing. She once escaped capture by jumping into water 10 metres below. Along with her gang of local youths, known as 'the young bucks', she is said to have ridden to the official stock holding yards while the police were away and stolen all the penned cattle. She was again brought to court in 1928 on cattle-duffing charges, but again walked free after the evidence mysteriously disappeared from police custody.

After a few quieter years of duffing, Jessie Hickman died of a brain tumour, possibly the result of a horse-riding accident, and was buried at Sandgate Cemetery in Newcastle. Her last resting place was a shared pauper's grave, with no headstone or other marking. Jessie's exploits, real and exaggerated, are said to have earned her the local nickname of 'The Lady Bushranger'. Her life and crimes have attracted the attention of writers and filmmakers, though she still remains little known outside the traditions of her local community.

As far as anyone knows, Jessie did not rob banks, mail coaches or gold escorts, but she certainly 'ranged the bush' and thumbed her nose at authority in the manner of earlier rural outlaws. While the classic periods of Australian bushranging were long over by the time Jessie hit her straps, she could perhaps be considered our last bushranger.

Lord of the Bush

Among its many astonishing holdings, Sydney's Museum of Applied Arts and Sciences (the Powerhouse Museum) has a rotating 'bush pantry'. It is made of a 44-gallon drum, flattened kerosene tins, agricultural water pipe and other salvaged oddments. The whole thing is painted blue with three large drawers at the top, twelve small drawers in the next two levels and a single curved compartment at the bottom covered in wire mesh to allow for ventilation. This cleverly crafted piece of make-do furniture was inspired by a professional product sold in Anthony Hordern's department stores in the 1920s. It kept a Queensland family's food supply safe from ants and vermin.

Make-do items like this, as well as cupboards, beds, chairs, tables and a range of other household furniture, have always been a feature of bush life. Dad, or Mum, or a worker around the place with a bit of skill, a few tools and a need would knock these items together out of whatever was available. After their service, often for many years as they were sturdily made, they were usually thrown away by a more affluent or less needy next generation. But some pieces were kept and were still in use when a flamboyant English lord arrived in Australia.

Robert Alistair McAlpine was born in 1942 into the wealthy McAlpine dynasty descended from his railway-building great-grandfather. His family lived in London's Dorchester Hotel, which they had built and owned. It is said that his first bottle was delivered by room service. After an uncertain start, he began to make money in building and construction in the 1960s, mainly in Western Australia. He was attracted to the northwest and the sleepy 'port of pearls', Broome. With a grand vision and a lot of money, he set about turning Broome and other parts of the northwest into a tourist destination. He built a zoo, a condominium, the Cable Beach Club and an international airport, and was involved in other enterprises that, sometimes controversially, led to the current tourist industry in that part of the country.

Lord McAlpine was also a great, if somewhat eccentric, collector, with an eye for previously unappreciated items which he bought cheaply and on-sold, or sometimes simply gave away. He became interested in the Australian bush make-do tradition of furniture building and set about forming a collection. He scoured the country for items, eventually amassing the largest collection ever assembled. In effect, he created a market by cornering much of the available supply, providing his collection with the veneer of respectable vernacular art and so exponentially increasing the value of items previously considered worthless. McAlpine may have been eccentric, but he was no fool. Suddenly, he was the owner of a most valuable collection of vintage Australiana. The revolving bush pantry is from his collection, as are many other items in museums, galleries and private collections.

In 2017, an early West Australian pine 'chiffonier'—you and I would probably call it a 'dresser' or a 'sideboard'—from McAlpine's collection was on sale for $3250, in original condition. It was built, very well, by Earnie Scott of Bullfinch, north of Southern Cross, possibly before 1900. The rapid escalation in value of bush furniture was assisted by several major exhibitions of McAlpine's collections in Sydney and Melbourne in 1990 and 1991. Two years later, pieces from Lord McAlpine's collection, together with items from other owners, were auctioned by the high-end auctioneers Sotheby's Australia in Armadale, Victoria.

After a colourful and eventful life as a staunch senior member of the British Conservative party, Irish terrorist target, extraordinary entrepreneur and passionate aquisitor of almost anything, Lord McAlpine of West Green, and 'Lord of the Bush' as his critics unkindly dubbed his Australian persona, died in 2014.

Lord McAlpine put Broome on the international tourist map and lost a large part of his personal fortune in the process, largely through the prolonged Australian airline pilots' strike of 1989. Probably he needed to recoup some of his enormous losses by selling his collections. But whatever his needs and motivations, he created awareness of a significant and previously neglected dimension of the bush tradition.

Men working to get a submerged vehicle out of the overflowing Mitchell River using a Spanish windlass, Mitchell River, Queensland, circa 1920–30.

3
Plagues and perishes

We fought the fires and we fought the floods,
We beat the droughts as well,
But we couldn't fight those city banks,
They beat us all to hell.

'A Hundred Harvests', Graham Seal

Bloody flies!

They have given us endless grief and two national icons—
the great Australian salute and 'Louie the Fly'. The bush fly
(*Musca vetustissima*) was troubling the First Australians long
before Europeans arrived and has been a legendary nuisance
ever since. And worse, according to the many myths they have
generated.

There have been reports of flies eating the eyes out of living
stock. It is said that they will suck human blood and carry
plague-level amounts of germs, among other nasty things. Most
of these beliefs are untrue or exaggerated. But even without
these horrors, there's no doubt that flies are a major issue of
bush life.

Colonial author Walter Spencer Stanhope Tyrwhitt described the battle he faced in southern Queensland in the 1880s:

The summer is very disagreeable on account of the tropical heat. In the hottest time thermometers rarely register less than 95deg. in the shade, and not unfrequently as much as 100 or even 110 degs. At this time of the year too mosquitoes of various kinds and other nocturnal insects make night hideous; but with all their powers of tormenting are quite unable to produce half the irritation that the common house-fly does. This insect in Queensland is of the most wildly aggravating nature, and at times he is enough to drive you mad. The numbers of these flies are such as are found in no other country, one would suppose, but it is not in their numbers that they are most objectionable. It is their deadly persistency. The very same fly will alight on the very same spot on your nose six or seven times in succession, and it is not until you have nearly killed him, that he will condescend to try another part of your face. As for your quite killing him he is generally too smart for that. When you have some hundreds of these wretches buzzing round you at once and all day, the effect may be easier imagined than described.

Early settlers developed an arsenal of anti-fly techniques. There were the herbalists who swore that growing basil, lavender, geraniums, marigold, rosemary, chamomile . . . the list goes on . . . would keep the pests away from the house. 'Blowies' (blow flies) used to be prevented by hanging tomato plants in doorways and windows or keeping a kerosene-soaked rag in the larder. A switch of tree branch was useful to shoo the pests away and some bush folk wore veils or even hats with strings hanging from the brim. The humble fly paper was in vogue for many years but simply couldn't cope with the problem. All of this was probably in vain due to the prevalence of the dunny: open earth closets and bins were, after all, great breeding grounds for flies.

And so was born the 'Australian salute'—the distinctive waving of the hand across the face to fend off the flies.

(The gesture has also been called the 'Barcoo salute', a reference to the thickness of the flies in that part of Queensland.)

Later, we got scientific, and proprietary brands of fly repellent and insecticide began to appear towards the end of the nineteenth century. Mortein (a combination of the French for dead—'mort' and German for one—'ein') appeared first as a powder in the 1870s. Many other brands have come and gone, but Mortein, like its one-time slogan of 'when you're on a good thing, stick to it', remains the best-known today. The famous pump-action fly sprayer introduced in the late 1920s allowed a much better spread of the poison but still the flies proliferated. It was enough to drive one to 'drink with the flies', meaning to drink alone, or to 'run around like a blue-arsed fly'.

When aerosol spray cans were introduced in the 1950s, a cartoon-fly named Louie was introduced as an advertising gimmick. Except for a few years absence, Louie the Fly has been promoting the brand ever since. He's 'bad and mean and mighty unclean/Afraid of no one 'cept the man with a can of Mortein'. So popular has Louie and his jingle been that 'Louie' became a generic term for a fly.

Widespread though the spraying of insecticides became, assisted by commercial rub-ons and spray-ons of all kinds, we still had a fly problem, made worse by the spread of cattle from the 1880s. More precisely, from the prevalence of cow dung. Local beetles were not adapted to deal with these and so flies were able to breed in even greater numbers. Enter the scientists.

Dr George Bornemissza of the CSIRO headed an international research project into dung beetles between 1965 and 1985. As part of a program of ongoing fieldwork and experimentation, different species of imported dung beetles were released in Australia from the late 1960s. Some established themselves, others did not. Some species were more effective at breaking down cow pats than others. But there was a noticeable decrease in flies in many parts of the country and it has been said that the Australian outdoor leisure culture has only been possible because of this work.

Yet in spite of all these innovations, the flies are still a permanent plague. And we haven't even mentioned the bloody mozzies!

Last of the nomads

There was cooking fire smoke on the far horizon. That could not be. The exploring expedition traversing the Gibson Desert in the mid-1970s was far from any known human habitation. When they returned to the mid-Western Australian town of Wiluna, they told the Mandiljara elders what they had seen. What did it mean? The elders knew.

Some time in the 1930s a young man named Warri and a woman named Yatungka fell in love. According to Mandiljara (Martu) custom, the two were not allowed to marry. Yatungka could only wed a man from her own skin group and Warri was already promised to another woman. That was the law. But the lovers were unwilling to accept it. One night they slipped away together to Budijara country where they received protection from the demands of their own people.

They were tracked by Warri's friend, Mudjon, tasked with bringing the couple back. He found them but they refused to return with him. Warri and Yatungka fled deeper into the desert country. They stayed there for the next thirty years, living as best they could off the sparse land. Naked, often hungry and in search of water, the lovers had only each other for company. The smoke seen by the expedition could only be from their fire.

In the years between, Mudjon became friends with Bill Peasley, a doctor and explorer with a deep interest in Aboriginal tradition. Mudjon persuaded Peasley, Stan Gratte, John Hanrahan, Harry Lever and Mark Whittome to mount an expedition in search of the missing couple. With a convoy of four-wheel drives the expedition set out in 1977. As they went, Mudjon lit fires and sent up smoke signals, hoping for an answer. Day after day he lit a fire and day after day there was nothing in reply. But eventually he did receive a response.

The expedition raced to the location and found the emaciated couple in the drought-ridden emptiness. They were in desperate straits but even so, they were afraid of the punishment they would receive for defying kinship law if they returned to their people. But Mudjon was finally able to reassure them that they would not suffer and they agreed to rejoin the Mandiljara, who forgave their breech of custom.

Bill Peasley, still alive at the time of writing, wrote a book about the story titled *The Last of the Nomads* (1983). A documentary film based on the story was made in 2007. In his book, Peasley ruminates on the ethical, practical and moral dimensions of his actions. Was it the right thing to do? Although the Mandiljara seemed willing to forgive the couple, there is no way of knowing if they were happier after being brought in than they were alone in the desert. Despite his close relationship with Mudjon and his knowledge of and sympathy for indigenous people, Peasley doubts that he, or anyone else who is not an Aboriginal person, can ever really understand the complexities and imperatives of traditional lore and the 'secret business' it often involves.

Within two years Warri, Yatungka and Mudjon were all dead. Warri died in April 1979. Yatungka did not wish to live without the companion of her long isolation. She died less than a month later. They are buried in the Wiluna Cemetery along with Mudjon who died in 1978. On their headstones Warri and Yatungka are described as 'The Last of the Nomads'. Mudjon is acknowledged as 'A Remarkable Man'.

There is a monument to the memories of Warri and Yatungka, just outside Wiluna on the Goldfields Highway. The couple is also commemorated in the Warri and Yatungka Hills, about 300 kilometres from Warburton.

A new chum is bushed

Out from England, the Oxford-educated Walter Spencer Stanhope Tyrwhitt, who later wrote the classic colonial book

The New Chum in the Australian Bush, was in the southern
Queensland bush for a year or two during the 1880s. This
was just long enough to pick up the basics of bushmanship
but not long enough to know how to use them. Out on a day's
shooting, all went well at first and the new chum bagged a
couple of wallabies, but then his problems began:

> Ten minutes more of scrambling through the scrub, and daylight
> is visible between the tree stems, and I come out into the open
> and throw myself down for a rest. I hear dropping shots from
> the others behind me, and wait for them. They do not come. The
> shots sound more distant, they must have turned back towards
> the horses. The wallabies being too heavy to carry, I cut off their
> heads and leave the rest. (Much I wished before nightfall, I had
> chosen a more nutritious part of the animal.) Into the scrub
> again to get back to the horses for lunch. Twenty minutes' more
> scrambling and another opening is visible between the branches.
> Ah! this must be where we left the horses; now for lunch and a
> rest. Why! they are not here; and now the disagreeable certainty
> dawns upon me that I have come in the wrong direction, and
> worse still, that I don't know the right one.

The new chum struggled on for another hour, following the
sound of shots from other members of the party:

> Another hour of vain endeavour to find our camping place, and
> occasional shots are heard, and I now begin to follow these,
> feeling sure of finding at least one of the party. A shot apparently
> close at hand, another that sounds miles off, shots from this side
> and from that, and after them I go, first in thick scrub, then in
> little paddocks surrounded by scrub, until I have to confess to
> myself that I don't know where I am or the way to anywhere. And
> then coming out into another opening, at last I get a view of the
> surrounding country. Not a sign of human habitation to be seen
> anywhere. I sit down to rest, and watch the sun set, in a blaze of
> colour; behind the furthest of the endless rolling ridges, that stretch

away to the horizon. Forest, forest, everywhere: nothing to be seen but miles beyond miles of tree tops, distinguishable as foliage for an immense distance in the exquisitely clear atmosphere, but melting at last into such a rich blue haze as can only be seen in a distant view in Australia. Most beautiful it certainly is, but with a wild, melancholy, and uninhabitable aspect of beauty. The most commonplace landscape in England though far inferior in grandeur would have seemed pleasanter to the eye. Nothing now to be done but camp for the night. To wander on in the darkness would be worse than useless. A clear pool of water on the edge of the scrub, surrounded by long reedy grass, suggests itself as a resting place, and there I stop, collect a few sticks, and make a fire; less for the sake of its warmth than its cheerfulness.

My dinner is a simple and unpretentious one, the head of a wallaby toasted over the fire, containing about as much meat as the head of a hare. This is followed by a long and comforting pipe, between the puffs of which I work out my plans for the morrow, whether to follow my own vague impressions of the right way or trust to some less fallible guide? 'Let me see, the sun sets behind our house, we have been riding away from it all day, consequently to keep the morning sun at my back should bring me to the creek before mid-day.' Rather this at any rate than wait to be found by a search party, who would very likely not find me till too late.

Alone in the complete darkness, the new chum recollected the stories he has been told of others lost in the bush. They are not comforting thoughts. He decides there will be 'time enough to think about starvation bye and bye' and the best thing to do is to get some sleep:

I curl myself up as comfortably as the awful hardness of the ground will permit, and try to sleep. No! impossible. Not 1000 counted backwards, not even 100 or more lines of Gray's Elegy repeated by heart, can produce the required slumbers. Nothing to do then but lie awake and listen to the uncanny noises coming from all parts of the scrub. The longdrawn howls of the dingoes (wild dogs), the melancholy wail of the curlews, and last, but by no manner of means least, the exasperating croak of the frogs; like the simultaneous sharpening of a hundred saws, effectually murder sleep. Ants too are a trifle familiar, not scrupling to crawl up the legs of one's trousers; well for me, that I did not settle myself near a nest of 'green heads,' or 'soldier ants' (an inch long, and with a bite like the sting of a hornet). At last it begins to get lighter, now for breakfast, the second wallaby's head. This toasted over the fire calls to mind the complaint of the English labourer's boy about his porridge, 'It's smoked, and it's full o' grit, and theer dang un theer bean't 'arf enough of un.' Breakfast finished, I plunge into the scrub without waste of time, keeping the sun at my back, as I had decided to do the night before. Half an hour's scramble and I pull up in disgust, seeing the sun right in front of me through an opening in the leaves. Rather discouraging to find I had been walking in a circle, however nothing for it but to be more careful. I stumble along for another hour, when at last I see daylight through the tree stems in front, and wonder whether it is the outside at last, or only another of the little paddocks that had so bothered me the day before.

The outside it was, and now being clear of the scrub walking was less difficult. Soon a mob of kangaroos appears, hopping among the trees in front of me, and I try to stalk them with a view to food; but cannot get near enough to them to justify firing my last two cartridges. Two more hours' climbing down the ridges, over ground getting gradually less steep and stony, and I catch sight of a line of fencing stretching away among the trees, and come down to an old sheep station, where I rest and pick a few mushrooms.

Mushrooms are not his favourite food and he barely manages to get them down. He knows he must keep moving:

Want of food and the heat of the day now make me feel rather faint, but being still far from home, and not knowing the right way, I am obliged to push on. I now come upon a small creek, but to my disgust can neither tell whether it is the one I am looking for, nor whether I am walking up or down it. After going wrong for a short time, common sense tells me to look and see which way the bushes along the bank grow, an infallible means of telling the way up or down a creek, when it is dry, as is generally the case. Another spell of walking, and I suddenly look up, and see on a low hill quite close to me, a selector's log hut, with, most delightful sight of all, a faint curl of smoke rising from the chimney. At the door I meet the proprietor's wife, who gives me a cup of tea and tells me the welcome news that I am within a mile of home. Ten minutes more and I am at the end of my troubles, and enjoy the first square meal I have eaten for more than thirty hours.

The new chum returns home and settles down to await the return of the search party:

Soon one of them gets back, and seems as pleased to see me as if I was a dead man brought back to life. At sundown another rides up, saying, 'Well, I can't see a sign of him anywhere,' and then stares in astonishment to see the very man he has been looking for all day.

Next morning he wakes up to find that he is famous:

. . . the report of a new chum bushed having spread over the country in all directions. Black fellows arrived offering to track me; the police sergeant, from the township 35 miles off, came up prepared to start on the search, and in short the report spread, as I subsequently discovered, even to Brisbane—the time I was out in the Bush, and the privations I endured, being of course magnified in proportion to the distance the news had travelled.

Walter Tyrwhitt was just one of many who were 'bushed' (lost in the bush), old hands as well as new chums. As he discovered the hard way, the skills needed for survival were only gained from long experience and from the nature of bush work:

Real bushmanship means not only that a man can find his way from point to point, where there is no track to guide him, but also that he can tell the whereabouts to a mile or so of a particular mob of cattle, and can follow them at full gallop for some distance, turning and twisting about all the time, and yet be able to pick up the right direction again without fail. Also he must be able to distinguish horse and cattle tracks at night, knowing whether they are fresh or not, to follow them and find the horses or cattle in question by means of them.

These were men, and sometimes women, born and bred to bush life. As the new chum himself became an old hand, he learned what all bushmen understood about bush skills: 'In nine cases out of ten a native of the Bush is better than a European, and a blackfellow better than a native.'

The emu wars

They could 'face machine guns with the invulnerability of tanks'. But they were not a new military weapon—they were a bunch of emus. How did a military commander come to describe a flock of birds in such dramatic terms?

In the early 1930s, the hard-hit soldier-settlers and other farmers in the eastern wheatbelt region of Western Australia had a problem. A big one. More precisely, a lot of big ones. After being promised government subsidies to increase their output in response to a booming world wheat market, the farmers were plunged into financial difficulty when prices plummeted in 1932. Bush people, like city people, were already struggling as the economic depression worsened and they needed no more bad news. But it came.

Flocks of emus migrating to the coast after their breeding season discovered cleared land and water sources provided by the farmers, along with fields full of self-service wheat. By October 1932 it was estimated that there was around 20,000 of the rangy birds ravaging the crops and destroying fences. Something had to be done.

Many of the farmers had served in World War I and were familiar with the devastating effect of the machine gun. They lobbied the federal government to supply the weapons in the fight against the emus. Surprisingly perhaps (though the Minister of Defence was a Western Australian MP), the request was agreed to as long as the weapons were only used by serving soldiers. It was, seemingly, not a bad idea. The troops would get some good firing practice, the farmers would get rid of the emus, and the Light Horsemen would get a bundle of new emu feathers for their hats. What could go wrong?

Hostilities began in earnest in November 1932 under the command of Major Meredith and with two gunners in charge of two Lewis guns. The first action was at Campion. The farmers tried to herd the birds into the line of fire but they broke into groups and scattered, making poor targets for machine-gun fire. The gunners did manage to kill a few birds but it was not until two days later that they had a real chance of mass slaughter. A flock of around a thousand emus was spotted near a waterhole and then began to advance right into the line of fire. The gunners opened up but the weapon jammed and only a dozen of the enemy died.

Four days later, a truce was called. Thousands of rounds had been expended but not too many casualties had been inflicted on the enemy. Some estimates were as low as fifty, while the farmers thought that anything between two hundred and five hundred birds had been killed. The operation was called off but the emus continued to cause havoc among the wheat farms and the farmers again requested help.

Less than a week later, Major Meredith and his machine-gunners were back in action. They blazed away for another month or so, taking out a claimed thousand-or-so emus after firing nearly ten thousand rounds.

Not surprisingly, news of these bizarre war games soon reached the national and international press. Reactions were predictably tongue-in-cheek, as they were in the House of Representatives of the Federal Parliament:

Mr Thorby (NSW): Who is responsible for the farce of hunting emus with machine guns mounted on lorries? Is the Defence Department meeting the cost?

Prime Minister Lyons: I have been told the Defence Department will not be paying the bill.

Mr James (NSW): Is a medal to be struck for this war?

Farmers again requested machine-gun assistance in some of the following seasons, though this was refused. The bounty system of trapping or shooting the birds proved to be far more effective, though the problem persisted. In 1953 the Western Australian government announced the erection of an emu-proof fence. It would be 135 miles long and would link up with the rabbit-proof fences at a cost of 52,000 pounds.

The news revived memories of the emu wars for the press. A 'Special Correspondent' to the Sydney *Sunday Herald* wrote:

This represented the opening of yet another major engagement in an unceasing war against an enemy as old as Western Australia itself. THIS war, ironically enough, is one being continually waged against a creature regarded at home and abroad as a national symbol of Australia. The enemy is the tough, prolific, gangling marauder of the sand plains whose species, ever since the beginning of agriculture in the State, has invaded, in a frenzy of hunger, some of the finest fields at the time of ripening of the harvest to shear off crops with voracious beaks and to trample with great webbed feet 100 plants into the earth for each one eaten. In such a way Australia's largest bird, the great 100 lb. non-flying native emu, has become for farmers a pest that has cost millions of pounds in lost production in recent years.

In Western Australia the emus, like the rabbit hordes, advance from the sandy, semi-arid vastnesses of the north and east . . . the experts now hope to pen them. They merely hope, for they know from experience that the emu is a tough and unpredictable adversary. The Western Australian Government and farmers for generations past have employed a variety of methods to control the menace, including poisoning, trapping, and shooting on a grand scale. These have met at best with mixed success, and even at times have resulted in such farcical and humiliating defeats that there are many officials and experts to-day in the State who cannot bear to be reminded of the outcome of some of their more ambitious efforts at emu destruction.

The article then went on to remind everyone in excruciating detail of the previous failures.

The emu fence is now part of the nearly 1200 kilometre-long State Barrier Fence system of Western Australia, which also contains kangaroos, dingoes, wild dogs and rabbits. Or not.

Black days

An unsuccessful stint in Australia produced one of the earliest novels of colonial life. It was written by Henry Kingsley, a failed Oxford student who arrived in Melbourne in 1853. Like almost everyone else at the time, he tried his hand at gold-digging and he may have been a policeman for a while. He was back in England by 1857, where he sat down to write the story of two Devonshire farming families whose fading fortunes forced them to migrate. The story was filled with dramatic scenes of bushranging and colonial life as the families achieve success and wealth in Australia. The book, titled *The Recollections of Geoffry Hamlyn*, was published in 1859 to great success in both Britain and Australia. It included a bushfire scene.

Although Kingsley's description is in a slightly old-fashioned style, there is no mistaking the terror of a raging fire, not only for humans but also for the wildlife and, in this case, a brave horse:

I had seen many bush fires, but never such a one as this. The wind was blowing a hurricane, and, when I had ridden about two miles into scrub, high enough to brush my horse's belly, I began to get frightened. Still I persevered, against hope; the heat grew more fearful every minute; but I reflected that I had often ridden up close to a bush fire, turned when I began to see the flame through the smoke, and cantered away from it easily.

Then it struck me that I had never yet seen a bush fire in such a hurricane as this. Then I remembered stories of men riding for their lives, and others of burnt horses and men found in the bush. And, now, I saw a sight which made me turn in good earnest. I was in lofty timber, and, as I paused, I heard the mighty cracking of fire coming through the wood. At the same instant the blinding smoke burst into a million tongues of flickering flame, and I saw the fire—not where I had ever seen it before—not creeping along among the scrub—but up aloft, a hundred and fifty feet overhead. It had caught the dry bituminous tops of the higher boughs, and was flying along from tree-top to tree-top like lightning. Below, the wind was comparatively moderate, but, up there, it was travelling twenty miles an hour. I saw one tree ignite like gun-cotton, and then my heart grew small, and I turned and fled.

I rode as I never rode before. There were three miles to go ere I cleared the forest, and got among the short grass where I could save myself—three miles! Ten minutes nearly of intolerable heat, blinding smoke, and mortal terror. Any death but this! Drowning were pleasant, glorious to sink down into the cool sparkling water. But to be burnt alive! Fool that I was to venture so far! I would give all my money now to be naked and penniless, rolling about in a cool pleasant river.

The maddened, terrified horse went like the wind, but not like the hurricane—that was too swift for us. The fire had outstripped us over head, and I could see it dimly through the infernal choking reek, leaping and blazing a hundred yards before me, among the feathery foliage, devouring it, as the south wind devours the thunder clouds. Then I could see nothing. Was I clear of the forest? Thank the Lord, yes,—I was riding over grass. I managed to pull up the horse, and as I did so, a mob of kangaroos blundered by, blinded, almost against me, noticing me no more in their terror than if I had been a stump or a stone.

Soon the fire came hissing along through the grass scarcely six inches high, and I walked my horse through it; then I tumbled off on the blackened ground, and felt as if I should die. I lay there on the hot black ground. My head felt like a block of stone, and my neck was stiff so that I could not move my head. My throat was swelled and dry as a sandhill, and there was a roaring in my ears like a cataract. I thought of the cool waterfalls among the rocks far away in Devon. I thought of everything that was cool and pleasant, and then came into my head about Dives praying for a drop of water. I tried to get up, but could not, so lay down again with my head upon my arm.

The lucky hero survives the fire but then there is the next fear:

It grew cooler, and the atmosphere was clearer. I got up, and, mounting my horse, turned homeward. Now I began to think about the station. Could it have escaped? Impossible! The fire would fly a hundred yards or more such a day as this even in low plain. No, it must be gone! There was a great roll in the plain between me and home, so that I could see nothing of our place—all around the country was black, without a trace of vegetation. Behind me were the smoking ruins of the forest I had escaped from, where now the burnt-out trees began to thunder down rapidly, and before, to the south, I could see the fire raging miles away.

So the station is burnt, then? No! For as I top the ridge, there it is before me, standing as of old—a bright oasis in the desert of burnt country round. Ay! the very hay-stack is safe! And the paddocks?—all right!—glory be to God!

Rarely does an Australian summer go by without at least one major blaze, often with catastrophic consequences for the environment, wildlife, stock and for humans. The station in

Kingsley's story was spared, but so many have not been as fortunate. Few bush families did not have survival stories, often with vivid details like that recounted by historian Don Watson's grandmother who survived the Gippsland fires of 1898. The home was destroyed, along with the few other dwellings in their hamlet. The terrified child, her siblings and her mother crouched in a clearing as the fire rushed by them. It was so hot that the mother's cheeks were scalded for months from the boiling tears that ran down her face. No one forgets a scene like that.

Bushfire stories are part of the lore of the land. Conflagrations like South Australia and Victoria's Ash Wednesday fires of 1983, Victoria's 'Black Thursday' of 1851 and the same state's 'Black Friday' of 1939 are among the worst. Tasmania suffered a 'Black Tuesday' in 1967. In February 2009 Victorians were visited by the deadliest blaze in our history on 'Black Saturday' when more than 170 people died and over 2000 homes were lost. These tragedies, along with numberless smaller but no less devastating blazes, are branded into the national psyche.

Unfortunately, not only the past and present are marred by these disasters. The future is likely to see more furious fires, seriously stretching the resources of professional firefighters and emergency services as well as the bravery of the state volunteer brigades. Together these people on the front line number in the tens of thousands, supported by even more spontaneous volunteers who donate time, energy and other resources in support of the annual war of flames.

Perishes

The arresting title of the newspaper column was 'Blood Drinkers'. As usual, the colourful newspaper *Smith's Weekly* had come up with another sensational headline in discussing whether or not drinking blood—your own or that of an animal—could save a lost person from dying of thirst:

In Dec. 1901, Jack Edwards, who attempted a dry stretch of 70 miles, between Blair Athol (N.Q.) and Alpha, drank his own blood from a cut wrist, and when found next day said he had got no relief from it.

Several have been found who perished quickly with a supply of animal blood inside them. Clarke, a Coongee stockman, left a mustering-camp for the homestead, 26 miles distant. A month later, his horse was found with its throat cut, and near his saddle a quart-pot of dried blood and a blood-stained pocket-knife; but the stockman's body was never found.

In December 1901, drover Harry Hopkins and his son left Loudan for Rankine River. Three months later, another drover found their bodies lying together, 18 miles from Austral Downs, and only six miles from water. Around them lay four dead horses, one with its throat cut; and a billycan showed that it had been used to catch the animal's blood.

A remarkable occurrence was the mail-coach disaster, between Powell's Creek (Old) and Anthony's Lagoon, in Jan. 1902. Whether Driver Stibe missed the road or turned off for water is not clear. A stockman reported meeting him, accompanied by a passenger named Hare, a lubra and a blackboy guide, all on foot, and facing a dry stage of 50 miles to Brunette Lakes. That was the last seen of them alive. On March 4, a search party found the mail, and with it seven dead horses, 130 miles from Powell's Creek, and 80 miles off the usual road. Three months later, the N.T. police found the remains of Stibe and the lubra, who, after leaving Hare and the blackboy, whose bodies were discovered in another part, wandered around, in circles, leading two packhorses. Then they cut the throat of one animal, and carried the blood along in a quart-pot. Finally, they perished beneath a tree, only six miles from water.

Smith's concluded the evidence suggested that drinking blood 'increases thirst and accelerates the craziness associated with its extreme form'.

Long before this, another traveller faced death in the bush on his way to the Mount Browne goldfield in 1881:

I went via Forbes to Condobolin, and then to Euabalong, where I heard that by going to Cobar I could get coach to Wilcannia, but found I could not, so I made my swag lighter and started to walk, the distance being 220 miles, which I accomplished. As the news was good from the diggings, and I learned the distance was 215 miles to Dippe Glen, I went right on that night to save coach fare, which was £6, and the weather being hot we walked at night, and lay in the shade all day. On the Tuesday morning we were at Dry Lake, 20 miles out, next morning 25 miles, and the following morning we were at Tin Hut or Bunker Hotel. On the Thursday evening we went six miles more, and camped a little off the road for water. At three o'clock on Friday morning we got up and made a start at a quarter to four for the road, but got into the desert, and wandered about without a drop of water until ten o'clock on Monday morning. The man who was with me I left two miles behind quite done up, but he revived and came up with me, or I would never have got up again. After the first day we threw away our swags and everything we had except our billies. Before Saturday we suffered much, but on Sunday we got a sleeping lizard and sucked his blood; I found three young ones in it and eat them with relish, but this did not relieve our pangs for long. Every night we pulled off our shirts and trousers, which were all we had left, to obtain relief. On Sunday night I thought I was dying, when I was mercifully rescued as you have heard.

Getting 'bushed' continues to be a surprisingly common misadventure considering the well-known dangers of travelling in the bush and outback. A British tourist went looking for the old telegraph station north of Alice Springs in September 2006. With no water and almost-dead mobile phone, he wasn't seen for three days. Fair enough, it's easy to get lost when you don't know the country, or the risks. But, even after he was found and received a crash course in outback survival from the local ranger, the same tourist did it all again less than a week later—less than 2 kilometres from where he got into trouble the first time. Four days and tens of thousands of taxpayers' dollars later, they found him wandering hopelessly in the wilderness.

In January 2018, two Americans hiking the Northern Territory's Larapinta Trail decided to climb Mount Sonder. On the way down, in 42-degree heat, they became separated around 2 p.m. Three hours later, the 33-year-old was found dead of dehydration.

Sometimes people have deliberately bushed themselves. In 1999 an Alaskan firefighter decided to test his faith in God. He thought that, like the Biblical messiahs, he should do it in the wilderness and selected outback Western Australia for his ordeal. He was not found for six weeks, badly emaciated and surviving on muddy water and plants. A 33-year-old, his impressive fitness had allowed him to last that long.

Even Aboriginal people can find themselves lost and in trouble. A group of five women from Wingellina, at the meeting of the South Australian, West Australian and Northern Territory borders, drove with their dogs into the desert one day in January 2013. They knew the country and the waterholes and where they could find good *punu* roots for carving. They had some radiator trouble but managed to reach their destination, collect the roots and load them into the car for the return trip. But their car would not start.

The women had some food and water then settled down for a night of unexpected camping. Next day they expected they would have been missed at home and someone would come looking for them. But by evening no one had turned up and they were out of food and water.

The following morning, three of the women walked to a rockhole but found it dry. The only place to get water was back at Wingellina or another distant location. They started walking, spying a spot of green in the distance. Two of the women made for that while the other three returned to the car. Here they remembered being taught how to drain the moisture from the *punu* roots and gained some relief until the collected water was lost through a hole in their water bottle.

The other women reached the green spot and found small desert finches known as *nyi nyi* birds, a sign of water. The sand was damp and they began digging with their hands and the few wooden implements they had with them. But the water was too deep. They would have to return to the car for heavier duty tools. On the way, they killed some perentie lizards, providing their first food for some days.

That night three of the women set out for the green spot with shovels and a crowbar. This time their digging reached the cold water spring deep beneath the desert. They filled their water bottles and returned to the car, their dogs discouraging the dingoes that followed them.

Back at the car they collected their friends and gathered up what they needed, including the rear-vision mirror from the car. Together the little group and their dogs trekked back to the spring and set up camp. By morning, they had now been in the desert for five days.

At Wingellina, people had realised they were missing and feared they were dead. But one of the women elders and a few others had been searching for them. As the missing women rested at their life-saving spring, they heard a car in the distance. They angled the rear-vision mirror into the sun, the flash alerting their rescuers to their location.

Safely home, the women, four of them in their fifties and one in her eighties, were in good condition. Their survival was due to a combination of traditional knowledge, as contained in the oral tradition of *tjukurpa,* and their own resourcefulness. Their story has since been incorporated into the tradition as a way of teaching the young how to survive in the desert.

The grave nomads

Yes, they are 'grey nomads' doing the Big Lap, but they have a very special interest in the dead. The bush and outback hold thousands of lonely graves and small cemeteries, the casualties of exploration, frontier expansion and perishes. Many of these final resting places are in danger of disappearing, taking with them the stories that link them to the past—and to the present. Now, some of the camper and caravan nomads travelling around the continent have taken up the challenge of recording and marking these poignant places.

An Outback Graves project has been started in Western Australia to encourage volunteers to find and mark burial places with whatever details of the deceased can be retrieved. Usually, these are few, but evocative: such as Ellen Moher who was just thirty-four when she died at Mt Anderson in 1885. She had been ill with fever, possibly aggravated by the actions of her husband, who beat and starved her.

A fatal mail coach journey took at least two victims in June 1902. When the coach arrived at Upper Levaringa on the Fitzroy River, James Marron was already dead of malarial fever and two other passengers were ill. They buried Marron and, six days later, another unnamed passenger. Members of the Outback Graves group placed memorial plaques beneath a boab tree near the two graves in 2015.

The old Fossil Downs homestead, a pioneering pastoral lease northeast of Fitzroy Crossing, holds a number of graves. Stationhand Michael Barry died there of influenza in 1893. In 1910, stockman Joseph Daroo succumbed to malaria, aged about twenty-five years. Labourer John West died of natural causes in 1923, and a man named Munro Martin died there in 1916; no further details known. Aged one year and fourteen days, little Maud Dunn was laid to rest on Fossil Downs in October 1904.

Through their work marking the graves, today's travellers have learned that there were many ways to die in the outback. Some died in accidents, of heat stroke, suicide or natural causes. Others became lost and died of thirst. Mail contractor Richard Palmer died of ptomaine poisoning in 1907 and was buried at the original Napier Downs Station. Occasionally they met their end more violently. Clive Palmer's grave is a few miles from Alice Springs. He died in 1870 and according to local tradition:

Palmer was a teamster for the Overland Telegraph in the days when they were making a mistake of erecting pine posts for the white ants to eat and which were subsequently replaced by iron poles. In those days most of the wagons were drawn by donkeys, who, small as they were, did in numbers draw enormous loads. Beyond a blackboy, they seldom had any company, and at the place where this man was camped is now known as the Wigley, a notorious waterhole, the home of various blacks. Just why he should make his camp in such a dangerous place is not known. What is suggested is that one morning the donkeys were not collected. On the side of a stony hill 1000 miles from civilisation, a body riddled with spear wounds, answered the last call.

In the Manning Valley of New South Wales, the local family history group has been working for seven years to identify 1500 unmarked graves in the area. And there are a lot more to go. In their work the researchers came across a note, seemingly from grieving parents notifying the local school teacher of the death of a young boy in their family of nine children: 'The little fellow is sick with the bad throat, he's the best one we've ever had . . . he didn't make it through the night, we've buried him in Kennedy's paddock.'

Excavating heritage stories like these and naming the lost has mainly been carried out by interested members of the public and through rural newspapers, though there is a Register of Outback Burials created and maintained by the South Australian Outback Communities Authority.

The 'Fergies' and the flood

The small but powerful Ferguson tractor is a legend of the bush. Developed by an English inventor and businessman, Harry Ferguson, in the 1940s, the nimble and adaptable workhorse was quickly taken to the heart and paddocks of rural Australia. With a 'Fergie' you could plough, pull, push, dig and almost anything else required with one or more of the snap-on tools the tractor supported. You just had to have a Fergie, and many farmers did.

Fergie stories are legion and, although long superseded by bigger and better equipment, the tractor is still fondly remembered and even celebrated. The town of Wentworth in New South Wales, about 30 kilometres from Mildura, sits right where the Murray and the Darling rivers meet. No stranger to flooding, it was in the big wet of 1956 when both rivers flooded together that Wentworth and districts produced one of the Fergie's finest moments.

A La Niña weather pattern developed over the years 1954 to 1957. Nobody knew this at the time because there wasn't today's technology to provide meteorological warnings. Not that the locals needed to be told. It just rained and rained. And then it rained again. The flood waters flowed slowly but inevitably down the Murray towards them for months. They knew it was coming.

So the predominantly soldier-settler farmers of the region fired up their Fergies. They worked the little tractors around the clock, heaping up earth levees and filling endless sandbags to defend their town from the worst flood since 1870. People who were there recall hundreds of Fergies rumbling through the night as the flood peaked, dropped and peaked again. Everyone pitched in, either driving tractors, filling sandbags, or preparing and delivering the huge number of meals needed to keep the effort going.

When the waters of the two rivers met, they covered the land for up to 30 kilometres. Then the water rose until it was well above the level of the town. Would the levee banks hold? They did—just. The Town Clerk reportedly proclaimed: 'By God and by Fergie, we beat the flood.'

But many properties were ruined by the salination brought by the flood waters, which took months to subside in this area. The torrent rolled on into South Australia, inundating the river towns along the way and causing even more damage to livelihoods and land.

Ever since the flood, the people of Wentworth have held a regular celebration of the gutsy little tractor and the community spirit that saved their town. The main street of the town is lined with grey Fergies and a festival of vintage machinery and related activities complements a monument to the tractor that beat the big flood of '56. The town's festival of July 2017 also saw a group of enthusiasts take twenty Fergies from Wentworth to Durham in Queensland, following the tracks of explorers Burke and Wills. At around 20 kilometres an hour, it was a slow trip of 2300 kilometres. But, as the president of the Harry Ferguson Tractor Club said, 'You see so much of the country.'

Influential anthropologists Baldwin Spencer (front right) and Frank Gillen (front left) on their 1901 expedition in the Northern Territory with (back from left) Purunda (Warwick), Mounted Constable Harry Chance and Erlikilyika (Jim Kite).

4

Pastimes and pleasures

There's time enough for everything in the Never-Never.

Jeannie 'Mrs Aeneas' Gunn in *We of the Never-Never*

The legend of the lost library

The origins of the remote port settlement of Borroloola in the Barkly Tablelands are uncertain. Even the name itself is swathed in mystery. Some say it means 'ti-tree' or perhaps a place where paperbark trees grow. Others say that it means 'the place of water' or that it is the local Aboriginal name for the area. This speck on the Northern Territory map about 1000 clicks south-east of Darwin and 50 kilometres up the McArthur River may have begun as a sly grog shanty, a droving route stopover or a convenient depot for the construction of the Overland Telegraph. However, or even whenever, it began, 'the Loo', as it was known to old timers, grew sufficiently in size and trouble to boast a senior constable by the mid-1890s. His name was Cornelius Power. From around this point in the story, even less is certain.

In accordance with the spirit of self-improvement that characterised this era, together with the do-it-yourself philosophy
of the bush, the citizenry of booming Borroloola aspired to
intellectual and cultural improvement. An 'institute' was opti-
mistically established and at some point early in the twentieth
century, policeman Power received a gift of books to form a
library. The gift may have arrived through the global philan-
thropy of the American squillionaire Andrew Carnegie, a great
believer in self-improvement with the money to do something
about it. Think Bill Gates in modern terms. Or it may have
been through the offices of Australia's first governor-general,
Lord Hopetoun. Or both. Or neither. Anyway, the Borroloola
library legend was born.

It was said that the library consisted of some three thousand
volumes, including the classics, great works of literature,
philosophy, science and anything else of consequence. The
riches of the collection were available to everyone. Not only the
hard-bitten residents of Borroloola and the harsh surrounding
country but also to footsore swaggies and any other battered
and weary travellers who fancied enlightenment or entertainment in that remote place. Even wayfaring scientists.

In 1901 the anthropologist Walter Baldwin Spencer and
his associate Frank Gillen mounted an expedition collecting
Aboriginal traditions. Beginning at Oodnadatta, they finished
at Borroloola. Baldwin Spencer described their approach
to the settlement 'over a miserable plain with gum trees and
grasshoppers and nothing else'. When they got there it was
'a drearily cheerless hot looking sun-stricken place'. But with
nowhere else to go, they made camp under the verandah of
the court house, planning to leave after a few days rest and
recuperation.

'The wet' put an end to that plan and they spent a couple of
months flooded in at Borroloola. To pass the time, they worked
their way through the books in the library. Gillen, in particular,
was an avid reader and by the time the two men were able to
leave he had devoured many of the novels in the library.

So, there was definitely a library of some sort at Borroloola in 1901, though there seems to be none of the classics and other learned tomes of the legend. In 1923 Bill Harney, the bushman and yarn-spinner, was in prison at Borroloola on a cattle-duffing charge. The charge was subsequently dismissed but while he was inside he claimed to have taught himself to read from the library which, at that stage, had apparently been transferred from the court house to the prison cells.

But by the 1930s Borroloola itself was on the wane. According to the journalist Ernestine Hill who visited briefly, there were only 'four men and one woman—the wife of the furthest-out police sergeant' left in the place. The library was now locked away and was still said to hold three thousand titles though these were fast fading under the remorseless effects of the humidity and the white ants. Hill would write about the library in newspapers and in her very popular travel books, each time further embroidering an already shaky story. She would eventually declare that the lost library of the Gulf Country was a kind of outback university where drovers, swaggies and lonely wanderers could save their sanity by borrowing poetry, the great works of history and those of William Shakespeare. They might also avail themselves of a copy of parliamentary debates, though it seems unlikely this title would have improved their mental balance. Hill would also make the unlikely claim that the library had produced 'more classic scholars than any university in Australia'.

Bill Harney was back there in 1949 and was once more given access to the library by the local policeman. By this time it seems that whatever books remained readable in the library were being sold after a cyclone destroyed their alleged home in the court house in the late 1930s. Harney would later publish his own recollections of the library, claiming that it contained the classics, as well as scientific and medical works. He said that the books had been distributed throughout the region and were fast disappearing, even being used to light campfires. He claimed to have read a volume of Plutarch that came from the library while he was in the lavatory of the local pub.

Later visitors and writers confirmed the steady decay of the library from its glory days, often quoting local identities who remembered the library or claimed to have read everything in it two or three times. In the 1960s a youthful David Attenborough of TV nature-documentary fame followed up with more local interviews, all reinforcing the myth of the library's termite-terminated greatness and claiming there was only one volume left. The Borroloola library, whatever its exact origins and contents, was gone.

But the legend lived on. Writer Nicholas Jose tried to track down what he could of the library and its last local keeper, the 'hermit of Borroloola', Roger Jose, a possible relation to Nicholas. *Black Sheep: Journey to Borroloola* was short-listed for the Age Book of the Year award in 2003, adding further to the mystique of the tale. Interest in the library and its extensive legendry is kept alive on the World Wide Web.

After many years of decline, Borroloola is now part of a thriving regional economy based around tourism. There is still a Borroloola Library, in name at least, and the council provides literacy and other community learning and support programs for a widespread, largely indigenous population. And if you visit the Old Police Station Museum you can inspect the last known book from the fabled library. It had been out on loan for quite a while before it came back, around eighty years later. The *Webster's Dictionary* was borrowed in the 1930s and the family of the borrower decided it was time to return the tome after it survived the 1998 Katherine floods.

So, despite the legend of its loss, the Borroloola Library is still providing access to education and information in one of the most remote parts of Australia.

The flying Viola girls

Towards the end of the nineteenth century there was a craze for hot-air ballooning. Individuals calling themselves 'aeronauts' lifted into the sky to perform all sorts of dare-devil stunts for the delight of the paying public below. One of the most intrepid of these adventurers was the Texan, Millie Viola. Often with her younger sister, Essie, and sometimes in partnership with a 'Professor Price', she barnstormed the country in the early 1890s.

The twenty-one-ish Millie and seventeen-year-old Essie were a drawcard wherever they went. Millie was at Broken Hill in July 1890 where, with Professor Price, they gave a half-benefit ascent for the local hospital. Millie was 'attired in a handsome tight fitting red silk costume'. At 3000 feet:

> ... beneath the balloon a parachute, which seems like a bell-shaped flower, gradually unfolds itself, until it forms a large dome. Suddenly the connection between the huge globe and this white dome is snapped as if by magic, and it begins to descend at first very slowly, but faster and faster as it approaches the earth. People hold their breath in amazement mingled with anxiety for the fate of the sylph-like figure swaying like a feather in the wind, and for an instant a thrill of something akin to terror runs through the crowd as the parachute is seen to career over as if threatening to capsize, but then is witnessed the fearless skill and self-possession of the aeronaut who corrects the flight by swaying from side to side. A few minutes more and she alights about a quarter of a mile south-west from the site of ascent, and gradually the balloon settles down, reaching terra firma some distance off. Then, after a delay of 10 minutes, during which the spectators exhaust all the vocabulary of delight and astonishment, the lady is driven back in triumph to the enclosure, and received with enthusiastic ovation.

Before Broken Hill, the flying dare-devils had thrilled crowds at Geelong and Ballarat, and they did good business in Sydney at the end of 1890. They were at Bairnsdale in February 1891, though failed to appear for the advertised show in Sale a few days later, disappointing a crowd of 600 as well as the 'dead-heads' who positioned themselves in trees, on chimneys and hills to avoid paying. But they were back in the air again in late June or early July 1893, with Miss Millie Viola performing in Young. Later that month she had 'a sensation in store for Goulburn'.

The Viola girls' act involved a balloon fitted with a trapeze and a parachute. Fired up with hot air, the balloon quickly ascended several thousand feet, then either Millie or Essie would spring from the balloon's basket on the trapeze bar and literally fly to another bar hanging from the parachute, which was originally attached to the side of the balloon. The weight of the aeronaut would then detach the parachute and an alluringly clad Viola would drift down towards an admiring crowd below. After several mishaps, though, this was deemed to be too dangerous even for the Viola girls so, as Essie explained in Rockhampton: 'Now we have what we call the life-line. The parachute hangs directly under the balloon, being attached to it by a patent lock capable of bearing pressure equal to 20cwt. The life-line moves a trigger by a six pound pressure which unlocks the bolt and detaches the parachute.' Perfectly safe.

By now, the antics and accidents of the Viola girls were being widely reported. One of these incidents took place in Fremantle, starring Millie. It was a moonlight show and all went well on the way up. But on the way down, Millie became entangled with the spire of a church steeple, said to be 300 feet high. 'There she swung with a very precarious hold by one of her feet and legs, no one among the large crowd beneath being able to reach her.'

The local police commissioner was in the crowd and sent for a very long rope from the circus then playing in Perth. Byron Hayes, circus proprietor and nimble chap, arrived with a long rope. By this time Millie must have been dangling for several hours. Byron lashed the rope around his waist and 'scrambled up the lightning rod, reached Miss Viola, and transferring the end of the rope from his waist to hers, lowered her down from the giddy height. Even then the rope was seen to be some 30ft too short, and Miss Viola was kept suspended, a la the Fleece, until ladders were procured and she was rescued from her dangerous position'.

It was stories like these, appearing in local papers across the country, that guaranteed the Violas large audiences as they travelled from town to town. The most thrilling account came from Gympie in April 1895, via a besotted journalist from the *Australian Star*. He described the event in detail, as Essie walked casually through the crowd to the waiting balloon, smiling, then:

> She at once took her place on the trapeze attached to the parachute. Every thing being ready, all the ropes were let go, and the lady prepared for her aerial flight, but at the moment a very strong gust of wind caused the huge fabric to sway heavily about, and displacing the damper used for regulating the flame, caused the latter to burst out, unfortunately catching the side of the balloon, igniting the same at the precise moment when everything was let go. Miss Millie tried to stay her sister, but the intrepid young aeronaut would not be stayed, and the balloon at once shot up like a rocket, Miss Essie, hanging by her feet, ascending to a height variously estimated, but we say not less, at any rate, than 2000ft., drifting away from the river. At this stage the balloon, which at the start was noticed to be on fire, became a blazing mass, extending towards the parachute.

The crowd went wild as the huge balloon descended in a mass of flames, 'with a frail girl waving her handkerchief in the most fearless manner':

> No help was possible until the earth was reached. Down, down the balloon came, and was watched with intense anxiety until the intervening trees hid the spirited young lady and her blazing chariot from view. Long before this numbers of people were doing their best to follow her to give all the assistance possible, foremost amongst them being Mr. S. Gamgee, who rendered good service by extricating Miss Essie from the burning mass as soon as she touched the ground.

Essie, in a 'most nonchalant manner, requested the bystanders to try and save her parachute'. The balloon was destroyed but waves of cheering erupted from the crowd on seeing that the brave young aviator was safe and 'a few gentlemen at once took up a collection for the benefit of the young lady who had gone through such a trying experience'.

When Essie was interviewed in Rockhampton the next month, the Gympie conflagration was uppermost in the journalist's mind (after admiring 'the prepossessing brunette'). She was asked if she was frightened during the incident, to which she replied: 'I was too angry to be frightened . . . When I saw the balloon catch fire I thought those around it would seize the ropes and prevent the ascension and I did not want to disappoint the public.' She went on: 'And, you know . . . I am just as happy up aloft as I am on terra firma—more so because, you see, when I'm in the clouds, and the balloon's moving rapidly, I have a lot of people running after me, and I don't when I'm on the ground.' She then produced 'an arch smile' and added 'not nice people like the Rockhampton newspaper men seem to be'. The young reporter concluded his gushing report: 'Then, in merciful consideration for the *Argus* representative's blushes, which this gigantic compliment called forth, Miss Essie went on to explain how the balloon and the parachute work.'

In the showbiz tradition, the show went on, fortunately with no more major mishaps.

The aeronauts were in Townsville in June and in Ipswich the following month. They departed in September and by December, Millie was in San Francisco with plans to go over Niagara Falls in a barrel dropped from a balloon. No more was heard of this feat but in January 1896 Millie had another accident, falling from an ascending balloon when a rope broke. She was sore but not seriously injured. A year later, Millie Viola was set to marry a local press agent under her real name of Ruby Horaker.

What happened to Millie and her sister Essie after that is unknown but they certainly made an impact in Australia.

Newspapers and authors were still recalling their adventures and dare-devil feats nearly seventy years after their departure.

Grog

There are many names for alcohol of one kind or another— 'the amber fluid', 'the creature', 'the hops', 'plonk' and so on. The most common term is probably just 'the grog', derived from the traditional rum, water, lime, sugar and mint drink of the Royal Navy. The grog runs through many yarns and almost any event and is the indispensable fluid of bush life and lore.

Clancy of the Overflow is a well-known character in one of 'Banjo' Paterson's most loved poems. The original poem has generated many anonymous parodies, one of which is known as 'Clancy's Overflow', depicting a man who could not abide to see even a drop of the amber brew wasted:

> Sure, the beer I love to taste it,
> But it breaks my heart to waste it,
> As the careless barman spills it
> And the bubbles rise like snow.
> For I somehow rather fancy
> That the barman thinks I'm Clancy,
> And the waste upon the counter
> Is Clancy's overflow.

In northern New South Wales during World War II, a local identity so frequently declaimed these beery lines in various watering holes that he was given the nickname 'Clancy'. Local legends about Clancy and his antics in different pubs were legion, such as the night when the barmaid served Clancy a beer with an enormous frothy head. He looked at it, then slowly removed the bow tie he happened to wearing and tied it around the beer glass. The barmaid watched in astonishment: 'Why did you do that?'

In tones of disgust, Clancy replied, 'A collar that size deserves a tie.'

Then there was the period when Clancy was seen to be ordering two schooners every time he breasted the bar. He would down them, swiftly, one after the other, saying that one was for himself and the other for his mate who was fighting in New Guinea. This went on for a while but then Clancy stopped ordering two schooners and returned to the usual practice of having one at a time. The publican delicately inquired if something had happened to Clancy's fighting mate. 'Oh no,' replied Clancy. 'That one is his drink, the doctor's ordered me off the grog.'

Another yarn tells of the inebriated Clancy reeling out of the pub and unsteadily making his way homewards, on and off the pavement. A car roared past and the driver asked in a colourful manner why Clancy didn't keep to the footpath. Clancy yelled back 'What do you think I am—a tightrope walker?'

There are, of course, countless legendary drinkers in bush lore of which much has been written. Another prodigious gulper of note, according to *Smith's Weekly*, was known as 'Jimmy the Swallower':

Years ago, an old swaggie, known everywhere as 'Jimmy the Swallower,' infested the St. George (Q.) district. He gained his sobriquet from his knack of swallowing a pint of beer at a gulp, and was always ready to show off his stunt, of which he was inordinately proud. One day he dropped into Billy Richardson's pub at Dirranbandi. A commercial was waiting there for the St. George coach, and his attention was called to Jimmy. Richardson went behind the bar and, picking up a couple of dead mice from a trap, threw them into a pint-pot, under cover of the counter. Filling the pot up with beer he said, 'Here, Jimmy, show this gent how you do it.'

Jimmy grabbed the pot, threw his head back, and, blinking a little, put the empty pewter on the bar. The amazed stranger gazed into the empty receptacle. 'Damn it, man,' he said, 'couldn't you feel anything?'

'Well,' replied James, 'maybe there was a 'op or two in it.'

Killing a kangaroo

Upper-class English artist Archibald Stirling spent some time in the Queensland bush during the 1880s. One day he went hunting in the manner that gentlemen chased down the fox back home. The hunters had a small pack of hounds, including 'Count', and their quarry was not the fox but the kangaroo.

> We had gone about seven miles, when I saw a regular mob of some twenty kangaroos feeding not more than fifty yards from the track; the dog at first did not perceive them, but when I began to canter, understood at once what was in the wind, and dashed straight at the whole mob. Amongst these kangaroos was an enormous 'old man,' who, as soon as his companions began to move, rapidly dropped into the rear; so slow was he, indeed, that in about three hundred yards the dog was close upon him, and finding flight not his strong point, the old gentleman deliberately turned round and came towards the dog. Count was not, however, in the least disconcerted, but rushed straight in and secured a firm grip on his hind leg. Several times the kangaroo shook the dog off, trying on each occasion, by falling upon him, to get him within the grip of his short fore-arms. Had he succeeded in this, I knew well—as probably did Count—that a single stroke from the powerful hind leg would have disembowelled my canine friend as effectually as a boar's tusk, or a bull's horn. Fortunately, however, before any harm was done, I came to my ally's assistance, and made a diversion in his favour.
>
> The 'old man' seemed in no way dismayed at the arrival of a fresh foe, but getting his back against a tree, he faced me boldly, every now and then disregarding the dog, and making as if he would attack me. I had not brought my waddy with me, and for some time tried by the help of one of my stirrup-irons to

administer the necessary blow; but finding this of no avail, and seeing plenty of wood lying about, I determined to get off and pick up a stick. Foolishly for myself, I did not move far enough away, and just as my leg was over the horse's back, the kangaroo, having shaken the dog off, made a couple of large hops towards me, and I was forced to flee ignominiously to a safe distance.

Stirling found himself a good stick, or 'waddy', and eventually managed to recapture his horse and return to the attack:

My object was to dodge behind the 'old man,' so as to get a fair blow at the back of his head; his to keep me in front of him, where I could do no harm. In one of his unsuccessful efforts to fall upon Count the enemy exposed himself to my stick. Nor did I neglect the opportunity. A single blow settled matters, and having cut off the tail and attended to a few flesh wounds that the dog had received, I proceeded on my way without more loss of time.

Stirling had come to learn the delicacies of bush tucker: 'The tail of the larger kangaroo is also a trophy not to be despised, making as it does a soup far richer and in every way better than the best ox-tail with which the European is acquainted.' But like most people of his era, he was oblivious to the savagery by which the meal was obtained and the slaughter of a whole animal for an entrée.

Painting the land

There is a utopia in the desert. It is an Aboriginal outstation of that name established as part of the movement which sought to return Aboriginal people to their ancestral lands. Like most of the outstation endeavours, the land on which it operated, around 250 kilometres northeast of Alice Springs, was subject to pastoral leases which had to be purchased from their holders.

From the 1880s, European settlers struggled to establish viable stations in the arid region, employing local Aboriginal people as stockmen and domestic servants. In the 1930s two German brothers took a lease on holdings in the area and, according to one tradition, named the place 'Utopia', a term for an earthly paradise, and possibly used ironically. The other story is that the name is an Anglicisation of *Uturupa*, an indigenous word referring to a large sandhill. Whatever the origin of the name, it was adopted when the Anmatyerr and Alyawarr people obtained freehold title to the land in 1979 through sale of the pastoral lease to the Aboriginal Land Fund Commission.

There are sixteen homelands within Utopia where members of the two main language groups are able to follow a relatively traditional lifestyle. This includes body painting and other forms of art associated with ceremonies. From the 1970s, various other forms of creative art were introduced to the community and in the late 1980s local artists began to paint, transferring traditional stories and motifs onto canvas. The best known examples of the art styles that developed from this work are usually called 'dot paintings', many of which now also refer to modern themes and imagery, though still preserving an unmistakable indigeneity. The Utopia artists are now famous around the world, with a number of noted practitioners. Their works capture the colours, myths and symbolism of the land in which they are painted.

Far away, in the southwest of Western Australia, another group of indigenous people created a little-known body of art that has only recently been rediscovered. Aboriginal children removed from their families and communities were housed at the Carrolup Native Settlement near Katanning in the 1940s where they received training in farm and domestic work. The children also began to draw and paint under the guidance of a teacher named Noel White and his wife, Lily.

The Whites were amazed at the relative sophistication of the work they encouraged the children to create from walks through the bush. The visual perception and accuracy of the images portrayed in the paintings was remarkable for children aged between nine and thirteen. The paintings depicted traditional culture as the children knew it, as well as native animals, trees, plants and landforms. The techniques used were Western, as taught to them by the Whites, but like the Utopia work the paintings are distinctively indigenous.

In 1949, word of this work drew an English woman named Florence Rutter to the settlement to see the art for herself. She was greatly impressed with what she saw and was given a number of paintings to promote the work internationally, which she did through the 1950s. A New York art dealer purchased all the known 120-or-so paintings in the late 1950s, donating them to Colgate University in New York state. Here they were stored and forgotten until 2004 when Australian National University academic, Howard Morphy, accidentally rediscovered them. After negotiations between the southwest Noongar community, Colgate University and Curtin University, the paintings were repatriated in 2013. Together with documents, the paintings are now in the care of Curtin University.

Although the Carrolup Settlement closed in 1950 and the artworks were lost for so many years after, the artistic skills of the children transferred to later generations of Noongar artists, leading to the formation of a recognised school of contemporary indigenous art.

Buckjumpers

Riding was a basic skill in colonial Australia. Anyone who could sit a bucking horse or steer was widely admired. Though, as Edward Sorenson observed by the early twentieth century, the ability to ride a horse was disappearing and those who could sit untamed beasts were mostly to be found in the back country:

There was a time when the native-born who could not mount a brumby and stick to him like wax to a blanket was an exception, who was not only chaffed and scoffed at by his fellows, but was viewed with surprise by visitors from other countries. His fame had travelled early. Even now the typical Australian, to foreign pens and brushes, is a horseman whirling several yards of stock-whip around while racing after long-horned cattle, just as the cowboy is considered typically American. But the horseman is merely one of a hundred types. He is more picturesque than the general run; the thrill of romance and adventure runs through his career, which appeals to the untameable blood that courses under the veneer of civilisation in the Anglo-Saxon; and he is seized upon with so much zest as to overshadow all other types, if not to entirely obliterate them in far-off places. The miner is grudgingly permitted to step on to the stage occasionally, and the shearer is briefly noticed in season; but the horseman is an evergreen.

At one time everybody rode, but closer settlement, railways, coaches, and steamers have so limited the usefulness of the hack that thousands of people in every State are as much out of place in a saddle as a Jack Tar, while the majority in big towns have never been on a horse's back in their lives.

On agricultural and dairy farms little riding is necessary. The farmer may ride to and from work, bareback, on the plough-horse, and his sons and daughters ride about the paddock or farm on quiet old mokes, but send them after half-wild cattle or brumbies on a scrubby run, put them on a cutting-out camp, or on a buck-jumper, and most of them would be hopelessly at sea.

Selectors, as a rule, shape much better, many of them being smart cattle-men and rough-riders. They work intermittently on neighbouring stations, and occasionally go droving. Girls ride bareback or in a man's saddle round the selection fences, muster their stock from the bush, riding at times full gallop through thick and thin. This was a simple matter to all of them in the days when the bush was wide. Marsupials and dingoes were plentiful, and so were wild horses in many places, and men and girls trooped forth on Sundays and holidays to hunt them, and the greater part of the day would be spent riding hard through thick timber and over rough country. On the road home they jumped their horses over logs and fences just for sport, or to see who had the best horse. Kangarooing was a fashionable pastime then.

The tactics of the town breaker make the old hand and the backblocker tired to look at. In their way a horse would be caught and driven round a few times with the mouthing reins, then ridden without loss of time. Of course they bucked, bucked hard and often; but the men were like sticking-plasters on their backs. The town breaker shuts his colt up for two or three days, with its head strapped back to its chest; then he pulls and twists it about for a week with clothes-lines, after which it is led around half the universe beside another horse, often with a dummy flopping and wobbling on its back. A bag on the end of a long stick is banged about its back and legs and drawn over its head to cure it of nervousness; dry cow-hides that make a great clatter are thrown against its heels, and every night it is turned out short-hobbled. When it is too dead to look round at an earthquake the breaker mounts it in a very small yard, or perhaps he will take it on to a sandhill or a boggy flat, where it would be extra hard to buck and a fall wouldn't hurt. It takes the unfortunate animal about two years to recover from the ordeal.

When the runs everywhere were wild and broad, with never a fence to block the movements of the half-wild cattle, every station had its coterie of brilliant horsemen. Horses were many, always fresh and ready for a set-to, and men had to ride. When one applied for a billet he was given a noted buckjumper to test his ability in the pigskin, and if he failed to sit him he was turned away with contempt. No other credentials were asked of him.

Australia can lay claim to the cleverest horsemen in the world, but you must go back on to the big cattle runs to find them in numbers. The riders have drifted farther out, passing and on with the march of civilisation. The Richmond and Clarence Rivers have always been noted for good horsemen, and likewise the Monaro country. When competing for buckjumping prizes at country shows it is common to see riders, seeking to excel one another, sitting bucking horses without bridle or saddle, having first thrown off the latter and then the former without dismounting.

And 'there were experts among women as well as among men', as Sorenson observed:

> I remember two sisters on the Richmond who could handle and ride a colt as well as the best—and though they used any kind of saddle, they mostly rode in the approved feminine fashion. Some men believe that a woman, jammed behind the horns of a side-saddle, should have less difficulty in sitting a buck than a man has in his saddle. But a little reflection will show that a woman, sitting comparatively on one side of the horse, hasn't the same advantage to follow its movements as the man has, who sits equilaterally and centrally over the animal. The sisters referred to rode bucks in either saddle.

The tea and scone ladies

Known affectionately rather than condescendingly as 'the tea and scone ladies', the Country Women's Association (CWA) is not only an icon of bush life but also one of Australia's most remarkable organisations. Established in 1922, the association grew rapidly, with branches in every state. The network and meetings filled a void in the lives of many rural women, fostering companionship, sharing and community work.

Early in World War II, the CWA of Tennant Creek, Northern Territory, played an important role in supporting the large numbers of troops travelling from Alice Springs to Darwin: 'This consists of tea, scones, rolls, cakes, sandwiches and other dainties made by branch members. Almost daily parties consisting of from 30 to 90 men have been catered for and to date thousands of men have been served and have greatly appreciated the hospitality of the women in the midst of their hot, dusty journey.'

Fundraising activities to support this work included soliciting donations from the local community, and running dances and bridge evenings at the CWA club room. The organisation also took part in the homefront activities supporting troops overseas.

But the CWA is not only a social network and comforts organisation, it has always been a lobby group, quietly advocating for rural causes and issues. One of its least-known but most important initiatives took place during the 1950s and 60s. In this period, CWA clubs in New South Wales sought to involve Aboriginal women in their activities. While indigenous women were not formally barred from membership of the CWA in that state, there was little incentive for them to join with white women in activities that were seen as largely irrelevant to their interests and concerns.

At first, the CWA hoped to encourage Aboriginal members into local clubs. But this developed into a push for separate clubs for Aboriginal women as these were felt to be better aligned with indigenous culture. There was a danger that this could be seen as segregation but, at the time, Aboriginal women were more likely to join a club of their own rather than one involved with the needs of white country women.

The first club specifically for Aboriginal women began at Boggabilla, New South Wales, in 1956, instigated by a male Aboriginal elder and a CWA member. Seeing an opportunity to develop a social life away from the usually remote stations where they lived and worked, Aboriginal women joined the branch.

In some of the more segregated towns, there was resistance to Aboriginal branches. At one branch on the mid-north coast, the progressive white CWA women joined the Aboriginal branch, leading community attitudes away from the prejudiced past.

Today, the CWA has updated the image many people may hold of the organisation. In 2017 the Queensland branch released its own perfume, featuring the bush scent of boronia, naturally. Planned government cuts to regional education ignited the first political action by the Western Australian CWA in the organisation's 94-year history. 'We're just angry,' said the state promotions coordinator. 'It's our kids and it's not fair.'

As well as making perfume and protesting, the CWA continues to make its legendary cookbook available in a form packaged by major publishers. The various branches of the organisation lead a busy life on social media and continue to do voluntary work for their communities and to support a diversity of charitable causes.

And, of course, the tea and scones are still being served wherever the CWA does its work. Here's their scone recipe—the proper one:

> Heat the oven to C 200 (400). You'll need three cups of sifted flour, one half to three-quarters of a teaspoon of baking powder and a pinch of salt. Top up half a cup of full cream milk with cream at room temperature. Mix the milk and cream with the flour, fold the dough lightly using a knife and empty onto a floured board. Give the dough a light knead and cut out the scones, patting them lightly into shape. Don't make them too big. Place in the oven and cook for 10–15 minutes.

I mean to get a wife!

From the earliest days of settlement, colonial Australia suffered an imbalance between the sexes. Particularly in the bush and outback, men had difficulty finding partners and in some parts of the country the problem of finding a marriage partner still exists. One favoured method was for bush bachelors to visit the city in search of a wife, a topic played for its humorous aspects in the ballad known as 'The Old Bullock Dray', which opens with a direct statement of the singer's intentions:

> Now the shearing is all over, and the wool is coming down,
> I mean to get a wife, my boys, when I go down to town,
> For everything has got a mate that brings itself to view,
> From the little paddy-melon to the big kangaroo.

The chorus offers an agreeable woman the opportunity to take her share of the assets, such as they are, in the form of 'the old bullock dray':

So roll up your blankets and let us make a push,
I'll take you up the country and show you the bush,
I'll be bound such a chance you won't get another day,
So roll up and take possession of the old bullock dray.

This ballad was popular in the bush from at least as early as the 1880s and probably dates from the period of 'free selection' when, in the wake of the goldrushes, colonial governments responded to pressure to open up the land. The gold era led to a massively expanded population in the eastern colonies, but most had not made their fortunes and needed employment. Offers of cheap rural land were made to those willing to take up agriculture or pastoralism. They and their families were expected to live and work on their 'selections', improve them and eventually to buy them from the government, creating what was often depicted as an Australian 'yeomanry', or rural middle-class of landholders, based on the British situation.

Most selectors struggled to make ends meet. Their blocks were often of poor quality and without access to adequate water or transportation to get any produce to markets. In some areas, settler life was no better than grinding poverty and was a contributing factor to rural crime, especially bushranging. It's little wonder that wives were in short supply, as evidenced by 'The Old Bullock Dray'.

The rest of the song elaborates on the less-than-appealing delights of marriage to a struggling free selector:

I'll teach you the whip and the bullocks how to flog,
You'll be my off-sider when we're fast in the bog,
Hitting out both left and right and every other way,
Making skin and blood and hair fly round the old bullock dray.

Good beef and damper, of that you'll get enough,
When boiling in the bucket such a walloper of duff,
Our mates, they'll all dance and sing upon our wedding day,
To the music of the bells around the old bullock dray.

There'll be lots of piccaninnies, you must remember that,
There'll be Buckjumping Maggie and Leather-belly Pat,
There'll be Stringybark Peggy and Green-eyed Mike,
Yes, my colonial, as many as you like.

The song ends with what the man believes to be an enticing picture of the idyllic life he imagines that he and his wife—together with their many children—might have if she does take possession of the old bullock dray:

Now that we are married and have children five times three,
No one lives so happy as my little wife and me,
She goes out a-hunting to while away the day,
While I take down the wool upon the old bullock dray.

It seems unlikely that the amorous male of this ballad attracted much interest in his offer.

*Photo by Arthur Upfield of camel turn-out at government Camel Station,
Western Australia, circa 1930.*

5

Wrongdoing

We'll take the whole damn country,
Says Dunn, Gilbert and Ben Hall.

'Dunn, Gilbert and Ben Hall'

We'll take the whole damn country

At one point in the 1860s, it was feared they might just do
that. Bushranger John Gilbert became the leader of a band of
Lachlan River wild boys that included, at various times, Frank
Gardiner, Ben Hall, John Dunn, John Vane and others. Together
and in one or other combinations, these men terrorised not only
their local area, the vast Central West of New South Wales, but
also threatened to attack the capital of Sydney. It was no idle
threat and people knew it.

Led by Frank Gardiner some of these men, including Gilbert,
had already carried off the nineteenth-century Australian
equivalent of the Great Train Robbery by holding up the gold
escort at Eugowra Rocks in June 1862. They got away with
large amounts of gold and cash. Gardiner went to Queensland
where he was later arrested. Ben Hall and others remained

in the Lachlan area and later began a crime spree unequalled until Ned Kelly and his gang raged through northeast Victoria and Jerilderie, New South Wales, in the late 1870s. Just as the Kellys posed a serious threat to law and order, the Gilbert gang quickly assumed the roles of local Robin Hoods, enjoying considerable sympathy and support from the poorer sections of the community.

Despite the trepidations and dire predictions appearing in the newspapers, locals delighted in the less violent antics of the gang. The outlaws would attend local dances and race meetings right under the noses of the police, including, on one occasion at the Wowingragong races, the district police inspector Sir Frederick Pottinger.

It began to look like Gilbert and company might be able to mount an attack on the capital when they occupied the town of Canowindra for three days and then raided the regional centre Bathurst in October 1863. A lively bush ballad, one of a number about the Gilbert gang, celebrated the Canowindra event:

> John Gilbert was a flash cove,
> And John O'Meally, too,
> With Ben and Burke and Johnny Vane
> They all were comrades true.
> They rode into Canowindra
> And gave a public ball,
> 'Roll up, roll up and have a spree',
> Says Gilbert and Ben Hall.
>
> They took possession of the town,
> Including public houses,
> And treated all the cockatoos
> And shouted for their spouses.
> They danced with all the pretty girls
> And held a carnival:
> 'We don't hurt them who don't hurt us',
> Says Gilbert and Ben Hall.

Then Miss O'Flanagan performed
In manner quite genteely,
Upon the grand pianner
For the bushranger O'Meally.
'Roll up, roll up, it's just a lark
For women, kids and all,
We'll rob the rich and help the poor',
Says Gilbert and Ben Hall.

Goulburn was reckoned to be the gang's next conquest:

'Next week we'll visit Goulburn
And clean the banks out there;
So if you see the peelers,
Just tell them to beware,
Some day to Sydney city
We mean to pay a call
And we'll take the whole damn country',
Says Dunn, Gilbert and Ben Hall.

These were the more publicity-friendly events among a long list of robberies, horse stealing, raids on stations and murders. The list of their crimes between 1862 and 1865 was lengthy, including more than forty armed robberies. Gilbert was outlawed with Dunn under the *Felon's Apprehension Act*, meaning they could be legally shot on sight with a price of 1000 pounds on each man's head. Gilbert was shot dead by a policeman at Binalong in May 1865. Dunn escaped but was later caught and eventually hanged. Ben Hall was betrayed and shot dead by a police party in May 1865, allegedly while he was asleep, at Goobang Creek outside Forbes.

Those deaths ended the threat, real or imagined, of Gilbert and his gang. Although some of them were murderers, their legend was strong in the bush. 'Banjo' Paterson, who grew up in the area and knew the strength of their popularity, wrote up the local version of the story in 'How Gilbert Died'. The poem ends with Gilbert trapped by police and facing up bravely to his inevitable fate as all outlaw heroes do in folklore:

> But Gilbert walked from the open door
> In a confident style and rash;
> He heard at his side the rifles roar,
> And he heard the bullets crash.
> But he laughed as he lifted his pistol-hand,
> And he fired at the rifle-flash.
>
> Then out of the shadows the troopers aimed
> At his voice and the pistol sound.
> With rifle flashes the darkness flamed—
> He staggered and spun around,
> And they riddled his body with rifle balls
> As it lay on the blood-soaked ground.
>
> There's never a stone at the sleeper's head,
> There's never a fence beside,
> And the wandering stock on the grave may tread
> Unnoticed and undenied;
> But the smallest child on the Watershed
> Can tell you how Gilbert died.

The death of Ben Hall

The death of bushranger Ben Hall in 1865 has always been controversial. Second only to Ned Kelly as a folk hero, Hall's real life and legend perfectly fitted the romanticised pattern of Robin Hood's. He was said to have been forced into outlawry by oppressive police actions, offered violence to no one unless provoked and was well thought of in the community of Lachlan River selectors to which he belonged. The manner of his death, betrayed and butchered by police bullets as he lay asleep, also contributed to his image as 'poor Ben Hall'. Long after the shooting and the parading of Hall's body strapped across a horse through the streets of Forbes, locals were giving their version of the story, as well as their interpretation of its significance.

John McGuire was married to the sister of Ben Hall's wife, Bridget Walsh, and was deeply knowledgeable about the activities of Hall and the other wild colonials he rode with, including Johnny Gilbert, John O'Meally and, of course, Frank Gardiner, mastermind of the Eugowra Rocks gold escort robbery of 1862. In 1911 McGuire's memoirs were published in the *Truth* newspaper:

I remember May 5, 1865. (I have particular occasion to remember this, for I was very sick at the time, and had been attended to by three doctors. I was suffering from a mishap caused from drawing water from a well on the Weogo Station). I was staying at the Montgomery Hotel, at the corner of Rankin-street, opposite William Jones' store. Jones was a lame man, and was known as 'Hoppy' Jones. I was sitting on the verandah front of the house on the morning of May 5, as above stated. I saw some troopers coming along down the hill with a black tracker from the Billabong. They passed the house where I was, Inspector Davidson leading the packhorse with apparently a very large swag on his back, with a black poncho thrown over it. I saw the legs of a man dangling down over the horse's shoulders. I soon discovered that it was Ben Hall, as I had seen his treacherous friend the day before (Coobong Mick).

The same evening Bill Hall (Ben's brother) came in to get his remains for to bury him. I went to the hotel where they took him to. I went to see him, and when he was stripped from head to foot he was a mass of gunshot wounds, principally the lower part of his body. Such a sight I never wished to see again, for he was literally torn to pieces like an old torn red rag, caused by the number of shots fired into him. We counted thirty-two gunshot wounds. This was the most cowardly and disgraceful business that could possibly be done by men who figured in society, as civilised men, especially to be called Englishmen. He must have been shot by five vollies after he was dead, for he offered no resistance, he being asleep at the time, for he was never a very desperate man.

One policeman, Jack Bowen, refused to fire, as he said, at a dead man. The diggers afterwards stuck to him for his humane treatment, and he was discharged from the force. The troopers and policemen must have been panic-stricken with fear. I moved from the place disgusted, with a horrible feeling for revenge. That was the last I saw of Hall. He was buried next day by the side of his brother-in-law, John Walsh (commonly called Warragal), and close to O'Mally [John O'Meally], whom Mr. Campbell shot close to Eugowra, close to where the gold escort was stuck up by the gang.

McGuire also provided one version of the story that evolved into the lyrics of a song that has since become famous as 'The Streets of Forbes':

Come all you highwaymen, a sorrowful tale I'll tell,
Concerning of a hero, who through misfortune fell;
His name it was Ben Hall, a chap of great renown,
He was hunted from his station, like a native dog shot down.
On the fifth of May, when parting from
His comrades all along the highway,
It was at the Wedding Mountains those three outlaws did agree
To give up bushranging, and cross the briny sea.
Then going to the billabong, which was his cruel downfall,
And riddled like a sieve was that hero, Ben Hall;
It was early in the morning, before the break of day,
The police, they surrounded him as fast asleep he lay.
The tracker, he was chosen to fire the fatal shot,
The rest then they rounded him to secure the prize they got;
They threw him on his horse, and strapped him like a swag,
And led him through the streets of Forbes to show the prize
    they had.

Hang him like a dog

The mob swore to 'hang him like a dog'. But what had so angered the Charters Towers' miners in November 1872? Butcher Adolphus Trevethan had put up the price of his meat.

There was already unhappiness among those seeking their fortunes at Charters Towers in northern Queensland. The goldrush was over-hyped by local businesses hoping for a retail bonanza and many hopefuls were broke. There were tensions over the management of the field by Commissioner W.S.E.M. Charters and disagreements over whether the township should be situated near the water or near the mines.

Attempts to raise the price of meat had already been foiled by threats from the miners. But the price cap did not last long. Trevethan jacked up his prices for a second time on Monday morning, November 2, and threatened to close his shop if the customers would not pay. It was his attitude as well as his prices that riled the miners. That night there was a 'roll-up', an assembly of miners who warned Trevethan to drop his prices. If not, they would destroy his shop the next night.

Unwisely, the butcher refused to reduce the price; it would now be 6 pence a pound instead of the 4 pence previously agreed.

On Tuesday night there was another roll-up outside Trevethan's closed and darkened shop. After some talk, cries were heard from the crowd: 'Pull the—house down; bring it down!' A rope was called for and passed around the wooden building. The crowd strained at the rope, which immediately snapped, probably cut. It was quickly readjusted, 'this time higher up, and after a few hearty pulls and a considerable amount of creaking and groaning on the part of the doomed house, down it came with a crash, amidst great applause. A lull now took place, and the rope was coiled for return, but some out-buildings were discovered, and after a little discussion they were next attacked, and brought down.'

Next morning the police made three arrests and placed

the men in the lock-up. The word was that the miners would forcibly release the arrested men on Wednesday night. Around 9 p.m. the miners assembled as threatened. The police were in the lock-up, armed. The police commissioner, Mr MacDonald, stepped out in front of the crowd and asked what they wanted:

> On a reply being made, he said he hoped those assembled would have more sense than to attempt a rescue. He very coolly told them that if they did so, they might expect the most serious results. He had been placed in his present position to maintain law and order, and to see that property was protected. It was, therefore, his duty to do so, and unless he performed his duty he was unfit for his position.

A voice in the crowd called out that the police were armed. MacDonald replied: 'Yes, the police have revolvers; but I hope you will give them no cause to use those revolvers.'

Many miners then stepped forward saying that they were as guilty as their mates, and they should all be locked up or the imprisoned miners freed. MacDonald coolly refused to comply with these demands.

Fortunately, the situation was defused when someone asked if the police would bail the miners until 10 a.m. on Friday. After a couple of minutes' consideration, MacDonald agreed and the men were freed to great applause. The miners repaired to the pub to celebrate and fixed another roll-up for 10 a.m. Monday morning when the bailed miners' case was tried.

As the case proceeded, there was so much noise from the 800-strong crowd that it was difficult to hear the witnesses. Then, just after 11 a.m., the noise increased and the crowd headed for a local hotel near which Trevethan was unwisely riding down the street.

Shortly after, a shot was heard. The mob was chasing Trevethan and wanted his blood: 'No sooner had he made his appearance, than the crowd began to hoot and groan at him. He rode on in defiance, and dismounting at the North Star, led his horse up to the verandah, and tried to fasten him to the verandah post. The horse, however, had become frightened, and he took him to the yard in the rear.'

By now the mob had swelled and continued cat-calling:

Trevethan turned on the crowd and presented his revolver, which he had drawn some time previous. Of course this only exasperated the men. Some of them, pushed on by those behind, jostled against him, and a bottle was thrown by someone in the crowd. This, if aimed at him, did not hit him. Trevethan again turned, and fired point blank into the crowd. A man close to Trevethan received a slight wound in the neck, the shot taking effect on King, who was immediately behind. The bullet entered his neck on the right side, and passed out behind, immediately above the blade-bone. King dropped at once, and a rush was made for Trevethan. His revolver was seized, and he was carried by the crush which followed into the street. Mr. Clohesy managed to reach him through the crowd, and after a great deal of difficulty and danger succeeded in wresting the revolver from Trevethan, who had retained hold of it, and was endeavoring to use it again. Owing to the crush little damage could be done to him, although many kicks and blows were aimed at him.

The police, assisted by Bishop Quinn, managed to get to Trevethan and take him back to the relative safety of the court house. 'He presented a most pitiable appearance; his head and face were bruised and bleeding, while from his rapid and difficult breathing it was evident he had just gone through a severe struggle.'

King was then carried into the court house, bleeding badly from his neck wound. They managed to staunch the blood flow and bandage him up. But the rumour spread rapidly through the crowd of miners that King was dead. The miners rushed the court house and 'swore they would have Trevethan out—that they would hang him like a dog, and for some minutes it looked very like as though they would be as good as their word. The police drew their pistols, but were driven back into the court, and things looked serious'.

The magistrate, Mr Jardine, pushed his way onto the crowded verandah and assured the angry miners that they had Trevethan in custody and that he would be charged with shooting King, who was alive. This, together with calming words from the bishop, satisfied the miners and the surly crowd broke up around 3 p.m.

The man after whom Charters Towers was partially named was, suspiciously it was suggested, taken ill the day the riots began. He was eventually removed from his position as a gold commissioner. Adolphus Trevethan never faced a court for the shooting of Joe King.

All in the family

The events in northeastern Victoria between 1878 and 1880 are well-known. A gang of bushrangers led by Edward 'Ned' Kelly defied and eluded the Victoria Police for almost two years, robbing banks and occupying homesteads, seemingly at will. The bushrangers had a lot of help from members of the community who shared their disaffection, justified or not, with the law and the social and economic circumstances of their time and place. Their greatest allies were the members of the Kelly family.

Ned Kelly's sister, Margaret or 'Maggie', was married to Bill Skillion (spelled Skillian here). He was in prison, along with matriarch of the family Ellen Kelly who had been arrested for the attempted murder of Constable Fitzpatrick, the confrontation that ignited the bushranging outbreak. Ned and younger brother Dan were outlawed and living in the bush with Steve Hart and Joe Byrne. As the eldest daughter, Maggie had to take over as head of the household and give what assistance she could to her brothers. Like other sympathisers she had some tricks to keep the police off the outlaws' trail, as Superintendent Hare, the man in charge of the pursuit, wrote many years later:

It was perfectly wonderful how all the trains were watched by Kelly sympathisers. You could tell them in a moment, they were to be seen on every railway station. It is not to be understood that all these men could communicate with the outlaws; my opinion is they trusted no one but their own blood relations, but the information concerning the police was sent to persons like Aaron Sherritt, there being perhaps three or four men in the whole district who could communicate to the outlaws' sisters any information that was obtained concerning the movements of the police. Hart had a brother and sister, and they were always on the move. Byrne had a brother and two or three sisters; the former was always riding about.

Maggie excelled in this game and was often seen riding through the bush at night, sometimes with large packs tied to her saddle:

A curious incident occurred one morning about daylight. Some policemen had got to Mrs Skillian's house about two o'clock in the morning, and were within a short distance of her place, and in some way she must have become aware of their presence there. She went into the paddock about three or four o'clock, caught her horse, saddled it and tied a large bundle on the saddle, mounted the horse, and started off towards the mountains, the three policemen following her, but without the slightest idea that she was aware of their presence. She made for a very steep gap in the mountains, the men following on foot, thinking they had a good thing on hand. The sun was nearly up when they reached the top of the gap, and the first thing they saw was Mrs Skillian sitting on a log facing them, and her two hands extended from her nose, and taking what is called a 'lunar' at them, with a grin of satisfaction on her face. They went up to examine the pack on the saddle, and found it to be an old table cloth wrapped up evidently to take a rise out of the police, who had been watching her.

Like all the sympathisers of her generation, Maggie was a superb horsewoman who used her skills to mislead and ridicule the police. Her mother, Ellen Kelly, had a different technique. Examined at her hearing for the attempted murder of the constable, Mrs Kelly was asked by the court:

> Having heard the evidence, do you wish to say anything in answer to the charge; you are not obliged to say anything unless you desire to do so; you have nothing to hope from any promise of favor, and nothing to fear from any threat which may have been held out to you, to induce you to make any admission or confession of your guilt; but whatever you say will be taken down in writing, and may be given in evidence against you upon your trial.
>
> Whereupon the said Ellen Kelly saith as follows: Nothing.

The Namoi horror

It began when a man's body was found in the Namoi River, near Wee Waa, in northwest New South Wales, in December 1908. The corpse was weighted down with the braking mechanism from a horse-drawn van and was not a pretty sight. Police went to the spot where the dead man, Johnston, had camped with his mate, Williams, a few days earlier.

According to a newspaper report: 'Hidden behind a log near the camp they found another piece of the brake, a pair of boots, a pair of trousers, and some clotted blood mixed with leaves. An attempt had been made to burn these things. A hammer with bloodstains on it was also found.'

Police were soon onto the dead man's companion and arrested Stanley Williams, who was about twenty years old, for the murder. He was carrying Johnston's bank book. Why one man murdered the other in such a bloody way for small gain and then concealed the body in such a grisly manner was a mystery. It seems that Williams was later tried and got off with ten years for manslaughter! If so, he must have had a good lawyer.

And that might have been the end of the story. Another bloody act of greed and violence in the bulging annals of bush crime. But then strange things began to happen.

A year or so later a correspondent to a local newspaper reported 'appalling happenings that have been experienced lately by persons living near to and strangers visiting the spot'. A local man, Arthur Perritt, camped, unwittingly, near the spot where Johnston's mate had beaten him to death. His horses 'showed a decided aversion to the locality' and broke from their tethers and ran away during the night. 'After passing a night of fearful sleeplessness, for which he could not in any way account', Perritt went in search of his frightened horses and found them some miles away.

On his next trip through the area, Perritt had to ask permission of local landowner Thomas Underwood if he could tether his horses in the paddock as they completely refused to return to the campsite. Underwood's own stock were also displaying a strong disinclination to go near the crime scene and a docile old horse his sons used to take them fishing 'smashed the winkers and galloped homeward in a perfect frenzy of snorting fear'.

One Sunday morning, the newspaper correspondent and Underwood visited the scene of the tragedy, which:

> . . . is a few yards from a steep bank of the river on the outer curve of a sweeping bend. An ideal camping ground, beautifully situated and well grassed with couch and trefoil. The exact position of the victim's tent was pointed out by Mr. Underwood, beneath a handsome well-grown Peruvian, the largest of a clump of similar trees which shelter the spot on the southwestern side. The position of the victim's head appeared to have been close to the tree, as he was supposed to be in the tent at the time of the tragedy, and after the crime had been discovered a patch of ground, about half the length of the dead man's body was found to have been saturated with blood. The tree was also dyed with blood and, even now, the dark sinister stain can be detected on the back of the tree trunk close to the ground. A startling fact that belies explanation is that although grass is growing luxuriantly, quite three inches long, all round the tree on three sides, that portion of the ground upon

which the victim is said to have been lying, is absolutely bare of grass, and Mr. Underwood says that no grass has grown there since the tragedy.

It was not only locals who reported incidents like these. People travelling through the district with no knowledge of the murder, camping in the pleasant riverside spot, also found their horses gone by morning. Just a few weeks earlier:

A man and his wife, strangers to the district, unyoked the horses near the spot and arranged to camp for the night. Soon after dark the horses were missing, and all through the night the woman went nearly raving mad, declaring, in her paroxysms of terror, that she was surrounded by, and struggling in, a sea of human blood. The poor man really thought his wife had lost her reason, and in the grey dawn made off to the nearest house he could find, which happened to be Mrs. M'Kenzie's. Here he related the experience of the night, stating that he was sure his wife was going to be very ill and asking for assistance. After being questioned as to where his camp was situated, the man was then told of the tragedy and he lost no time in vacating the dreaded spot. Immediately after leaving the place, his wife began to recover, and by nightfall on the succeeding day she was almost in her normal state of health, being utterly at a loss to account for her frenzy of the previous evening.

Another unwitting visitor camping at the spot declared 'he would refuse all the gold of the Empire rather than go through a similar experience again'. The visitor swore that 'all night long some unseen power was trying to pull the bed clothes off his bunk, and that terrific agitation was going on in the river, just below him, where, he has since found out, the body of Johnston, with the heavy brake bar attached to it, was hurled down the steep bank into the river'.

The unnamed correspondent, no slouch with words, concluded his report with a masterful flourish:

Any reader doubting the fear that dumb animals have for this lonely and beautiful spot on the river has only just to visit the place at sundown any day of the year, and he will see the stock, both cattle and horses, silently and swiftly hurrying away. As the shades of night close round the portion of the reserve, which is rapidly earning an unenviable reputation, when the extreme stillness of everything and the absence of all animal life is borne in upon the silent, lonely watcher, a chill of sheer fear creeps over him, and he wonders not that this portion of the river is spoken of in hushed whispers over the firesides of the homes of the settlers along the river.

Murder by the book

Arthur Upfield was the creator of the fictional detective Napoleon Bonaparte, known as 'Boney' (originally spelled 'Bony'). These who-dunnits were immensely popular from the 1920s to the 1950s and were usually set in the bush. One of Upfield's books featured a perfect murder, a crime that was copied in real life—and death. Not only that, but the author was himself implicated in the crime.

Born in Britain in 1890, Arthur came to Australia, reportedly at his father's strong suggestion, in 1911. He took immediately to bush life and became one of the many casual workers wandering around the country, drifting from job to job and getting by as best he could. He saw extensive service during World War I, then married and returned to Australia and his former life after the war.

He began writing in the 1920s and scored an early success with his part-Aboriginal Detective Inspector Napoleon Bonaparte of the Queensland Police. Boney was a highly efficient detective who used his tracking skills and knowledge of the country to hunt down malefactors and bring them to justice. In 1929, Upfield wanted to write another detective story in which there would be no body. He needed to devise a plot that included a very clever way to get rid of the evidence. But he was stumped. So he turned to his mates working with him as boundary riders along Western Australia's Number 1 Rabbit-proof Fence. Any ideas?

George Ritchie had one. Why not burn the body along with that of an animal, then get rid of any remaining metal pieces, such as belt buckles and boot nails, along with the bones in a vat of acid? Smash anything leftover into powder and let the wind blow it all away across the desert. Genius!

But there was a problem. This was too efficient. How would even the great Boney ever find the remains? This topic seems to have been the basis for widespread discussion among the few people inhabiting the rabbit-proof region, no doubt a welcome diversion from the usual basics of bush life. In any case, Ritchie's body disposal method soon became known to all.

From December 1929, local men began to disappear. This was not unusual, people came and went with the wind, so they were not missed. Until May 1930. In that month, New Zealander Louis Carron collected his final pay cheque at Wydgee Station and left in the company of a man known as 'Snowy Rowles'. Not too long after, Rowles cashed Carron's cheque in Paynesville. When Carron's friends did not hear from him as usual, they contacted the police.

Detectives arrived to investigate and soon heard about the perfect murder plot of Upfield's planned novel. The locals also remembered that two other men who had earlier vanished were last seen in the company of Snowy Rowles. It wasn't long before they found Carron's body at the 183-mile hut on the rabbit-proof fence. Rowles was arrested and tried for the murder of Carron. It was certain that he had also murdered the other men but he disposed of their bodies using the technique that George Ritchie originated and which was so lightheartedly discussed by all the locals. He failed to complete the process with Carron's body.

Among what was left of the dead New Zealander, police found a distinctive gold wedding ring that, at one time, had been poorly repaired. At the trial, it was the final piece of evidence identifying Carron and leading the jury to find Rowles guilty of murder. He was sentenced to death and hanged for Carron's murder in June 1931.

Upfield was called to give evidence at the trial and later did write his novel using the Ritchie body disposal method. It was called *The Sands of Windee*, published in 1931. A few years later he also wrote an account of the 'Murchison Murders', as they became known, some of the most unusual bush crimes ever committed—in reality or on paper.

Arthur Upfield went on to a career in journalism and wrote many more detective stories, becoming an international success. He said he was 'a story teller first and last' whose familiarity with the bush flavoured his stories. He died in 1964. The last of his twenty-nine Boney books was completed by other writers and published as *The Lake Frome Monster* in 1966. A successful television series based on the novels was produced in the 1970s and another in the 1990s, along with a telemovie. An enthusiastic fan base and committed publisher keeps some of the books in print today.

Murderer's bore

'Well, that's the end of it; those are old Bill's bones in the bore hole; I killed him but I am no murderer.' These contradictory words were spoken to a detective sergeant from Cunnamulla by Jim Callaghan on 5 December 1941. Callaghan would go on to describe in chilling detail how he had disposed of the body of his offsider, Bill Groves, at a bore on Boorara Station a few weeks earlier.

James Callaghan was sixty at the time of the incident. He had been sinking bore holes in the Great Artesian Basin underneath New South Wales and Queensland for almost forty years. It was hard, dirty work in often atrocious conditions, and did not pay well. He was receiving only 10 shillings a foot from the manager of Boorara and was deep in debt to the station and local businesses for supplies, equipment and costs.

William Groves had been working with Callaghan for the nine years he had plied his trade in Queensland and the two men were well known in the sparsely settled region. Callaghan said he was 'steady going and did not want to get away on a "booze" like a lot of other fellows'. Despite this, evidence was given at the trial that Groves was in fear of Callaghan. The reason was that he knew Callaghan was cheating Boorara Station. Instead of boring to a depth of over 900 feet, as he told the manager, Callaghan's rig had reached only half that deep.

When people began to notice that Callaghan's co-worker did not seem to be around anymore, Callaghan said he had paid Groves the 160 pounds of wages owed him and that he had taken off for Charleville. But Groves had earlier complained about his boss to a local union representative and told him, 'The old——is mad. He is always trying to quarrel with me. I would not trust him. He might do you in.'

The police were called in and at first Callaghan stuck to his story that Groves had left: 'I know you fellows think I have done something to old Bill, but you'll find him either in Charleville or Cunnamulla.' But later, under questioning, his defence and logic began to unravel and he told the police:

> I'm——if I know what to do about this. I can see now that my story has more holes in it than a sieve, and I'm trying to think of a way out. It is a serious business. The first barrel misfired and the second has got to be word perfect . . . You won't find old Bill. I know you fellows think I killed old Bill. I have thought out about three or four stories which I thought might be all right. I even put myself in the witness box and cross-examined myself and——myself every time.

By now, the police had discovered the remains of a fire near the drilling camp, including some burned buttons. They asked Callaghan to start up the sand pump in the bore, but he replied: 'You don't think I would put him in my drinking water and the water that you fellows have been using. Anyhow you have no chance of starting the engine. It hasn't been going for weeks, and is out of order.'

But the engine was found to be operational and Callaghan reluctantly lowered the sand pump into the bore hole. He tried to sabotage the proper workings of the machine but eventually the pump produced charcoal and bones. Knowing the game was up, Callaghan walked away and sat down, muttering that 'I must have been—well mad.' As more bits of burned bone came to the surface, he told his grisly tale:

> Old Bill and I got back here about 3 o'clock on the afternoon of November 7. Next day Bill put water into the truck's tank instead of benzine, and the truck would not go. After I found out what the trouble was we packed the tucker box and set out for Boodeheree bore. After crossing the creek he let the clutch in suddenly and chewed off a key in the drive shaft. We came home and I started to make a new key at the bench near the camp. I told Bill that he could not drive a wheel barrow, and he made a hit at me with his left fist, and I hit him with my left fist. His head bumped the anvil above his left ear and he became unconscious. He lived for about 20 minutes.

After that, Callaghan said he 'got panicky' and decided to get rid of the body:

> I built a fire at the back of the cooking galley and I burnt him. I started the fire about 10 o'clock that night, and at 3 o'clock next morning he was burnt practically to nothing I dumped some water on the coals and collected the bones at sunrise, and dropped them down the bore hole. I poured kerosene on the coals and what was left of some of the burnt bones, and let them burn to powder. A severe dust storm blew everything away. After that I burnt charcoal on two occasions where the fire was. Bill was wearing a pair of overalls and old slippers when I burnt him. I raked the buttons and other things from the fire, and put them in another fire. I was still panicky when I told the first story to the police.

Callaghan admitted that he broke up the burnt bones before he put them in the bore hole: 'I put old Bill on a heap of mulga about three or four feet high. There is a hell of a heat in mulga, and the bones were well and truly burnt. I cracked some by walking on them with my boots.'

When asked what he thought had caused Groves's death, Callaghan responded: 'I don't know. I suppose he cracked his skull.'

The hearing and subsequent trial was a sensation in Cunnamulla, and beyond. The chillingly familiar manner in which Callaghan described the disposal of his mate's remains was horrifying and widely reported in the press. Callaghan was found guilty in May 1941 and sentenced to life imprisonment. The grotesque murder was soon forgotten as the threat from the military forces of Japan became a reality after the bombing of Pearl Harbor barely six months later.

The conviction is said to be the first in Australia to be based completely on forensic evidence, and is still alive in local memory. Now known as 'Murder's Bore', the crime scene features in the outback eco-tourism business of Kilcowera Station.

A dingo's got my baby

The newborn baby was found lying across the overland railway line near Carrabin in Western Australia. It was the height of summer in January 1925 and the child was thought to have lain there for up to twenty-four hours. He was sunburned, wounded on one ankle and had suffered a broken leg. The area was a known dingo haunt and it was assumed that the wound had been inflicted by a wild dog dragging the child from the sun-baked ground to the relative shade of the rail line. There was no other explanation for such a miraculous survival. It was assumed that the baby had been born on the train and flung out of a window.

The State Children's Department took the child into care and presented him as a neglected child at the Children's Court a month later. Department Inspector, Mrs MacLagan, held the infant in her arms and explained how they had come to name him Raymond St. John Weston:

> The nurse who attended him in hospital hit upon Raymond, because he was able to withstand the rays of the hot sun. Following the same line, another hit upon St. John, because of the belief on the part of many that the Apostle of that name was able to look at the sun without blinking. The surname was suggested by the proximity of the mining centre of Westonia to the spot where the newborn babe was found.

The police had been unable to trace Raymond's mother and he was committed into the care of the state.

More than fifty years later another story about a dingo and a baby plunged the country into rabid division and our most notorious travesty of justice.

On 17 August 1980, the campsite at Uluru (then known as Ayer's Rock) was busy with travellers preparing evening meals. The Chamberlain family were cooking theirs and nine and a half weeks old Azaria was in the tent not far away.

Then Lindy Chamberlain screamed: 'A dingo's got my baby!'

A desperate hunt for the baby and dingo found nothing definite but a nation-wide debate erupted about whether a wild dog could or would take a human child. Those who believed it to be possible, even likely, lined up against those who thought it was impossible. 'The dingo did it' became a catch-phrase for those who did not accept the other possibility, that Lindy Chamberlain had murdered her daughter in the family car and then, somehow, disposed of the body.

A coronial inquest into the disappearance was opened in December of the same year and in February 1981 concluded that a dingo or wild dog took Azaria from the tent, not a human. Later that year, the Northern Territory administration initiated another police investigation involving new evidence and in November the findings of the first inquest were quashed.

A new inquest began in December in Alice Springs and in February 1982 Lindy Chamberlain was committed for trial for the murder of Azaria, and her husband Michael Chamberlain was committed as an accessory after the fact. The trial began in Darwin in September with Lindy Chamberlain seven months pregnant. In October, both Michael and Lindy were found guilty. Lindy was imprisoned for life and Michael received an eighteen-month suspended sentence. In November Lindy gave birth to a baby girl, Kahlia, in Darwin Hospital and was released on bail pending her appeal to the Supreme Court, which rejected the appeal in April 1983 and sent her back to jail. Lindy Chamberlain's subsequent appeal to the High Court was rejected in February 1984.

In November 1985, the Northern Territory government refused to order a judicial inquiry into the Chamberlain case in defiance of mounting public pressure, and later that month rejected an application for the release of Lindy Chamberlain on licence. In February 1986, a baby's knitted matinee jacket, believed to be Azaria's, was discovered at Uluru and four days later the Northern Territory government released Lindy after remitting her life sentence. The Chamberlains were exonerated by subsequent inquiries, including a Royal Commission, though have not, as yet, received an apology from the Northern Territory government.

Throughout these momentous events, the popular image of the dingo was discussed more intensely than ever before. On the one hand, the dingo is seen as a lean marauder, able to survive in the harshest environment. In folk speech, a 'dingo's breakfast' is 'a piss and a good look round'. But on the other hand, the dingo's cunning, stealth and killing efficiency, well-known to pastoralists, are captured in insults like 'He's a low dingo', meaning that the person described should not be trusted under any circumstances. These contradictory views were expressed in a seemingly endless circulation of dingo jokes related to the Azaria case. A form of 'sick joke', in which serious matters like death are treated for laughs, they reveal the deep divisions and discomforts brought about in Australian society by the outback events of 1980 and after.

These jokes were swapped at a party in an inner-city Sydney suburb in January 1981, during the period of the Azaria Chamberlain inquest at Alice Springs:

What's worse than a bull in a china shop?
A dingo in a tent.

What kind of droppings have pink booties?
A dingo's.

In October 1981 this variant of the first quoted dingo joke appeared: 'What's worse than a bull in a china shop? A dingo in a maternity ward.' Together with: 'What runs round Ayers Rock on its back legs with its arms in the air? A dingo doing a victory lap.' and 'How should you bring up children? Kick a dingo in the guts.'

In November of the same year, this joke significantly linked two naggingly persistent mysteries of the recent Australian past: 'Have you heard that they've re-opened the Harold Holt case? They're looking for a dingo wearing a wetsuit and flippers.'

When the Australian media announced the news of the imminent arrival of an heir to the British throne in late 1981, this joke appeared: 'What is the definition of anticipation? The dingo sitting on the steps of Buckingham Palace.'

As the trial of Lindy and Michael Chamberlain for the murder of their daughter proceeded, a number of fresh jokes were created to suit the occasion and most of the old ones continued to circulate as well. Among the new items were:

Did you hear the bookmaker's odds on the trial?
1/10 Lindy
1/1 Michael
10/1 Kids
20/1 Dingo
500/1 Suicide

When the news was revealed that Lindy Chamberlain was pregnant, the jokes adapted: 'A rumour has spread through Darwin that Lindy Chamberlain is not really pregnant—she just swallowed the evidence.'

And soon after the child was born in jail: 'Did you hear what Lindy named her new son? Mandingo.' (A reference to a telemovie then screening, based on the book of the same name.)

In 2012 the Northern Territory Coroner found that a dingo, or dingoes, did indeed take baby Azaria from the family tent. Despite many definitive legal declarations of innocence, some still believed Lindy Chamberlain murdered Azaria. Some still do. Even today, the case and its consequences are considered to be of profound national significance. Some of Azaria's clothing is held by the National Museum of Australia. The National Library of Australia also holds a large collection of letters sent to Lindy Chamberlain during the numerous legal proceedings she endured. The case has also generated many books and articles, an opera and the Hollywood movie, *Evil Angels*, based on the book of the same name by John Bryson.

Azaria Chamberlain's body has never been found.

*Australia's 'bard of the bush', Henry Lawson,
in Sydney, 1915.*

6

Where the dead men lie

Out on the wastes of the Never Never—
That's where the dead men lie!
There where the heat-waves dance forever—
That's where the dead men lie!

'Where the Dead Men Lie', Barcroft Boake, 1891

Unhallowed graves

The 'perish' has always been a constant possibility in the bush and outback. Even today people are frequently 'bushed' or lost while holidaying or travelling. Mostly they are rescued, but not always.

In 1891, the bushman, tobacco addict and emerging poet, Barcroft Boake, published a near-apocalyptic poem on the horrors of death in the emptiness. Even today it makes for confronting reading and conveys the author's over-intense involvement with his topic. Boake was born in Sydney and received an excellent education, but at the age of eighteen he rejected city life and began working in the bush as a surveyor's assistant. His experiences in the Snowy Mountains and as a drover and boundary rider in the Monaro district and in western Queensland familiarised him with the perils of bush life and death. He eventually found a way to get them down on paper:

Out on the wastes of the Never Never—
That's where the dead men lie!
There where the heat-waves dance forever—
That's where the dead men lie!
That's where the Earth's loved sons are keeping
Endless tryst: not the west wind sweeping
Feverish pinions can wake their sleeping—
Out where the dead men lie!

Where brown Summer and Death have mated—
That's where the dead men lie!
Loving with fiery lust unsated—
That's where the dead men lie!
Out where the grinning skulls bleach whitely
Under the saltbush sparkling brightly;
Out where the wild dogs chorus nightly—
That's where the dead men lie!

Deep in the yellow, flowing river—
That's where the dead men lie!
Under the banks where the shadows quiver—
That's where the dead men lie!
Where the platypus twists and doubles,
Leaving a train of tiny bubbles.
Rid at last of their earthly troubles—
That's where the dead men lie!

East and backward pale faces turning—
That's how the dead men lie!
Gaunt arms stretched with a voiceless yearning—
That's how the dead men lie!
Oft in the fragrant hush of nooning
Hearing again their mother's crooning,
Wrapt for aye in a dreamful swooning—
That's how the dead men lie!

Only the hand of Night can free them—
That's when the dead men fly!
Only the frightened cattle see them—
See the dead men go by!
Cloven hoofs beating out one measure,
Bidding the stockmen know no leisure—
That's when the dead men take their pleasure!
That's when the dead men fly!

Ask, too, the never-sleeping drover:
He sees the dead pass by;
Hearing them call to their friends—the plover,
Hearing the dead men cry;
Seeing their faces stealing, stealing,
Hearing their laughter, pealing, pealing,
Watching their grey forms wheeling, wheeling
Round where the cattle lie!

Strangled by thirst and fierce privation—
That's how the dead men die!
Out on Moncygrub's farthest station—
That's how the dead men die!
Hard-faced greybeards, youngsters callow;
Some mounds cared for, some left fallow;
Some deep down, yet others shallow.
Some having but the sky.

Moncygrub, as he sips his claret,
Looks with complacent eye
Down at his watch-chain, eighteen carat—
There, in his club, hard by:
Recks not that every link is stamped with
Names of the men whose limbs are cramped with
Too long lying in grave-mould, cramped with
Death where the dead men lie.

('Moncygrub' is a made-up name, denoting the grasping squatter whose wealth and position depends on the labour and, in this case, the death of the bushman.)

Boake was one of the writers of the late nineteenth century who contributed to the powerful idea that the bush, its people and lifestyles reflected and shaped a characteristically Australian identity. His relatively few poems are all on bush themes and he had long hoped to compose this particular poem, as he wrote in a letter:

If I could only write it, there is a poem to be made out of the back-country. Some man will come yet who will be able to grasp the romance of Western Queensland . . . For there is a romance, though a grim one—a story of drought and flood, fever and famine, murder and suicide, courage and endurance . . . I wonder if a day will come when these men will rise up—when the wealthy man . . . shall see pass before him a band of men—all of whom died in his service, and whose unhallowed graves dot his run— the greater portion hollow, shrunken, burning with the pangs of thirst.

Barcroft Boake suffered from 'melancholia', or what we would call depression, all his life. This made him what was often called in those days 'unsteady' and his affliction undermined his commitment and focus. As the editor of his posthumously collected verse, A.G. Stephens, wrote:

His temperament was sluggish. He was a dreamer and procrastinator—quick to perceive, slow to act—executing task-work reluctantly and mechanically, though developing plenty of fitful energy when spurred by appropriate stimuli. Of this dreaming habit, apart from his general delicacy of constitution, the chief curse was a weak, slow-beating heart—often met among children reared in the moist and depressing climate of Sydney. And Boake further slowed his slow heart by the excessive use of tobacco.

Faced with unemployment and a host of family problems, Boake hanged himself at Middle Harbour with a stock whip in 1892. He was twenty-six.

The tree from which the poet was found hanging became known locally as 'the hanging tree'. It was replaced with a new tree, planted in 1991 or 92 by the North Shore Historical Society and the local council. It grows on what is now a roundabout on Cammeray Road and Cowdroy Avenue, Cammeray, and bears a commemorative plaque which tells the reader that Barcroft Boake is buried 'not far from here at St Thomas Cemetery, West Street, Crows Nest'.

A lady explorer

She rode from Normanton in northern Queensland to Darwin—side-saddle. Her name was Emily Caroline Creaghe, Australia's only female explorer. The year was 1883 and Caroline, as she was known, accompanied her husband on an expedition led by the explorer Ernest Favenc designed to extend knowledge of this then little-known part of the country. Favenc's wife also accompanied the group at first, but became ill and had to return to Sydney before the adventure began.

Caroline kept a diary in which she recorded experiences and reactions. The journey finally began in April. The small party was immediately tormented by flies which were 'something dreadful' and suffered beetles in plague proportions. In the searing heat, it did not take long for the rations to be reduced to 'nasty, dirty, hairy, dried salt beef, dark brown sugar (half dust) and hard damper'.

At Carl Creek Station, Caroline was introduced to the ways of the frontier. A Mr and Mrs Shadforth lived there with ten children in a four-roomed hut. Many of the chores were performed by Aboriginal women and while Caroline was there she witnessed Mr Shadworth's introduction of a new servant to the enterprise: 'He put a rope around the gin's neck and dragged her along on foot, he was riding. This seems to be the usual method. They call her Bella. She is chained to a tree and is not to be loosed until they think she is tamed.'

After this sort of treatment, it is not surprising that a white man was found killed by Aborigines. Caroline and her companions were armed with pistols and rifles in case of attack, though the Aborigines they soon encountered as the days became even warmer were not hostile. They had never seen white people before.

By mid-May, the meat was all gone and the party had been without water for more than two days. The horses were knocked up and one had to be shot. They were soon out of food altogether and in danger of dying. Just in time they came across the Overland Telegraph wire linking the south of the continent with the north, not far from Powell's Creek. They recuperated here for some days then pushed on north along the secure route of the 'OT'. From here, their journey was relatively comfortable and safe, although they passed through much sparsely inhabited country where those few white people living there had frequently not seen another white person for years.

Caroline's diary expressed her enjoyment of much of this part of the expedition and of their time in Darwin after they reached it in August. She commented on the multicultural character of the town and enjoyed socialising with the leading citizens. A ship took them back to Queensland.

Caroline Creaghe's journey stands out from the otherwise completely masculine history of Australian exploration.

Despite publication of her diary in 2004, her unique achievement remains barely known.

The lost boy

The annals of the bush are full of lost children. Sometimes these tales end well, often they do not. In a section of Joseph Furphy's great novel, *Such Is Life*, the characters are sharing stories of children lost in the bush. Stevenson, a tank sinker, tells his sad tale:

> There was a pause, broken by Stevenson, in a voice that brought constraint on us all:
>
> 'Bad enough to lose a youngster for a day or two, and find him alive and well; worse, beyond comparison, when he's found dead; but the most fearful thing of all is for a youngster to be lost in the bush, and never found, alive or dead. That's what happened to my brother Eddie, when he was about eight year old. You must remember it, Thompson?'
>
> 'Wasn't my father out on the search?' replied Thompson. 'Tom's father, too. You were living on the Upper Campaspe.'
>
> 'Yes,' continued Stevenson, clearing his throat; 'I've been thinking over it every night for these five-and-twenty years, and it seems to me the most likely thing that could have happened to him was to get jammed in a log, like that other little chap. Then after five years, or ten years, or twenty years, the log gets burned, and nobody notices a few little bones, crumbled among the ashes.
>
> 'I was three or four years older than Eddie,' he resumed hoarsely 'and he just worshipped me. I had been staying with my uncle in Kyneton for three months, going to school; and Eddie was lost the day after I came home. We were out, gathering gum—four of us altogether—about a mile and a half from home; and I got cross with the poor little fellow, and gave him two or three hits; and he started home by himself, crying. He turned round and looked at me, just before he got out of sight among the trees; and that was the last that was ever seen of him alive or dead. My God!

When I think of that look, it makes me thankful to remember that every day brings me nearer to the end. The spot where he turned round is in the middle of a cultivation-paddock now, but I could walk straight to it in the middle of the darkest night.

'Yes; he started off home, crying. We all went the same way so soon afterward that I expected every minute to see him on ahead. At last we thought we must have passed him on the way. No alarm yet, of course; but I was choking with grief, to think how I'd treated the little chap; so I gave Maggie and Billy the slip, and went back to meet him. I knew from experience how glad he would be.

'Ah well! the time that followed is like some horrible dream. He was lost at about four in the afternoon; and there would be about a dozen people looking for him, and calling his name, all night. Next day, I daresay there would be about thirty. Next morning, my father offered £100 reward for him, dead or alive; and five other men guaranteed £10 each. Next day, my father's reward was doubled; and five other men put down their names for another £50. Next day, Government offered £200. So between genuine sympathy and the chance of making £500, the bush was fairly alive with people; and everyone within thirty miles was keeping a look-out.

'No use. The search was gradually dropped, till no one was left but my father. Month after month, he was out every day, wet or dry, and my mother waiting at home, with a look on her face that frightened us—waiting for the news he might bring. And, time after time, he took stray bones to the doctor; but they always turned out to belong to sheep, or kangaroos, or some other animal. Of course, he neglected the place altogether, and it went to wreck; and our cattle got lost; and he was always meeting with people that sympathised with him, and asked him to have a drink—and you can hardly call him responsible for the rest.

'However, on the anniversary of the day that Eddie got lost, my mother took a dose of laudanum; and that brought things to a head. My father had borrowed every shilling that the place would carry, to keep up the search; and there was neither interest nor principal forthcoming, so the mortgagee—Wesleyan minister, I'm sorry to say—had to sell us off to get his money. We had three uncles; each of them took one of us youngsters; but they could do nothing for my father. He hung about the public-houses, getting lower and lower, till he was found dead in a stable, one cold winter morning. That was about four years after Eddie was lost.'

Stevenson paused, and restlessly changed his position, then muttered, in evident torture of mind:

'Think of it! While he was going away, crying, he looked back over his shoulder at me, without a word of anger; and he walked up against a sapling, and staggered—and I laughed!—Great God!—I laughed!'

That was the end of the tank-sinker's story; and silence fell on our camp.

The great heat of '96

It was 120 Fahrenheit (50 degrees Celsius) in the shade at Bourke. There was 'fearful heat' at Cunnamulla and the papers ran articles advising on how to avoid 'heat apoplexy'. The blast of heat that scorched much of southern Australia in the summer of 1896 may have been worse than Victoria's Black Saturday fires of 2009. It certainly affected a much larger area of the country and killed more than four hundred people.

In South Australia, it was 'Too hot to read, too hot to eat, and too hot to sleep'. By the time those words appeared in print in February, the worst was over, though it was still blisteringly hot in much of Western Australia, Victoria, New South Wales and Queensland. The heatwave seemed endless.

Through it the papers frequently published death rolls. Only fifty-one years of age, the publican of the Royal Hotel in Singleton dropped dead. A 26-year-old in Jerilderie died and six children in Goulburn were dead by mid-January. A man cut his own throat in the bush near Collarenabri, thought to have been driven mad by the raging heat. A young girl died at Mount Hope, and at least a dozen fatalities were reported in and around Bourke. Five people died on one day in Wilcannia and there were more in Angledool, Moree, Condoblin, Crookwell and Young. A woman was 'brought to the Bulli Hospital in a demented condition, suffering from sunstroke. She was tramping the roads, with her husband, two days before, when she was prostrated by a sunstroke. Her husband carried her through all the sweltering heat to Bulli, taking two days over the journey'.

These and many more tragedies generated a growing sense of panic as the unrelenting heat burned on, day after day. People sought relief by escaping in special trains to cooler climes in the Snowy Mountains and the Riverina. But it was too late for some. A young boy sent to the mountains died just as the train arrived there. More trains were provided for those desperate to survive.

And still the deaths by heat were tolled through the columns of local and city newspapers. Eight dead in Wilcannia, three in White Cliffs, one in each of Gnalata, Wonnamint and Tongo. Old Larry Keogh was found dead in his hut near Goodooga. A hairdresser, too hot to work, shot himself in the chest. By the end of the month, the papers were reporting that the inland regions of the southern colonies were 'under fire', as yet another heatwave rolled through. There were occasional cool changes but these only made the return of the heat and the violent electrical and dust storms that accompanied it even less bearable.

More deaths were reported in Brewarrina, where even at midnight on 22 January it was still 109 degrees Fahrenheit. More people died there. The postmaster at Cunnamulla reported on 23 January:

> The heat of the past month here has been unprecedented in my experience of nearly fifteen years' residence, both for intensity and continuance. Observations taken at Grosvenor Bank, situated immediately over one of the main holes of the Warrego River, show a shade maximum temperature of over 110 deg. daily since the 31st December, except on three days, when 106 deg.

was touched or exceeded. Yesterday 120.5 deg. was reached, and today 123 deg., the average daily temperature from the Ist instant exceeding 114 deg. . . . Much sickness prevails, and heat prostration is common, four fatal cases having occurred within the week. All fruit crops in the Chinese gardens, and all the grapes, melons, peaches, and figs are destroyed. Cool water is unobtainable for drinking purposes, the canvas water bag proving ineffectual in the temperature prevailing. In rain water tanks placed under the house with spouting, as commonly seen in Brisbane, the water acquires a temperature of 103 deg. At present time of writing (3.00 p.m.) the thermometer stands at 112.5 in my office.

By this time more than forty people were declared dead of heatstroke in Bourke alone. Hospital wards began to fill with victims of sunstroke or fever. Rivers stopped running, crops withered and stock perished in vast numbers and as the water supplies ran low the risk of typhoid increased. Farmers and graziers and their stock and crops suffered badly: 'the feed being withered up, tanks dry, and horses, sheep, and cattle dying by hundreds, and many settlers' homes have been destroyed by the bush fires. Never in the history of New South Wales has such a continuance of fierce heat been known.'

Cities and towns also suffered, of course, but the effects of the heatwave were more savage in the bush. Towns and regions continued to report oppressive and sometimes deadly heat until temperatures began to ease in February.

Nobody knew what caused the scorching weather of 1896. It was not global warming, but the inferno was a frightening glimpse of what summer in Australia might look like if climate science turns out to be correct. The relative severity of the event and the accuracy of temperature measurement at the time has been the source of some controversy in the debate over climate change. While it seems certain that there have been warmer years, the great heat of '96 was one of the most disastrous in terms of lives lost and the amount of crops and stock destroyed.

The union buries its dead

Henry Lawson was the great sardonic bard of the bush. His determinedly unromantic stories and verse capture the often-harsh realities of those who lived and died making ends meet and getting by as best they could. In this sparse tale, he most perfectly depicts the taciturn mood of the bushman:

While out boating one Sunday afternoon on a billabong across the river, we saw a young man on horseback driving some horses along the bank. He said it was a fine day, and asked if the Water was deep there. The joker of our party said it was deep enough to drown him, and he laughed and rode farther up. We didn't take much notice of him.

Next day a funeral gathered at a corner pub and asked each other in to have a drink while waiting for the hearse. They passed away some of the time dancing jigs to a piano in the bar parlour. They passed away the rest of the time skylarking and fighting.

The defunct was a young Union labourer, about twenty-five, who had been drowned the previous day while trying to swim some horses across a billabong of the Darling.

He was almost a stranger in town, and the fact of his having been a Union man accounted for the funeral. The police found some Union papers in his swag, and called at the General Labourers' Union Office for information about him. That's how we knew. The secretary had very little information to give. The departed was a 'Roman,' and the majority of the town were otherwise—but Unionism is stronger than creed. Liquor, however, is stronger than Unionism; and, when the hearse presently arrived, more than two-thirds of the funeral were unable to follow.

The procession numbered fifteen, fourteen souls following the broken shell of a soul. Perhaps not one of the fourteen possessed a soul any more than the corpse did—but that doesn't matter.

Four or five of the funeral, who were boarders at the pub, borrowed a trap which the landlord used to carry passengers to and from the railway station. They were strangers to us who were on foot, and we to them. We were all strangers to the corpse.

A horseman, who looked like a drover just returned from a big trip, dropped into our dusty wake and followed us a few hundred yards, dragging his packhorse behind him, but a friend made wild and demonstrative signals from a hotel veranda—hooking at the air in front with his right hand and jobbing his left thumb over his shoulder in the direction of the bar—so the drover hauled off and didn't catch up to us any more. He was a stranger to the entire show.

We walked in twos. There were three twos. It was very hot and dusty; the heat rushed in fierce dazzling rays across every iron roof and light-coloured wall that was turned to the sun. One or two pubs closed respectfully until we got past. They closed their bar doors and the patrons went in and out through some side or back entrance for a few minutes. Bushmen seldom grumble at an inconvenience of this sort, when it is caused by a funeral. They have too much respect for the dead.

On the way to the cemetery we passed three shearers sitting on the shady side of a fence. One was drunk—very drunk. The other two covered their right ears with their hats, out of respect for the departed—whoever he might have been—and one of them kicked the drunk and muttered something to him.

He straightened himself up, stared, and reached helplessly for his hat, which he shoved half off and then on again. Then he made a great effort to pull himself together—and succeeded. He stood up, braced his back against the fence, knocked off his hat, and remorsefully placed his foot on it—to keep it off his head till the funeral passed.

A tall, sentimental drover, who walked by my side, cynically quoted Byronic verses suitable to the occasion—to death—and asked with pathetic humour whether we thought the dead man's ticket would be recognized 'over yonder.' It was a G.L.U. ticket, and the general opinion was that it would be recognized.

Presently my friend said: 'You remember when we were in the boat yesterday, we saw a man driving some horses along the bank?'

'Yes.'

He nodded at the hearse and said 'Well, that's him.'

I thought awhile.

'I didn't take any particular notice of him,' I said. 'He said something, didn't he?'

'Yes; said it was a fine day. You'd have taken more notice if you'd known that he was doomed to die in the hour, and that those were the last words he would say to any man in this world.'

'To be sure,' said a full voice from the rear. 'If ye'd known that, ye'd have prolonged the conversation.'

We plodded on across the railway line and along the hot, dusty road which ran to the cemetery, some of us talking about the accident, and lying about the narrow escapes we had had ourselves. Presently someone said: 'There's the Devil.'

I looked up and saw a priest standing in the shade of the tree by the cemetery gate.

The hearse was drawn up and the tail-boards were opened. The funeral extinguished its right ear with its hat as four men lifted the coffin out and laid it over the grave. The priest—a pale, quiet young fellow—stood under the shade of a sapling which grew at the head of the grave. He took off his hat, dropped it carelessly on the ground, and proceeded to business. I noticed that one or two heathens winced slightly when the holy water was sprinkled on the coffin. The drops quickly evaporated, and the little round black spots they left were soon dusted over; but the spots showed, by contrast, the cheapness and shabbiness of the cloth with which the coffin was covered. It seemed black before; now it looked a dusky grey.

Just here man's ignorance and vanity made a farce of the funeral. A big, bull-necked publican, with heavy, blotchy features, and a supremely ignorant expression, picked up the priest's straw hat and held it about two inches over the head of his reverence during the whole of the service. The father, be it remembered, was standing in the shade. A few shoved their hats on and off uneasily, struggling between their disgust for the living and their respect for the dead. The hat had a conical crown and a brim sloping down all round like a sunshade, and the publican held it with his great red claw spread over the crown. To do the priest justice, perhaps he didn't notice the incident. A stage priest or parson in the same position might have said, 'Put the hat down, my friend; is not the memory of our departed brother worth more than my complexion?' A wattle-bark layman might have expressed himself in stronger language, none the less to the point. But my priest seemed unconscious of what was going on. Besides, the publican was a great and important pillar of the church. He couldn't, as an ignorant and conceited ass, lose such a good opportunity of asserting his faithfulness and importance to his church.

The grave looked very narrow under the coffin, and I drew a breath of relief when the box slid easily down. I saw a coffin get stuck once, at Rookwood, and it had to be yanked out with difficulty, and laid on the sods at the feet of the heart-broken relations, who howled dismally while the grave-diggers widened the hole. But they don't cut contracts so fine in the West. Our grave-digger was not altogether bowelless, and, out of respect for that human quality described as 'feelin's,' he scraped up some light and dusty soil and threw it down to deaden the fall of the clay lumps on the coffin. He also tried to steer the first few shovelfuls gently down against the end of the grave with the back of the shovel turned outwards, but the hard, dry Darling River clods rebounded and knocked all the same. It didn't matter much—nothing does. The fall of lumps of clay on a stranger's coffin doesn't sound any different from the fall of the same things on an ordinary wooden box—at least I didn't notice anything awesome or unusual in the sound; but, perhaps, one of us—the most sensitive—might have been impressed by being reminded of a burial of long ago, when the thump of every sod jolted his heart.

I have left out the wattle—because it wasn't there. I have also neglected to mention the heart-broken old mate, with his grizzled head bowed and great pearly drops streaming down his rugged cheeks. He was absent—he was probably 'Out Back.' For similar reasons I have omitted reference to the suspicious moisture in the eyes of a bearded bush ruffian named Bill. Bill failed to turn up, and the only moisture was that which was induced by the heat. I have left out the 'sad Australian sunset' because the sun was not going down at the time. The burial took place exactly at midday.

The dead bushman's name was Jim, apparently; but they found no portraits, nor locks of hair, nor any love letters, nor anything of that kind in his swag—not even a reference to his mother; only some papers relating to Union matters. Most of us didn't know the name till we saw it on the coffin; we knew him as 'that poor chap that got drowned yesterday.'

'So his name's James Tyson,' said my drover acquaintance, looking at the plate.

'Why! Didn't you know that before?' I asked.

'No; but I knew he was a Union man.'

It turned out, afterwards, that J.T. wasn't his real name—only 'the name he went by.' Anyhow he was buried by it, and most of the 'Great Australian Dailies' have mentioned in their brevity columns that a young man named James John Tyson was drowned in a billabong of the Darling last Sunday.

We did hear, later on, what his real name was; but if we ever chance to read it in the 'Missing Friends Column,' we shall not be able to give any information to heart-broken mother or sister or wife, nor to anyone who could let him hear something to his advantage—for we have already forgotten the name.

The Never Never

The seemingly endless distance beyond the narrow band of coastal settlement has been called the 'Never Never' probably since the 1850s when the phrase begins to appear in newspapers. It is a term that well captures the isolation and emptiness of the outback and has often been used in literature. Before that, it was in the mouths of colonists. One gave some idea of the problems of Never Never life in a letter to the editor of a Queensland newspaper in 1861. This man signed himself 'Superintendent' and was probably the manager of a station. He was pretty cranky:

SIR,—I hope you will take up the cudgels on behalf of us unhappy outcasts situated on the wrong side of the Balonne River, opposite Surat. It is now two months since I and my employer arrived here from Ipswich; we have sent to Ipswich on three several [*sic*] occasions. I also sent one letter to the D. D. G., but suppose as we have received no answer that the letter never came to hand. Are we not men and brothers in the Never Never Country? We hear floating reports which, I expect, are shouted across the rivers, and carried up here by wandering travellers, of what is going on in the civilized districts, but letters or newspapers we never get.

Seriously speaking, the mail service is a perfect farce. I have here a letter dated September 10th from Dalby, but no Ipswich letters, although I am sure there have been letters sent, and week after week we are put to the trouble of sending to Surat for no purpose. The answer is 'the mail has not arrived'.

And on the superintendent's letter went:

There are people on stations here, literally without flour, tea or sugar, owing to the drays being delayed through the disgraceful state of the roads and rivers, the latter being frequently up, the drays have to wait on the bank until they go down again . . . It was said some time since that if the English were to evacuate India they would leave nothing but their empty beer bottles behind them to mark that they had ever been there, but if we were to leave this country, owing to the parsimony, or something worse, of Government, we should leave nothing at all behind us.

An early use of the term was in the title of a book on northern Queensland published in the 1880s. The author, A.W. Stirling, said that the Never Never land was 'all that portion of it [Queensland] which lies north or west of Cape Capricorn' but 'how and whence it got its name I know not'. Wherever it originated, the name was not meant to be a compliment. But by then it is likely that the term was already being applied more broadly to other isolated parts of Australia and it naturally

attracted the interest of poets and writers. Henry Lawson
published 'The Never-Never Country' in 1901:

> By homestead, hut, and shearing-shed,
>   By railroad, coach, and track—
> By lonely graves of our brave dead,
>   Up-Country and Out-Back:
> To where 'neath glorious clustered stars
>   The dreamy plains expand—
> My home lies wide a thousand miles
>   In the Never-Never Land.
>
> It lies beyond the farming belt,
>   Wide wastes of scrub and plain,
> A blazing desert in the drought,
>   A lake-land after rain;
> To the sky-line sweeps the waving grass,
>   Or whirls the scorching sand—
> A phantom land, a mystic land!
>   The Never-Never Land.
>
> Where lone Mount Desolation lies,
>   Mounts Dreadful and Despair—
> 'Tis lost beneath the rainless skies
>   In hopeless deserts there;
> It spreads nor'-west by No-Man's Land—
>   Where clouds are seldom seen—
> To where the cattle-stations lie
>   Three hundred miles between.
>
> The drovers of the Great Stock Routes
>   The strange Gulf country know—
> Where, travelling from the southern droughts,
>   The big lean bullocks go;
> And camped by night where plains lie wide,
>   Like some old ocean's bed,
> The watchmen in the starlight ride
>   Round fifteen hundred head.

And west of named and numbered days
   The shearers walk and ride—
Jack Cornstalk and the Ne'er-do-well,
   And the grey-beard side by side;
They veil their eyes from moon and stars,
   And slumber on the sand—
Sad memories sleep as years go round
   In Never-Never Land.

By lonely huts north-west of Bourke,
   Through years of flood and drought,
The best of English black-sheep work
   Their own salvation out:
Wild fresh-faced boys grown gaunt and brown—
   Stiff-lipped and haggard-eyed—
They live the Dead Past grimly down!
   Where boundary-riders ride.

The College Wreck who sunk beneath,
   Then rose above his shame,
Tramps West in mateship with the man
   Who cannot write his name.
'Tis there where on the barren track
   No last half-crust's begrudged—
Where saint and sinner, side by side,
   Judge not, and are not judged.

Oh rebels to society!
   The Outcasts of the West—
Oh hopeless eyes that smile for me,
   And broken hearts that jest!
The pluck to face a thousand miles—
   The grit to see it through!
The communism perfected!—
   And—I am proud of you!

The Arab to true desert sand,
    The Finn to fields of snow;
The Flax-stick turns to Maoriland,
    Where the seasons come and go;
And this old fact comes home to me—
    And will not let me rest—
However barren it may be,
    Your own land is the best!

And, lest at ease I should forget
    True mateship after all,
My water-bag and billy yet
    Are hanging on the wall;
And if my fate should show the sign,
    I'd tramp to sunsets grand
With gaunt and stern-eyed mates of mine
    In the Never-Never Land.

As always, Lawson located the hallowed mateship 'Up-Country and Out-Back'.

Other writers used the term, the most influential probably being Jeannie Gunn in her *We of the Never Never* published in 1908. The 'Never Never' is now heard in Australian speech alongside 'past the black stump', 'Bullamakanka' and simply 'out to buggery' as terms for anywhere thought to be a long way away. As the bushman informed the new migrant who asked how to get to the outback: 'Outback is away out west, out in the never-never where the crows fly backwards; it's away out west 'o sunset and right outback o' beyond; it's away outback o' Bourke in the great open spaces where men are men and women are few and far between; it's right away out—well, it's away out back, yer can't miss it.'

The stockman's last bed

Maria and Bessie, Colonel Grey's two daughters, were fond of music, especially the hit of the 1840s known as the 'Last

Whistle', a tear-jerker parlour ballad about an elderly sailor
doing his duty to the last:

> Whether sailor or not for a moment avast
> Poor Jack's mizzen topsail is laid to the mast,
> He'll never turn out or will more heave the lead.
> He's now all a back nor will sails shoot a head,
> Yet tho' worms gnaw his timbers his vessel a wreck,
> When he hears the last whistle he'll jump upon deck.

And the sad tale only got worse from there!

Maria and Bessie correctly thought they could improve on
this and use the song as the basis for one of their own on a
more local theme. They came up with a song destined to be
a musical icon of the bush—'The Stockman's Last Bed':

> Whither Stockman or not for a moment give ear
> Poor Jack's breathed his last, and no more shall we hear
> The crack of his whip or his steed's lively trot,
> His clear go a-head and his jingling quart pot
> He rests where the wattles their sweet fragrance shed,
> And tall gum trees shadow the stockman's last bed.
>
> When drafting one day he was gored by a cow,
> Alas, cried poor Jack, it's all up with me now;
> I'll no more return to my saddle again,
> Or bound like a wallaby over the plain.
> I'll rest where the wattles their sweet fragrance shed
> And tall gum trees shadow the stockman's last bed.
>
> My whip must be silent, my steed he will mourn,
> My dogs look in vain for their master's return,
> Unknown and forgotten, unheeded I'll die,
> Save Australia's dark sons none will know where I lie.
> I'll rest where the wattles their sweet fragrance shed
> And tall gum trees shadow the stockman's last bed.

In one form or another, this bush classic has been with us ever since. It was often printed in newspapers and magazines, many of which circulated widely in the bush. It was released in sheet music form and, of course, was widely sung in many different versions. By the 1860s it had grown a new final verse:

> Now, stockmen, if ever on some future day,
> After the wild mob you happen to stray,
> Ride softly the creek beds where trees make a shade,
> For perhaps it's the spot where poor Jack's bones are laid.

By the 1870s the ballad was so well-known that the image of a sick or dying stockman had become firmly romanticised as a standard scene of bush death, preferably beneath a wattle or gum tree. Adam Lindsay Gordon's famous poem 'The Sick Stockrider' also cemented the idea in the 1870s. By the 1890s there was no escaping the image or the song, also known as 'The Stockman's Lone Grave'. As a writer in the *Australian Town and Country Journal* put it in 1893:

> The shearers at Paik held a little concert the other day in the woolshed, and among the songs were 'The Stockman's Lone Grave' and 'The Used Up Stockman'. Australian poets seem to have selected the stockman and boundary riders as objects at which to pelt all sorts of pathetic situations. The stockman of the songs is generally experiencing something depressing, and enough songs and poems have been written about lonely graves to smother all the lonely graves in Australia.

The song remained popular into the 1940s and 50s when visiting American folk singer, Burl Ives, took it up. Although the bush song tradition has all but died out, 'The Stockman's Last Bed' can still be heard today at folk festivals and on numerous recordings.

Vic Summers, champion tree-feller
and axeman, Gympie.

7

Hard yakka

How we suffered grief and pain,
On the banks of the Barron cutting cane

'The Cane Cutter's Lament'

The overlanders

By the time Chips Rafferty starred in the 1946 film, *The Over-landers*, the days of pushing big mobs of cattle or sheep across the country were coming to an end. But Harry Watt, a British film producer tasked with producing a propaganda piece on Australia's contribution to the war effort, heard of a recent large drove. With a feared Japanese invasion of the north expected at any time, 100,000 head of cattle were overlanded 3200 kilometres into Queensland in 1942.

The film was released too late to be of any use to the war effort, but it was a great box office success and helped to romanticise the overlanders. Not that they needed much help. The lusty legend of the overlanders was as much a part of the bush tradition as billy tea, damper and the drover's dog, and had been for a very long time.

159

As soon as the country began to open up and settlements
of any size became established, there was a need to move
stock, either to market or to establish pastoral business on
new frontiers. When South Australia was settled by Europeans in 1836, it opened a possible market for stock travelled
from Victoria and New South Wales. In 1838, 300 cattle were
overlanded to Adelaide and sheep were overlanded there the
following year.

Mobs continued to arrive, driven through what was at first
hostile Aboriginal territory. The first overlanders had good
relations with the indigenous groups, but as the impact of
large numbers of animals on hunting and gathering increased
and as settlement moved out from Adelaide itself, so tensions
grew. Dogs, stock and some drovers were speared and these
attacks were met with heavier and heavier reprisals resulting in the death of many Aboriginal people. An undeclared
colonial war was effectively being waged along the stock
routes. Fighting did not end until the mid-1840s by which
time disease and population losses had destroyed the indigenous resistance.

Stock were also being moved in other parts of the country
and droving was a trade followed by many. In 1872 some
400 bullocks were shifted 2500 kilometres from Charters
Towers to Palmerston, near Darwin, by D'Arcy Wentworth
Uhr. In the early 1880s, the Duracks walked over 7000 cattle
and 200 horses from southwest Queensland to the Ord River.
Often considered the greatest of the drovers, Nat 'Bluey'
Buchanan moved perhaps 20,000 head from Queensland to
the Victoria Downs Station in the Northern Territory between
the late 1870s and the early 1880s. The longest drove of
all began in March 1883 when a group of Scots Australian families in New South Wales headed north with nearly
800 cattle, horses and bullocks to establish a station almost
6000 kilometres away in the Kimberley region, arriving there
in mid-1886.

The men who drove the stock across the often-great

distances became known quite early as 'overlanders'. They also became known early as troublemakers. The rough and ready life in the saddle was akin in some ways to that of the cowboy in the American west and it bred a similar masculine attitude to work, life and social relations. The many ballads of the over-landers are rich in carousing, womanising and skiting:

There's a trade you all know well,
It's bringing cattle over.
On ev'ry track,
To the Gulf and back,
Men know the Queensland drover.

CHORUS:
Pass the billy 'round boys!
Don't let the pint-pot stand there!
For tonight we drink the health
Of every overlander.

I come from the northern plains
Where the girls and grass are scanty;
Where the creeks run dry,
Or ten foot high,
And it's either drought or plenty.

There are men from every land,
From Spain and France and Flanders;
They're a well-mixed pack,
Both white and black,
The Queensland overlanders.

When we've earned a spree in town
We live like pigs in clover;
And the whole year's cheque
Pours down the neck
Of many a Queensland drover.

As I pass along the roads,
The children raise my dander,
Crying 'Mother dear,
Take in the clothes,
Here comes the overlander!'

But the punishing life was anything but romantic. The reality was hard and dangerous work in appalling conditions. Perhaps that was why the overlanders had a reputation as very hard drinkers.

Trouble on the diggings

In the summer of 1853 Lancashire school teacher George Dunderdale reached the goldfields at Bendigo together with his mate, Philip: 'a Young Irelander, and therefore a fighter on principle.' Like most others on the goldfields, Philip was armed, in his case with a pistol and a Bowie knife, which he knew how to wield. Not that it was much use, it was a British imitation of the famous American frontier blade that 'would neither kill a man nor cut a beef-steak'.

Like everyone else, the two men came to seek their fortunes on the diggings. But the signs were not good. As they approached the goldfields they met parties of disappointed diggers returning from wherever they had come from, looking to sell cheaply the gold licences they purchased with such high hopes and at such high prices only months earlier. In this atmosphere of blighted hopes and harsh conditions, the already established ways of the bush were sharpened and toughened, as Dunderdale would later describe in *The Book of the Bush*:

While we stood in the track, gazing hopelessly over the endless heaps of clay and gravel covering the flat, a little man came up and spoke to Philip, in whom he recognised a fellow countryman. He said:

'You want a place to camp on, don't you?'

'Yes,' replied Philip, 'we have only just come up from Melbourne.'

'Well, come along with me,' said the stranger.

He was a civil fellow, and said his name was Jack Moore. We went with him in the direction of the first White Hill, but before reaching it we turned to the left up a low bluff, and halted in a gully where many men were at work puddling clay in tubs.

After we had put up our tent, Philip went down the gully to study the art of gold digging. He watched the men at work; some were digging holes, some were dissolving clay in tubs of water by stirring it rapidly with spades, and a few were stooping at the edge of water-holes, washing off the sand mixed with the gold in milk pans.

Philip tried to enter into conversation with the diggers. He stopped near one man, and said:

'Good day, mate. How are you getting along?'

The man gazed at him steadily, and replied 'Go you to hell,' so Philip moved on. The next man he addressed sent him in the same direction, adding a few blessings; the third man was panning off, and there was a little gold visible in his pan. He was gray, grim, and hairy. Philip said:

'Not very lucky to-day, mate?'

The hairy man stood up, straightened his back, and looked at Philip from head to foot.

'Lucky be blowed. I wish I'd never seen this blasted place. Here have I been sinking holes and puddling for five months, and hav'n't made enough to pay my tucker and the Government license, thirty bob a month. I am a mason, and I threw up twenty-eight bob a day to come to this miserable hole. Wherever you come from, young man, I advise you to go back there again. There's twenty thousand men on Bendigo, and I don't believe nineteen thousand of 'em are earning their grub.'

'I can't well go back fifteen thousand miles, even if I had money to take me back,' answered Philip.

'Well, you might walk as far as Melbourne,' said the hairy man, 'and then you could get fourteen bob a day as a hodman;

or you might take a job at stone breaking; the Government are giving 7s. 6d. a yard for road metal. Ain't you got any trade to work at?'

'No, I never learned a trade, I am only a gentleman.' He felt mean enough to cry.

'Well, that's bad. If you are a scholar, you might keep school, but I don't believe there's half-a-dozen kids on the diggin's. They'd be of no mortal use except to tumble down shafts. Fact is, if you are really hard up, you can be a peeler. Up at the camp they'll take on any useless loafer wot's able to carry a carbine, and they'll give you tucker, and you can keep your shirt clean. But, mind, if you do join the Joeys, I hope you'll be shot. I'd shoot the hull blessed lot of 'em if I had my way. They are nothin' but a pack of robbers.' The hairy man knew something of current history and statistics, but he had not a pleasant way of imparting his knowledge.

The men joined the other hopefuls and started digging, barely making enough for 'tucker' from their labours.

In those times it was customary to attend church. The diggings were crowded with men and women from many countries and faiths, but there were few clergy available. One was a no-nonsense Catholic priest:

Father Backhaus was often seen walking with long strides among the holes and hillocks on Bendigo Flat or up and down the gullies, on a visit to some dying digger, for Death would not wait until we had all made our pile. His messengers were going around all the time; dysentery, scurvy, or fever; and the priest hurried after them. Sometimes he was too late; Death had entered the tent before him.

He celebrated Mass every Sunday in a tent made of drugged [coarse woollen fabric], and covered with a calico fly. His presbytery, sacristy, confessional, and school were all of similar materials, and of small dimensions. There was not room in the church for more than thirty or forty persons; there were no pews, benches, or chairs. Part of the congregation consisted of soldiers

from the camp, who had come up from Melbourne to shoot us
if occasion required. Six days of the week we hated them and
called 'Joey' after them, but on the seventh day we merely glared
at them, and let them pass in silence. They were sleek and clean,
and we were gaunt as wolves, with scarcely a clean shirt among
us. Philip especially hated them as enemies of his country, and the
more so because they were his countrymen, all but one, who was
a black man.

The people in and around the church were not all Catholics.
I saw a man kneeling near me reading the Book of Common Prayer
of the Church of England; there was also a strict Presbyterian, to
whom I spoke after Mass. He said the priest did not preach with
as much energy as the ministers in Scotland. And yet I thought
Father Backhaus' sermon had that day been 'powerful,' as the
Yankees would say. He preached from the top of a packing case
in front of the tent. The audience was very numerous, standing in
close order to the distance of twenty-five or thirty yards under a
large gum tree.

The preacher spoke with a German accent, but his meaning
was plain. He said:

'My dear brethren, "Beatus ille qui post aurum non abiit".
Blessed is the man who has not gone after gold, nor put his trust
in money or treasures. You will never earn that blessing, my dear
brethren. Why are you here? You have come from every corner
of the world to look for gold. You think it is a blessing, but when
you get it, it is often a curse. You go what you call "on the spree";
you find the "sly grog"; you get drunk and are robbed of your
gold; sometimes you are murdered; or you fall into a hole and are
killed, and you go to hell dead drunk. Patrick Doyle was here at
Mass last Sunday; he was then a poor digger. Next day he found
gold, "struck it rich," as you say; then he found the grog also and
brought it to his tent. Yesterday he was found dead at the bottom
of his golden shaft, and he was buried in the graveyard over there
near the Government camp.'

My conscience was quite easy when the sermon was finished. It would be time enough for me to take warning from the fate of Paddy Doyle when I had made my pile. Let the lucky diggers beware! I was not one of them.

After one sermon, Father Backhaus stepped down from his packing-case pulpit and offered Philip a job as a school master. He took the offer of a secure job and George dug on alone until he gained a new partner. One morning around ten o'clock, he heard a rumbling coming from Bendigo Flat:

The thunder grew louder until it became like the bellowing of ten thousand bulls. It was the welcome accorded by the diggers to our 'trusty and well-beloved' Government when it came forth on a digger hunt. It was swelled by the roars, and cooeys, and curses of every man above ground and below, in the shafts and drives on the flats, and in the tunnels of the White Hills, from Golden Gully and Sheep's Head, to Job's Gully and Eaglehawk, until the warning that 'Joey's out' had reached to the utmost bounds of the goldfield.

There was a strong feeling amongst the diggers that the license fee of thirty shillings per month was excessive, and this feeling was intensified by the report that it was the intention of the Government to double the amount. As a matter of fact, by far the larger number of claims yielded no gold at all, or not enough to pay the fee. The hatred of the hunted diggers made it quite unsafe to send out a small number of police and soldiers, so there came forth at irregular intervals a formidable body of horse and foot, armed with carbines, swords, and pistols.

This morning they marched rapidly along the track towards the White Hills, but wheeling to the left up the bluff they suddenly appeared at the head of Picaninny Gully. Mounted men rode down each side of the gully as fast as the nature of the ground would permit, for it was then honeycombed with holes, and encumbered with the trunks and stumps of trees, especially on the eastern side. They thus managed to hem us in like prisoners of war, and they also overtook some stragglers hurrying away to right and left. Some of these had licenses in their pockets, and refused to stop or show them until they were actually arrested. It was a ruse of war. They ran away as far as possible among the holes and logs, in order to draw off the cavalry, make them break their ranks, and thus to give a chance to the unlicensed to escape or to hide themselves. The police on foot, armed with carbines and accompanied by officers, next came down the centre of the gully, and every digger was asked to show his license. I showed that of William Matthews.

The diggers were arrested, forced to march to the police camp and fined 5 pounds plus another 30 shillings for the licence they had been unable to produce. The men 'were outraged, and they burned for revenge'. It was the beginning of the protests and agitations that led to the Eureka Stockade the following year.

The blades that felled the bush

In the days before power tools, the bush was cleared by hand. English axes were soon found to be ineffective against many Australian timbers, especially the hardwoods. Axes with longer and narrower blades were favoured and these began to appear in Australia around the middle of the nineteenth century, imported from America. Local axes of similar design also began to appear around this time. By the end of the 1800s, Tasmanian axemen armed with tools of this kind were renowned for making cuts as clean as any machine. As well as being experts with these single-bladed axes, they were also famed for their skills with the double-bladed broad axe.

With a history like this, it is not surprising that, according to legend, woodchopping competitions began in Tasmania in 1880. A couple of woodsmen—their names vary from version to version—bet on which one could chop the fastest and competitive woodchopping was born. True or not, within a decade competitive woodchopping—or just the 'woodchop'—was well established and has been ever since. It is a standard event at agricultural shows and also in timber community festivals and celebrations, and is seen as a characteristically Australian sport.

One of its early champions took the event to America, becoming largely responsible for the international growth of the sport. Peter McLaren was born near Melbourne in 1882 and by the age of twenty-four was a noted champion in Victoria and Western Australia. In or around 1910, he went to the United States of America. Here he promoted wood-chopping and, in particular his favourite Plumb brand axes, by giving demonstrations and teaching boy scouts and others how to do it. None could do it as well as McLaren, though. It was claimed that he could split a small chip with an axe—a Plumb, of course—from a distance of 12 metres.

In 1947, Peter McLaren was described in an American newspaper as the 'world famous axeman and woodchopping champion' and became popularly known as 'America's Champion Chopper'. Even in later life, this legend of the axe was still capable of doing some serous chopping. There seems to be something about woodchopping and woodchoppers that keeps them going well past the age when most people have moved to a retirement home.

In 2012, Vic Summers stumped up to the Gympie Show woodchop event and lined up with the rest of the axemen. So what? Vic was ninety-three years old. He began cutting timber at the age of fourteen, ring-barking up to 1700 trees a day. With his father and two brothers, Vic lived mainly on damper and corned beef and was paid 1 shilling a day for his labour. His skills with an axe made him a champion from 1947 to 1961 at the Coffs Harbour Show and many other gatherings. Vic was the world tree-felling champion eight times from 1940. He once won a competition after dropping his standing board from the top of the tree; he climbed down, retrieved the board and continued cutting his way down the tree to victory.

Even after retiring from competitive chopping five times, Vic couldn't keep away from the sport. He came last in the scoring at Gympie in 2012, but that wasn't the point.

Vic died in 2015 at the age of ninety-six, but not before he'd taken up what he said was an easier wood sport, sawing.

The same Gympie Show also saw another veteran woodsman in competition. Ian McGinniss travelled from Tasmania and although, at eighty-two, he was only a youngster compared with Vic Summers, Ian came third in his event.

Other woodchopping champions of the past include Tom Pettit who was once the only man ever to hold world titles for chopping and sawing. Charlie O'Rourke was so fast that he would not need to take off his coat and start chopping until his competitors were well into their pace. It is said that on one such occasion an irate Irishwoman among the spectators shouted at him: 'Ah, you big ugly brute, no wonder you always win—you wait till those other poor fellers get tired before you start.' Tom Kirk was known as 'Bulldozer' because his swings were so powerful that he kept breaking axes.

Probably the best-known axeman now is another Taswegian, David Foster, who has won so many competitions and titles that he may be the most awarded athlete in history. Like many axemen, Foster is part of a family of choppers and a well-known spokesman for men's health, community relations and LGBTQ rights.

There is one important thing to remember when comparing the impressive feats of modern-day axemen with those of the past. Today's logs used in competition are considerably thinner. A 600-millimetre piece of tree was the norm then; most competitive events now chop about half that width.

Bush cooks

Someone has to do the cooking. No matter how tough they are, even shearers and drovers need to eat and the 'babbling brook', as these bush chefs are known in rhyming slang, have always been the butt of bush humour. He—and in those days it was always a 'he'—did not have an easy job, especially when it rained:

> The cook, who has charge of the camp-ware and drives the wagonette, has an unenviable time in wet weather. The roads are boggy, banks slippery, and gullies and creeks flooded. It takes him pretty well all day to zigzag his team along, and now and again he has to dig himself out. Horses knock up, a breakdown occurs, or he is left stranded in a sea of water. When he gets to camp he has to make a fire with sodden wood, and cook supper in the wet, up to his boot-tops in mud. On the black-soil plains I have seen him come in after dark and make a pile of wet earth to build his fire on, with a drain round it to run the water away. The tents are pitched near the fire, and the men spread bags on the ground where they make their naps to keep out some of the damp. In the morning the blankets are wet and muddy, and if it is still raining they are rolled up in that condition; yet, though the men may get drenched through the day, their clothes may dry on them and get drenched again, and they sleep in them on wet ground, they seem to suffer no effects from it. Summer and winter they go through it, and are nearly always free from colds—which in itself is evidence in favour of open-air life.

A steady stream of bush balladry suggests that the stereotype of the bush cook has at least some truth behind it, as this lament for disappointed expectations suggests:

> The song I'm going to sing to you will not detain you long,
> It's all about a station cook we had at old Pinyong,
> His pastry was so beautiful his cooking was so fine,
> It gave us all a stomach-ache right through the shearing-time.

Edward Sorenson saw many cooks in his bush years and devoted a whole chapter to the species in his classic *Life in the Australian Backblocks*:

Of bush cooks there are many classes, each following his own
particular line, the shearers' cook, station cook, drovers' cook,
&c. Among the nondescripts, who treat all as fish that comes
to their net, one encounters some hard characters. I made the
acquaintance of one at a wayside hotel out west, an under-sized,
wizened-faced man, who smoked prodigiously while kneading,
and included tobacco-ashes and whatever else fell into the sponge
as a matter of course. He had a clever knack of turning pancakes
by tossing them into the air and catching them, cooked side up,
in the pan. He was an economical worker, but the principle was
carried a little too far. For instance, when he had soup to make
and a plum-duff to cook at the same time, the duff was always
boiled in the soup.

Sorenson told the tale of one 'Long Mick' who 'cooked
abominably' but punched out anyone who complained. As
the season wore on, the food got worse and the beatings more
frequent until the shearers all threw in ten quid to bring in
'a noted fighter of the bulldog breed', known as 'Bandy Ike'.
There wasn't a lot of Ike, but he made up for his slight stature
with his impressive muscles, developed from woodcutting. Ike
arrived Saturday afternoon but said nothing at dinner time.
At breakfast 'he made a scurrilous remark on the chops'. Long
Mick bounced in with fire in his eye, and in one minute he had
thrown off his cap and apron and said, 'Come outside!' And
it was on:

All hands rushed out to see the battle, which was fought behind
the woodheap. For the first three rounds Ike never struck a blow;
he was dodging, feinting and running round, and taking headers
between the long fellow's legs. The latter began to blow hard;
then Ike went to work with his sledge-hammer fists, and at the
end of five minutes we carried Long Michael in and laid him on
his bunk. Every one knew how to beat him now, and several were
willing to have a cut later on; but Long Mick rolled his swag
two days later, and left without saying goodbye.

The down-to-earth democracy of shearers was legendary and was applied to cooks as well as to their union representative, as in this introduction to yet another poem about culinary criminals, 'The Song of The Shearers' Cook':

When a station is about to start the shearing, the roll is called. Then the men elect a representative, who looks after their interests throughout the shearing, acting on behalf of the A.W.U as intermediary between the men and the boss. Then the rep. says to the shearers:

'Now, men, the next thing you will have to do is to elect a cook. Here you have half a dozen candidates'—there may be more or less. 'Here is the "Berlin Bun," and here is the "Jack o' Diamonds." There you see "Old Thargomindah Mike," "Bullaroras Terror," "Scotch Mist," and not forgetting "Boxing Biddy" (a six-foot lubra weighing 13 stone, and a good cook), and you can have whichever you require.'

He then makes the candidates stand apart in a row against the shed wall, and their respective supporters go over to them, like boys picked at rounders, and the magnet who draws best wins. They have previously ascertained the rate of pay demanded by each, of course, perhaps 10/ a week per man engaged in shearing, but varying with the number of men to cater for; the more, the lower the individual rate. Some cooks are good and some are, well, listen to the following:

There's a little shed called Springfield,
Down among the hills;
Where the shearers sit and curse the cook,
And talk of tucker-bills.
The pouring rain doth make them growl,
The machinery doesn't suit;
The boss, he growls about the cut,
But, he isn't game to 'shoot.'
The poor old rep., he looks done up
For want of food to eat;

For, though he often fed on snake,
He dares not touch the meat,
For the 'floaters' which the cook serves up
Are something just a treat.
There's Paddy Harris who never swore,
Or said a thing unkind;
But when he saw our food dished up,
And served at dinner time,
His temper fused that blessed day,
And he cried: 'We'll sack him straightaway.'
So now he's gone we thank the Lord;
And the morning that he fled;
Old Mike McMahony for us at Mass,
Prayed, 'Kill the rotter dead.'

The image of the bush cook was immortalised in this classic bush yarn, known in many forms:

The shearers had been suffering under an especially crook cook for weeks. Eventually, there was a showdown. The sullen shearers—some looking a little green around the gills—the boss and the cook gathered together to sort things out. The boss defended the cook, after all, he had hired the man. But the shearers were having none of it and expressed their unhappiness in the traditional voluble manner:

'Who called the cook a bastard?', the boss demanded to know.

'Who called the bastard a cook?' came the swift response from the crowd of shearers.

Ploughing time

It is April 1880. Ploughing time. A journalist for *The Argus* newspaper travels through northeastern Victoria interviewing hard-pressed selectors 'where hopefulness was coupled with rough living and plenty of work'. This part of Victoria was settled early by squatters then, in the aftermath of the goldrushes, by 'free selectors', allowed by the government to 'take up' blocks of land, pay a minimal rent, improve the block and, ideally, finally own them as viable farming enterprises. It was tough going, and many struggled to survive.

When the journalist arrived at a small selection, the husband was out ploughing and 'the wife was occupied in "burning off" which meant hauling small logs and boughs to the heaps of dead timber, and keeping several fires in a state of activity'. He observed that, 'The children, too small to be of any use, were amusing themselves picking up sticks, and following their mother about. They were very poorly clad all of them and had evidently not worn new clothes for several seasons.' He duly interviewed the husband, who was 'very glad to leave off ploughing to have a consultation' and explain how he came to these dire circumstances:

> With his friend and adviser the bailiff, he took up 320 acres in February, 1877, beginning with a capital of £200. He had fenced all the land in, and was now getting 70 acres ready for sowing. Last season the crop was good, but the season before he did not gather in a single bushel.
>
> Nothing looked better in the summer of 1878–9 than the standing corn but owing to the rust the grain never formed in the ear. He was depending on the harvest of 1879 for the means of clearing off liabilities and did not realise a penny. In this instance the selector had bought a stripper, on bills, in anticipation of the harvest. Having no means of meeting the bills he had to make arrangements with his storekeeper for an advance. In 1878 the account against him stood at £64 and though he sent £154 worth of corn to his storekeeper in January last, there was still a heavy balance against him in the books. The storekeeper was dealing very fairly with him, charging 12 per cent on the bills, which were renewed from time to time and threatening no pressure. The lease was due, but the selector could not take it up until he paid £96 in rent—i.e. £64 arrears under the licence, £16 under the lease, and £16 more coming due. Should the harvest of 1881 turn out a

good one, he would be able to clear off his debts and raise enough money on the lease to carry him on for the future. Just now he was in doubt how to act. Having only paid £32 (one year's rent), ought he to forfeit the amount, as some advised, and start afresh under the Act of 1878 paying only £16 a year instead of £32?

So long as he was without the lease, no one except the Crown could dislodge him; but he saw no hopes of being able to pay rent, or any of his other obligations, before next February. The horses and plant were covered by bill of sale, and there was nothing on which he could just now raise any money. He bought 100 sheep on credit for £44 some time ago, but they got out through the fences, and 80 had been lost. It was likely when a muster took place at the station that most of them would be recovered. The man he bought the sheep off would take them back, and if they fetched within £10 of what was due on them probably he would be satisfied. Sheep had fallen in price since the purchase of this flock. He had two horses before beginning to plough but one took ill and he was obliged to borrow £5 to buy another.

This was the case of a man absolutely destitute of ready cash, with 10 borrowed months before him, no means of raising any funds, and carrying on only by the forbearance of the storekeeper, whose long bill was produced for our inspection. The first half of the account was contained in one line—'account rendered,' and the remainder filled two pages of foolscap. No item in it looked unreasonable, and the goods supplied consisted chiefly of requisites for earning on farming.

As well as the building debts this selector was incurring, the living conditions for himself and family were minimal:

The family lived in a bark hut, divided into two apartments by a partition. The inner room, where all the family slept, was not lighted by any window. Indeed, but for two doors the whole place would have been dark. A mud floor worn into holes and dusty, walls with a few paper decorations, some sacks of wheat kept for seed, a wide fireplace, a kettle swinging over the fire, a table, and a piece of dried meat hanging in a smoky place—these were the only noticeable features of the interior. In the old gold-digging times rough men would have been contented with similar lodging but it could not be said that the place was a suitable one for bringing up three children, shortly to be increased to four. The children being under six, were too young for school but in a year or two it would be safe to let them walk by themselves across the bush to the schoolhouse.

The journalist was impressed by the stoicism and industry of this man and his family:

It cannot be said that selectors in distress have failed for want of industry. Here was this one, out first thing every morning with his horses ploughing, preparing the ground for a harvest 10 months distant, and his wife (who would not be equal to field work long) helping him in the afternoons at 'burning off.' Everything in this instance was depending on the results of the harvest of 1881, and favourable weather in the meantime—on a fall of rain at proper intervals, dry days at ripening time, a good yield, assistance in money from the storekeeper at reaping and threading (for the harvest labourers must be paid in cash) and a good market when the grain is ready for sale—a good market depending on the state of affairs in Europe as well as on the condition of things here. And when the corn is being threshed out, the storekeeper will be standing by to make sure of the bags of grain. Until his account is squared up there will be nothing available for the payment of arrears of rent or for the purposes of another season's preparations. If anything, the facts of this case have been understated.

Blackbirds

Sugar cane cultivation began in Queensland and northern New South Wales in the 1860s. The industry grew quickly and depended heavily on large numbers of cutters performing hard and dirty work in hot and humid conditions. To increase

the workforce, the Queensland government sanctioned a form
of indentured labour that was to become notorious under the
term 'blackbirding'.

South Sea Islanders, and some Aboriginal people, were
offered paid work planting and cutting sugar cane and other
crops in Queensland and in northern New South Wales. They
agreed to a period of living and working on the farms, at
the end of which they could return to their homes or, if they
wished, sign on for another term. Some islanders accepted these
offers and worked reasonably happily in the sugar industry,
often returning voluntarily for further terms. But the numbers
of willing recruits were always far too small for the demand
and the indentured labour operations quickly became kidnap-
ping and transportation of unwilling 'Kanakas', as the island
workers were known, to the canefields and also to other forms
of cultivation. This practice was known as 'blackbirding' and
the often-ruthless ship masters and crews who carried it out
were 'blackbirders'.

Even where Kanakas were relatively well treated, they
suffered discrimination and hardship. Their wages were well
below those paid to Europeans for their work and they were
generally housed in segregated shanty areas at the edge of
towns or in a kind of feudal estate on the farms themselves.
The colonial government attempted to regulate and improve
the trade but was generally unsuccessful. It is estimated that
around 60,000, possibly more, individual Kanakas were
brought to Queensland and New South Wales between 1863
and 1904.

According to a journalist who went undercover aboard a
'recruiting schooner', by 1892 the excesses of the early decades
of blackbirding had passed:

> In recruiting, the master who attempted to kidnap or cheat the
> islanders, and the Government Agent who tolerated any wrongful
> act, would be bold to recklessness and foolish in the extreme. The
> natives, nowadays, understand all about the business, and are not

to be taken by force or fraud, and the idea of stealing them is so out of date that it was rare to meet with a tribe that betrayed any shyness in meeting the recruiter unarmed. The natives know exactly what they are wanted for—how many seasons make three years. If some of them cannot tell how many shillings there are in a pound they know that their wages are to be at least equal to what comrades they desire to imitate got for their first term of service, and they soon learn to say, 'Six pound one year,' and to see that they get it.

As far as the journalist could see, the young men on the *Helena* were 'recruited of their own free will and as a matter of choice, and that the recruiter had no power to influence them unduly'. He also observed: 'As for their treatment on board ship, judging from their high spirits and happy demeanour, the voyage must have been without exception one of the happiest chapters in their lives.'

They might not have been so happy when they arrived. A well-known song among the cane-cutters casts a darker light on the kind of working life that all in the sugar industry experienced:

How we suffered grief and pain,
On the banks of the Barron cutting cane,
We sweated blood, we were as black as sin,
And the ganger he put the spur right in.

The greasy cook with sore-eyed look,
And the matter all stuck to his lashes,
He damned our souls with his half-baked rolls,
And he'd poison the snakes with his hashes.

The first six weeks, so help me Christ,
We lived on cheese and half boiled rice,
Mouldy bread and cat's meat stew,
And corn beef that the flies had blew.

The cane was bad the cutters were mad,
The cook had shit on the liver,
And I'll never cut cane for that bastard again,
On the banks of the Barron River.

So now I'm leaving that lousy place,
I'll cut no more for that bugger,
He can stand in the mud that's red as blood,
And cut his own bloody sugar.

Those islanders who settled in Australia formed relationships and had children, creating distinctive communities along the coastal rivers and plains. But as the country moved towards Federation at the end of the nineteenth century, it became clear that Kanakas would no longer be welcome in the kind of 'white Australia' envisaged by the framers of the Constitution. They were to be repatriated to their islands of origin to make way for white workers. The Kanakas resisted this racist imposition, petitioning governments. While there were eventually exemptions of various kinds, including marriage to an Australian, all but around 2000 were deported by 1908.

Those who were allowed to remain because they satisfied one or more of the exemption requirements now became a distinctive group in Queensland society, often marrying into Aboriginal communities, though they continued to suffer discrimination up to the present day.

The descendants of the Kanakas have many, often bittersweet, stories passed down through their families. Interviewed for the National Library of Australia in 2017, Aunty Mabel Quakerwoot spoke of her grandfather who was stolen from Vanuatu to work around Mackay. He was whipped like a slave and worked hard. But, eventually, he married an Irish woman and was later given the land on which he had laboured. Today, the South Sea Islanders, as they have been officially known since 1994, are a little-known group. Even though they have been formally recognised by the Queensland and New South

Wales governments, there is little acknowledgement of their historical contribution to Australia. In 2017, a fourth-generation South Sea Islander became the first of that community to be elected to an Australian parliament, in Queensland, representing the seat of Mirani for the One Nation party.

The boundary rider

As bush and outback land was increasingly fenced with wire from the 1840s, so the new occupation of boundary rider was born. Whether the boundary rider patrolled the fencelines of a private property or any of the government's supposedly vermin-proof barriers like the dog fence or rabbit fence, it was a hard and lonely life, repairing breaks, putting out 'strangers', or strays, and avoiding the many hardships and dangers involved in 'doing all that may pertain to keeping his master's stock on his own land, and everybody's else [*sic*] out of it'.

Some of the difficulties faced by boundary riders and outback dwellers were graphically described in 1919:

> Almost anywhere west of Broken Hill you will find, trees standing on the ends of their roots, the soil having been swept from under. Here and there you see a few inches of the tops of a buried fence, and the boundary rider tells you there's a second fence beneath it, and sometimes another under that, the three having been erected one on top of the other and successively buried by drifting sand. On many runs men follow fences with shovels, occasionally with teams and scoops, all through summer, breaking up hard banks and scattering the stuff through the wires so that winds will carry it on. It is remarkable that a single wire a foot or more off the ground will cause a bank, to gather till the wire is covered. Netting fences are burled quickly in places. In other parts, instead of fences being buried, the ground is cut from under the posts till they topple. I have seen several chains lying flat at a stretch, from 18 to 20 in. of earth having been carried away to get under the posts. Where the ground was very hard, the earth round the

uprights had been whisked out by strong winds, leaving them toppling. Ploughs and scoops had to be used round some of the houses to prevent doors and windows being blocked. Sand-breaks were built at tanks, walls and troughs, and some homesteads were walled in. It was cheaper to thus fortify your house against the besieging storms than to be eternally removing the sandhills they dropped at your doors. At Morney Plains (Q.) a new £500 drafting-yard was entirely burled at the end of 1901. In such country you are never sure of your landscapes for long.

The term 'boundary rider' also came to be used for one of the essential tools of the trade, the wire strainer needed to tighten the fence to its required tension:

There are various devices and gadgets advertised and employed for straining wires in a fence. If you haven't got one of them there's no need to worry—the old forked stick, the 'boundary-rider', is as good as any and perhaps better than most. It's so delightfully simple; it's easy to get and to make it costs nothing other than the time spent in finding a suitable tree, cutting it and fixing it with your own fancy notions . . . You cut a forked stick, and your own judgment directs you to size and strength . . . You leave a spur at the fork about a foot or so long.

A typical example of bush economy—why invent another term when the one you already have will do nicely?

These skills are needed on the world's longest fence. The dingo (or dog) fence, zig-zags through the country from eastern Queensland to the South Australian coast, a distance of 5500 kilometres, give or take. It was started more than a century ago and still protects livestock across three states from predators.

Maintenance of the wood and wire wonder is a never-ending task entrusted to patrol officers who monitor and repair large stretches of the fence. They get a helping hand from volunteers who follow the bush tradition of doing it yourself. Taylah Smith lives in Mintaro, South Australia. She is the fourth generation of her family to drive almost ten hours a few times a year out to Lake Frome, where the South Australian, New South Wales and Queensland borders meet. Here, with her family, Taylah camps out and helps rebuild a stretch of the dingo fence. All in a day's work outback.

Wilhelmina and Winifred Rawson with their goats at The Hollow, Queensland, 1880.

8

Stringybark and greenhide

Stringy bark and green hide, that will never fail yer!
Stringy bark and green hide, the mainstay of Australia.

'Stringybark and Greenhide', George Chanson, 1866

I was by no means an exception

If you were unhappy with your freckles in the nineteenth century, you could try to eradicate them with horseradish and sour milk or cucumber and skim milk. At least, you could according to Mrs Lance Rawson's *Australian Enquiry Book of Household and General Information*, published in 1894. Mrs Rawson provided plenty more homely help and advice about making the best of bush life, domestic hygiene and cooking, especially using native Australian ingredients.

Mrs Rawson was a writer and cook whose full name was Wilhelmina Frances Rawson (nee Cahill) known, not surprisingly, as Mina. Born in Sydney in 1851, much of her childhood was spent in the New South Wales bush where she learned self-reliance and bush skills.

Mina married Lancelot Rawson in 1872 and moved with him and other extended family members out west of Mackay, Queensland, then an extremely remote location. On the isolated cattle station and later on a cane plantation near Maryborough, she had close contact with indigenous people and with indentured Melanesian labourers, becoming familiar with what were then exotic foods. Later the Rawsons were the first Europeans to settle Boonooroo near Wide Bay, where they were involved in the local fishing industry.

Through these experiences, including raising four children, Mina had the opportunity to further develop the techniques needed to live the bush life as comfortably as possible. There was not much money coming in so the Rawsons needed to do as much for themselves as possible. They made their own furniture, boots and even hats of plaited paper and seaweed. Mina crafted muffs, or hand warmers, from pelican breasts, as well as feather pillows, selling these in town. She won a contract to provide seaweed mattresses for a local hospital. Somehow, she also found time to write fairy tales for publication and contribute to local newspapers, often being the main provider of income for the family.

Mina's culinary prowess was derived mainly from these needs and her willingness to learn from others and experiment herself. When her last-born daughter failed to thrive, she developed a diet of oysters that restored her health. She worked out how to cure bacon made from dugong—from which she also made soap—and from the Pacific Island labourers she discovered how to cook flying foxes: 'Cut off the wings—the part that smells—and burn them. Skin the fox, cut it up, and having scooped out a pumpkin, fill it with the cut-up pieces and bake the pumpkin in the ashes for two or three hours.' Mina added onions, herbs, seasoning and a cup of gravy or water. 'I am sure no one could have had a nicer dish,' she recollected.

She committed much of this expertise to paper, publishing a number of books on household advice, home medicine and cooking. In one of her early books, the no-nonsense Mina pointed out that her work was for the middle classes and 'those people who cannot afford to buy a Mrs Beeton or a Warne', particularly the young housewife living in the bush with little access to markets or shops. She urged women to do it themselves and provided examples from her own make-do efforts turning kerosene tins into ovens and preserving jam in beer bottles.

As well as the more common dishes of kangaroo and wallaby, Mina had recipes for bandicoots and parrot soup. She also had a couple of suggestions for iguana, ranging from a straight grilling on a fire to an iguana-tail curry. She said the cooked lizard tasted like spring chicken. She even showed how it was possible to bake bread in an improvised oven:

Who would bake their bread in a kerosene tin oven made there and then while the dough was rising? But I did it once . . . I had done a regular fools' trick the previous night in setting a batch of bread without 'counting the cost'—in fact seeing if there was an oven to bake it in. There was none, and my own men were mean enough to jeer at me. 'That's nothing,' I said grandly, 'I'll soon have an oven.' But they still smiled. However, I gathered my materials round me, consisting of about 20 bricks and a couple of kerosene tins. I cut the top out of one of them, and, having made a hole in the sand to hold the tin, I fixed it on bricks, so that heat could get all round. Then I made a fire, to produce plenty of ashes . . . and I worked hard at it till we had plenty, enough to roast a bullock.

The dough meanwhile was being kind, and was rising to the occasion . . . I knew all about bread baking, as regards the heat, and that saved me, as it happened. I had my tin in place on the bricks, and just enough ashes to give the loaves their first attempt at a rise. I'd got two fair-sized loaves into my oven. The door of the wretched thing was a trouble. I was using the top of the kerosene tin, having improvised a long handle fixed to the ring that is in the centre, meant for lifting or carrying them. The first time I went to look at my bread the ring melted off, and, fearing my bread would burn, I seized a big cloth and lifted the oven bodily out of the fire on to the beach. But it was doing beautifully, both loaves had risen to the top and I very quickly put oven and all back, and regulated the heat again . . . The bread was perfectly cooked, but I was not anxious to continue baking in a kerosene tin oven.

Lance Rawson died in 1899 and Mina later married Colonel Francis Ravenhill who had been her husband's partner at Boonooroo. This marriage freed her of financial need, allowing her to continue writing, including her memoirs. She died in 1933. Among her many achievements, she was the first female swimming teacher in Central Queensland and strongly advocated teaching all children to swim.

Towards the end of her memoirs, Mina reflected on the experience of bush women in her era: 'There used to be hundreds of things done in the bush, in those days by both men and women whose inventive faculties only came to light through absolute necessity. I was by no means an exception; hundreds of women were just as clever as I was, though my pen was possibly an unusual gift.'

The gum leaf bands

In 1945 the *Adelaide Advertiser* published an article titled 'The Music of Strange Bands'. It was a knowledgeable account of 'bush' bands using mainly homemade musical instruments like gum leaves, spoons, cigar box fiddles, kerosene tin drums and banjos made from old tennis racquets. These 'found' and improvised instruments were often played in combination with 'proper' commercially produced instruments, mainly the button accordion, harmonica, tin whistle, concertina and triangle, among others.

The author, using the pseudonym 'Eureka' and obviously well-travelled, also described a large family band of teenage children and their parents: 'It had two concertinas, two accordians [*sic*], a cigarcione (a bush violin made from a cigar box, wallaby sinews and bits of timber), a tin whistle, a bush-made flute, a drum, gum leaves and several mouth organs. All instruments, except the accordians, concertinas and mouth organs, were home-made. The drum was a section of a hollow log with wallaby skins stretched over the ends.'

Such instruments were once fairly common in rural Australia in the era when people had to make-do for most things, including their entertainment. A description in the New South Wales gold town of Gulgong in the early 1870s gives a picture of a lively street music scene:

> The Queen Street, Gulgong, camp was the most crowded thorough-fare in Australia. It was a blaze of light at night. The pubs were doing a roaring trade, so also the shanties up and down the street. The click of the billiard balls were heard on every side and the ear was charmed (or otherwise) by the playing of concertinas, accor-dions, jew's harps, tin whistles, flutes etc., at every fancy goods store, where patrons were 'trying before buying'. Occasionally a good player would come along, and, urged by the proprietor, would stand on the doorstop and play popular airs to an audience of some hundreds in the street. Music had charms even in those sordid days, and a good concertina could cast a spell over the crowd by playing Home Sweet Home or Hard Times Come Again No More and so on. And then, when the player was tired and handed the instrument back to the proprietor or perhaps to an intending purchaser, the big crowd would give a cheer, while some of them would almost carry him off to the nearest pub for a 'wet of the wire'.

But apart from the rare recording, we now have no evidence of the sounds that these—or any other ensembles of the pre-recorded past—actually made. They have become 'ghost music'. The ignoring of this powerful and authentically Australian musical tradition, as Eureka complained, meant that we have little idea today of what this bush music might have sounded like.

The point of Eureka's article was to draw attention to the invisibility of these ensembles and to advocate the formation of an Australian 'bush band' using these instruments: 'If these novel bush instruments were gathered together to form an Australian bush band I believe that we would see and hear something outstanding.' The article accurately observed that 'Had these bands been in America they would have been featured in films and on the radio'.

One of the other 'strange bands' mentioned was the Wallaga Lake Gum Leaf Band, a famous Aboriginal ensemble formed at least as early as the 1920s. Research shows that Aboriginal players of the gum leaf can be traced to at least the late nineteenth century and groups have been identified in all mainland states and territories.

Basic though a gum leaf may be, it is possible to play relatively complex music using a surprisingly large array of techniques. Some of these techniques can emulate bird calls which may have a spiritual significance for players. Roseina Boston, a Gumbaynggir woman, used her gum leaf to imitate the sounds of storm birds, cockatoos and rain birds, spiritual totems from the ancestors and strongly related to identity. Roseina also produced the call of her own totem, the kookaburra. When Roseina played out of doors, birds would gather around her and she would talk with them.

The origin of gum-leaf playing is not known. It seems likely that it was a pre-settlement Aboriginal tradition and that groups and bands developed under the influence of Western popular music. Initially this would have been homemade settler music, mainly for dances, though later the rural touring of British and American entertainers, including minstrel shows, brought a wider range of popular music. As with many other Western influences, Aboriginal people were quick to adapt elements that appealed and make them their own.

Aboriginal gum-leaf bands had a vogue in the 1920s and 30s. The Wallaga Lake band played at the opening of the Sydney Harbour Bridge in 1932 and one such ensemble featured in Ken

G. Hall's 1933 sound movie *The Squatter's Daughter*. Non-Aboriginal people also learned to play the gum leaf, though it is particularly associated with indigenous bush music. While a rare treat, the gum leaf is still sometimes heard today.

Bush carpentry

Improvised structures have a long history in Australia. Aboriginal people often constructed dwellings by stripping bark from trees and using it for walls and rooves. The early settlers quickly adopted this technique, producing the basic bark hut. Because they had steel axes and saws, settlers were also able to slice lengthy sections from felled trees to form slabs, a more solid refinement of the basic bark structure, forming the slab hut. Basic buildings of this type were the common housing for generations and were sometimes satirised in bush songs such as 'The Old Bark Hut'. A few verses provide the picture:

> In the summertime when the weather's warm this hut is nice and
>   cool,
> And you'll find the gentle breezes blowing in through every hole.
> You can leave the old door open or you can leave it shut,
> There's no fear of suffocation in the old bark hut.
> In the winter-time preserve us all! to live in there's a treat ,
> Especially when it's raining hard and blowing wind and sleet,
> The rain comes down the chimney and your meat is black with
>   soot,
> That's a substitute for pepper in an old bark hut.

Tenting, or camping, was a common way of life in the bush and required a make-do approach:

> Tent furniture is made on the spot. For a stretcher, two poles are
> thrust through a couple of bags and laid on forked uprights a foot
> or so off the ground. Some merely lay the poles on the ground,
> filling the space between with leaves or grass. This is not a safe

bunk in a snake country; it also harbours centipedes, scorpions, and other undesirables. Four stakes and a square piece of bark complete the table. The usual light is a slush lamp. When a candle is used it is held between three upright nails on one corner of the table, or in a slit at the top of a stake, or in a jam tin partly filled with sand. On windy nights the candle is covered with a glass bottle, the bottom of which has been evenly taken off. This is accomplished by first tying some kerosene-saturated twine round the bottle, then burning it and plunging the bottle into cold water.

The tools for these constructions were of the most basic and limited kind. As a minimum, nineteenth-century migrants were advised to take into the bush an axe, an adze, a hand saw, a chisel, augurs (drill bits), wedges, ruler, chalk line, a square and a plumb bob. With these tools (often with fewer), little skill and a lot of ingenuity, people built homes for themselves and their families, as well as animal houses and any outbuildings needed for the kind of subsistence and basic market farming many practised. Some of them are still standing, testament to the durability of the local materials used, mostly hardwoods, and the efficiency of such basic building techniques.

When nails were unavailable, wooden pegs might be used or even 'greenhide' made from cured strips of animal skin and simply tied around whatever needed to be kept together. Later, fencing wire became an invaluable item of the bush carpenter's toolbox with the famous 'Cobb & Co. hitch'—an allegedly simple way to tie and tension two pieces of wood together—being used around the country to fasten posts and bearers in a very effective and lasting way. Slab walls might, or might not, be plastered with local clay. Hessian was used for walls and sometimes soaked in pitch or tar as a roofing material.

Henry Lawson gave a good description of this style of living:

The dairy is built of rotten box bark—though there is plenty of good stringy-bark within easy distance—and the structure looks as if it wants to lie down and is only prevented by three crooked props on the leaning side; more props will soon be needed in the rear for the dairy shows signs of going in that direction. The milk is set in dishes made of kerosene-tins, cut in halves, which are placed on bark shelves fitted round against the walls. The shelves are not level and the dishes are brought to a comparatively horizontal position by means of chips and bits of bark, inserted under the lower side. The milk is covered by soiled sheets of old newspapers supported on sticks laid across the dishes. This protection is necessary, because the box bark in the roof has crumbled away and left fringed holes—also because the fowls roost up there. Sometimes the paper sags, and the cream may have to be scraped off an article on dairy farming.

A lady in the bush

Katherine Kirkland (nee Hamilton) was one of the first pioneers in the Western District of Port Phillip. With her husband Kenneth Kirkland, their baby daughter, her two brothers and another couple, this well-educated middle-class Scotswoman settled at what they hoped to make a successful sheep station at Trawalla, 40 kilometres west of Ballarat, in 1839. At the time, Geelong was a spattering of tents, shacks and three shops. Katherine claimed to have been the 'first white woman who had ever been so far up the country'.

After their first day of travel towards their new home, Katherine and her companions camped on an earlier settler's failed run. Here, the Wathaurong people were friendly and the newcomers were treated to a corroboree:

They had about twenty large fires lighted, around which were seated the women and children. The men had painted themselves, according to their own fancy, with red and white earth. They had bones, and bits of stones, and emu's feathers, tied on their hair, and branches of trees tied on their ankles, which made a rushing noise when they danced. Their appearance was very wild, and when they danced, their gestures and attitudes were equally so.

> One old man stood before the dancers, and kept repeating some words very fast in a kind of time, whilst he beat together two sticks. The women never dance; their employment is to keep the fires burning bright; and some of them were beating sticks, and declaiming in concert with the old man.

In return, the Wathaurong wanted to see how the white people made a corroboree. They were entertained with Scottish dancing and a lively poetry recital. Apparently, they were pleased.

Pregnant with a son, wearing too much clothing and unused to the bush, Katherine made the journey to Trawalla in an open bullock dray. She suffered from the heat and lack of water, but the biggest challenge was negotiating new relationships. Katherine was living right at the pointy end of occupation.

The station was far inland and on the country of the Moner balug clan of the Wathaurong people. Although the previous owners had sold out through fear of Aboriginal resistance, most of Katherine's interactions with the original inhabitants were friendly. But there was always an underlying fear that matters could turn violent, as they would in the 1840s. One day she was alone with the other Scotswoman in the slab hut that served as home when a group of 'seven wild natives' ran past. Both women went for the pistols they kept loaded and handy. They spent the next hour guarding their hut, though had no need to use their weapons.

In her rugged new life, Katherine learned to adjust and to get on with what needed to be done. Her main task was feeding her family and workers. The staple diet on the frontier was mutton, black tea and damper, with little variety. But Katherine took cookery tips from the local Moner balug people. She adapted the food they ate and, for a blistering New Year's Day dinner in 1841, served up: 'kangaroo-soup, roasted [wild] turkey well stuffed, a boiled leg of mutton, a parrot-pie, potatoes, and green peas; next, a plum pudding and strawberry-tart, with plenty of cream . . . [and, later] currant-bun, and a large bowl of curds and cream.'

She also learned from Aboriginal women how to carry her infant son in a basket slung at her side, leaving both hands free to do her work.

Drought and an economic depression forced Katherine and her family to move to a small farm. By mid-1841 they were in Melbourne, where Katherine's husband gained government clerical work and she ran a short-lived school. In September 1841, Katherine returned to Britain with the children. She was in poor health as a result of her efforts to fight a bushfire. Her husband remained behind long enough to declare insolvency and sell up their colonial holdings. Friends had to pay his passage home.

Once again, Katherine adapted to new circumstances. She wrote a memoir of her time in the Australian bush, one of the few forms of publication deemed appropriate for women at that period. Another child was born in December 1843 and Katherine was widowed some time after this. Possibly influenced by her acquired knowledge of indigenous foods, Katherine began to publish successful vegetarian cookery books. She died in 1892.

Building the Barcoo Hotel

The Barcoo River in western Queensland is famous in story and verse, even recognised by 'Banjo' Paterson in his 'Bush Christening':

> On the outer Barcoo where the churches are few,
> And men of religion are scanty,
> On a road never cross'd 'cept by folk that are lost,
> One Michael Magee had a shanty.

While a 'shanty' was usually a place that sold 'sly grog' from unlicensed premises, Paterson may have had Blackall's Barcoo Hotel in mind. This licensed establishment was once owned by the champion hand-blade shearer, Jacky Howe, and has seen many big nights and big fights, almost from the very first day it opened for business.

A 'Captain Tomalin' played a role in the building of the Barcoo Hotel, and subsequently the first pacification of its patrons. After being sacked from his shepherd's job due to falling asleep and losing some of the flock, the Captain took up an offer to travel to the Barcoo River and help build a pub in the newly settled region. After a dry journey, he arrived at his destination:

Next day, after looking around for timber, we came across a fine clump of trees, which we felled and split up in slabs about nine feet long, six inches wide, and two inches thick, suitable for building purposes; the bark we laid out in eight feet lengths to dry in the sun, in order to make ready to put them on the top of the building for a roof.

It took us three weeks to get the timber, etc., ready on the ground and erect the structure, which we named 'The Barcoo Hotel.' It contained three rooms fourteen feet by sixteen and a kitchen twenty feet by ten, separate from the hotel, about six yards away to the rear and thee hundred feet from the bank of the Barcoo River.

I shall never forget the time when all hands began to build this hotel; eight men, including myself, were armed with crowbars, shovels, etc. and worked away for dear life, in the burning sun. From an architectural point of view I have seen far better piggeries erected at home; there was no glass in the windows, only shutters; nothing but an earthern [sic] floor; no lining or ceiling to the rooms, and, in fact, many of the iron bark slabs were two inches apart. The furniture consisted mainly of cases of liquor, English bottled ale, stout, etc.; the bar-counter, seats and bedsteads were made of saplings and empty cases; but nevertheless it answered the purpose for which it was intended.

In due course the house warming took place, and a right merry time we had; the chair was occupied by the proprietor, and he was supported by Dr.—, J.P., on his right and by Mr. C— on his left. Two toasts only [were] given: 'Success to the Barcoo Hotel,' proposed by Dr.—and responded to by the proprietor, the other was from me, and ran:

Here's to all as good as you are
And here's to me as bad as I am,
For as bad as I am and as good as you are
I'm as good as you are, as bad as I am

Despite the toasts, opening night went well, but not so the next evening:

About 7.30 an impromptu concert took place, much to the delight of all concerned, the choruses resounding over the bush as they were roared out, with perhaps more vigour than taste, while all the time the flowing bowl was merrily passed around. About 11 p.m. the proprietor rushed into the kitchen, where the widow and I were sitting, exclaiming:

'Great Scott! What are we to do? The guests have completely taken possession of the bar, Dr. B—, the priest, and I are quite powerless to control them, and in a minute there will be a free fight.'

It was then a happy thought struck me: Said I:

'Leave it to me, strategy is better than force.'

I procured a sack full of empty butter, meat and jam tins, swung it over my shoulder and, taking a lighted candle in my hand, darted into the midst of the mob and jumped onto the counter with a WHOOP that would have done credit to a Sioux Indian. In a moment silence fell on the struggling, swearing throng; they stared at me in wonder, knowing not what was up and probably thinking that I had suddenly become bereft of my senses. Taking advantage of the momentary hush I shouted:

'Now, you roughs, you want trouble and by thunder you shall have it (shaking my sack of tins). I have here about eight pounds of gunpowder; I'm going to set light, and blow this shanty and you, every mother's son of you, to kingdom come.'

So saying, I thrust the lighted candle into the sack and hurled it amongst them, the crash of the tins on the floor was tremendous, and as I burst into a demoniac peal of laughter those valiant revelers fled through the doors and the windows, hustling and jostling each other to get away from the fearful explosion they anticipated, falling over one another, curing, fighting, struggling until not a soul was left.

The bar was cleared in the quickest time on record.

Going by this stirring account, Captain Tomalin could qualify as a colonial superhero.

The Barcoo Hotel burned down at least twice and has been rebuilt a few times during its long and beery history, but it is still in business serving locals and tourists to the region. The area is famous in bush lore and history for many things. It is part of what is now known as 'Matilda Country' from its proximity, in bush distances, to Winton, the area where 'Waltzing Matilda' was composed and first became popular. The region appears in the droving folksong 'A Thousand Miles Away' in the lines 'on the far Barcoo where they eat nardoo, a thousand miles away'. Nardoo is a nutritious paste that the Yandruwandha people make from a fern. In bush slang, the 'Barcoo rot' is a scurvy-like condition, leading to the 'Barcoo spews'. The 'Barcoo salute' is the local version of the 'great Aussie salute', as futile a gesture here as anywhere else in the country.

Gum trees and gumsuckers

Tough, wiry and plentiful, gum trees cover most of Australia's landscape. There are said to be more than 900 species of eucalypts, almost all of them endemic to Australia. At least one species, the rose gum, found in coastal Queensland and New South Wales, is well over 100 million years old. Aboriginal people made use of the tree for medicine, shelter, canoe-building, cordage and smoking ceremonies. The near-uniqueness of the three genera of eucalypts (*Eucalyptus*, *Angophora* and *Corymbia*) to this country and their dominance made the gum tree a likely candidate for the national symbol it has become.

But, at first, most colonists saw the gum tree as a nuisance rather than a benefit. Gums had to be cleared from the land that settlers hoped to cultivate. They were notoriously resistant to the axe and regrew very quickly if not completely rooted out. And, like the rest of the Australian environment, the gum was initially seen to be ugly in comparison to the soft greens of the British countryside. Early attempts to accurately render gum trees in art produced some oddly gothic paintings in which these trees sprouted eerily creeping branches.

From the middle of the nineteenth century, attitudes began to change as settlers discovered many uses for the plentiful gum trees. Their timber could be used for furniture, floor tiles and all kinds of building. When properly extracted and prepared, the oil from the leaves could be used for cleaning, fumigation and healing wounds.

From at least as early as 1840, the term 'gumsucker' was in use to describe native-born Australians who were not Aboriginal. Australians came increasingly to see the prolific gum trees of the continent as a unique and powerful symbol of collective identity.

Towards the end of the century, artists, writers, poets and the general public adopted the gum tree as the country's own icon. As the search for an Australian identity developed, people looked towards the bush for inspiration. The wattle tree and its flowers was an early favourite, while stringybark, ironbark and, in the west, jarrah trees were all invested with an aura of national, regional and colonial identity.

May Gibbs produced her first book featuring the gumnut babies, Snugglepot and Cuddlepie, in 1916. The previous year, the landing of Anzac troops and the following campaign at Gallipoli was hymned by C.J. Dennis in his immensely popular *The Moods of Ginger Mick*, whose poetic letters home to the Sentimental Bloke of Dennis's earlier bestseller, celebrated the birth of the authentic Australian hero we now know as 'the digger'. When the previously unreflective and disaffected Mick gets to Gallipoli with 'the little AIF', he meets people from all walks of life, far beyond his narrow larrikin street world, and discovers that he is part of a nation:

> There is farmers frum the Mallee, there is bushmen down frum
>   Bourke,
> There's college men wiv letters to their name;
> There is grafters, an' there's blokes 'oo never done a 'ard day's
>   work
> Till they tumbled, wiv the rest, into the game—
> An' they're drillin' 'ere together, men uv ev'ry creed an' kind.
> It's Australia! Solid! Dinkum! that 'as left the land be'ind.

And later:

> But the reel, ribuck Australia's 'ere, among the fightin' men.

Images and icons of faraway Australia feature frequently in
Mick's growing awareness of national identity, including gum
trees, of course, as Mick's mate on the homefront mentions
in one of his return letters:

> I 'ave written Mick a letter in reply to one uv 'is, Where 'e arsts
> 'ow things is goin' where the gums an' wattles is.

By the end of the war in 1918, the gum tree and its leaves were
firmly established as the predominant floral icons of Australia.
People now make jewellery in the form of gum leaves, and gum
nuts (technically fruits) are themselves used for jewellery as
well as decorations. Dried branches of eucalypts may be used
as 'Christmas trees' and you can even play a tune on a gum leaf,
if you know how. Eucalyptus oil is still a good cleaning agent
and a common ingredient of both folk and patent remedies for
coughs, colds and wounds. A very useful tree, it is possibly the
only one to have its own national day—23 March.

Slippery Bob and other delights

Feeding and maintaining the human frame was a big challenge
in modern Australia's early days. People had to eat and they

also needed to be able to treat—or try to—a range of minor and major afflictions and injuries, many of which often proved fatal. Some of the cooking could also fall into this category.

The 'Bushman's Diet' was described in 1843 as 'mutton, tea and damper, three times a day' and settlers continued to refer to the monotony of this diet for decades. A 'Darling Sandwich' was said to be a goanna between two sheets of bark, and very tasty, too, no doubt. A 'Murrumbidgee Sandwich' was a wild pig in between two bags of flour, while a 'Stockman's Dinner' was a 'smoke and a spit'.

With these challenging dishes as the staples of bush food, some of the recipes of the past must have been comparatively delicious. Cow heels were boiled with vegetables then baked in breadcrumbs for 'a nice luncheon dish cold', according to *The Antipodean Cookery Book* of 1895. The same useful kitchen companion provided the recipe for jugged wallaby. Kangaroo minced pies were recommended in the *Australian Journal* of 1870. Based on diced 'roo steak, the resulting gunk could be stored in preserving jars until next Christmas.

The standard sweet treat of bush life was a sticky light treacle: 'Cocky's joy' was golden syrup, four times cheaper than jam in 1909 and, provided in 2 pound tins, much more portable: 'Every boundary rider's camp was littered with half empty tins of it,' according to journalist Charles Bean who also provided a description of 'a bushman's climax of misery': 'When I got back to my camp it had been raining. My tent had blown down, and my fire was put out. There was a wet kangaroo dog in my blanket, a crow had run off with my soap, and my cocky's joy was full of ants.'

On the same bush journey along the Darling River to Ivanhoe, Bean reported on the 'meat' situation:

In these immense spaces, where men are so few, though towns have no butchers; and at some of the hotels they discreetly offer you 'meat,' without particularising. Through the window you can see big herds of goats poking around the back yards—and

when they speak of 'ration sheep' you silently understand. It is
said that some time since, when the Governor came through, they
sent 70 miles to find a sheep, and gave it up; but returning killed
a pig and shot some galas—roast pork and pigeon pie. The local
policeman did enjoy himself. It was the first time for 18 mouths he
had eaten anything but goat.

A dish that strikes the modern palate as especially objectionable was known as 'Slippery Bob'. It was a mixture of possum
brains and emu fat and was a favourite, along with parrot pie
and possum curry. Pumpkin and bear—koala, that is—were
the staple food of hard-up cocky farmers.

Food was not the only thing that needed to be improvised
from whatever was available. Sickness and injury were everyday
occurrences in the bush, where there was often no chance of
proper medical attention. People simply had no choice but to
find remedies and treatments in the bush itself.

Aboriginal people had developed an extensive array of medicines from their environment, and settlers eventually learned
some of this bush medicine. Eucalyptus oil could help with
fevers, chills and pain. Kangaroo apple was good for swollen
joints. The antiseptic properties of ti-tree oil were valuable in
a paste for wounds and as a tea for sore throats, while desert
mushrooms could be sucked for mouth infections and billy
goat plum, or Kakadu plum in that part of the country, was
rich in vitamin C. Sores and cuts could be treated with the
antibiotic properties of emu bush, while the right kind of mud,
sand and termite dirt helped wounds to resist infection.

Many of these treatments were specific to the local environment in different parts of the country. In Victoria, New South
Wales and southeast Queensland, the bark of hickory wattle
was used to make a treatment for skin problems.

Over time and through experience, these ancient but effective medicines found their way into the first-aid kits of bush
folk. They also had a few treatments of their own, not necessarily efficacious. Kerosene was universally applied to wounds,

stings, ticks and anything else irritating. It was also good for keeping ants from food stored in containers by standing the containers in tin cans full of 'kero'. Even more dangerous was a small dab of strychnine on the tongue to relieve the DTs from too much grog. A favourite of the old hands.

With little medical expertise available or affordable, people relied on Aboriginal knowledge, on folk remedies and, increasingly, the pharmacist. As populations soared in the wake of the goldrushes, pharmacies sprang up in town and country, offering a range of treatments or 'patent medicines'. Some were based on medical knowledge, though many were not. The Spartan conditions and general medical ignorance of the colonial era was a happy hunting ground for charlatans and purveyors of quack medicines. These purported to cure everything from headache and 'melancholy' to loss of teeth and major chronic illnesses. Most were useless, or worse, often containing opium or similar addictive or dangerous substances legal in those days. These dubious medicines became colloquially known as 'snake oil'.

Some of the major health problems were diarrhoea and dysentery, sometimes severe enough to be fatal. There were many pills and potions available for relief, including 'Jayne's Carminative Balsam' and 'W Harris's antibilious mixtures'. As one manufacturer of these concoctions put it: 'No inhabitant of the bush, no digger, nor "anyone" subject to laxity of the bowels should be without a bottle.' Judging by the number and variety of 'snake oil' bottles dug up by archaeologists, few were.

The swagman's story

As the Great Depression of the 1930s ground on, Thomas Willis wrote to a Queensland newspaper objecting to the use of the Americanism 'hobo', then being applied to the large numbers of men tramping bush ways in search of scarce work. Willis argued that in America hoboes were 'loafers, wasters and men who will do anything rather than work'. The swagman, or bagman, by contrast, was a genuine worker down on his luck and looking for honest employment. The main aim of anyone 'waltzing Matilda, humping bluey, or carrying the swag hundreds of miles' was to find a job, not to avoid one. He then gave an account of his own wanderings during the industrial troubles and economic depression of an earlier era:

Early in 1894 I was in Coolgardie, W.A., where condensed water was 1s. a gallon, where men hung out their blankets when any sign of a storm appeared so as to get them wet and by wringing them out, if sufficient rain came, to obtain water to get a wash, and where men who died of typhoid, if in luck's way, had some sort of a coffin, with the brands of the merchandise still showing on the timber. I spent what money I had and was forced to leave before capital had opened up the goldfield.

There was absolutely no work in WA for 't'othersiders', as men from the Eastern States were termed, and by considerable ingenuity I got back to Sydney. At this time there were hundreds of unemployed in Sydney. Hotels gave out their refuse food at 9 o'clock each night and the rush for it was known as the 9 o'clock rush. Men were sometimes injured in the wild scramble for this food. A good meal, with a varied menu to choose from, at half-a-dozen or more eating houses was obtainable for 4d or one dozen meal tickets for 3s. 8d could be purchased in Sydney then if one had the cash.

Every day hundreds crowded any place where work was offering when only half-a-dozen or so men were wanted. The New South Wales Government were giving a free pass on the railways to miners who would go to any goldfield, old or new, and I took advantage of this and got a pass to Mudgee. I left Sydney without a penny, after purchasing half a blanket, a billy can and one or two other things, and for food one loaf of bread. I arrived at the end of the train journey about midnight and cleared off into the darkness. Being winter it was bitterly cold, but, I laid down and slept. At daylight I was frozen out and found I had slept just outside the cemetery fence. My loaf of bread [rhyming slang for 'head'] was at a loss how to get food.

I decided I must have food. I would ask for it first, and then if refused I must get it. The first store I came to gave me willingly flour, tea and sugar and I started to walk back to Longreach and take any work offering along the route. I had sufficient sense to get hold of the axe first when I saw a heap of wood and axe near it or a woman cutting wood and I was never refused food and often got it without asking when travelling in farming or cocky country. When I reached the sheep country I got among the travellers called swagmen then and later bagmen. To be a proper bagman it was necessary to have three sets of bags with very long necks, so that a supply of empty bags was ready for any 'hand out', and the long-necked bags made anything put in them look small and a good-natured station storekeeper might give a little more. It was necessary to be alive to all this or you went hungry, as work was very scarce and local men got the preference. Good bushmen capable of doing any kind of bush work could not get work.

My boots wore out and I mended them with greenhide—at that time classed with stringy bark as the mainstay of Queensland.

When I reached Goodoga, a township towards the Queensland border, I found a shearers' strike on. I got into a strike camp. As I was not a shearer I could not have got work had I been willing to take it. Eventually the station owners connected with this particular strike camp and came to terms. I was engaged as a roustabout, the first work I had been offered or obtained in my journey almost across the centre of New South Wales. I made the most of it. I agreed with both shearers and roustabouts' cooks to kill and dress all the meat they required after working hours for 2s. 6d, a week each. I built an oven out of a 400-gallon ships' tank and other jobs to get enough money to purchase horses and give humping the swag best.

This shearers' strike brought the riff-raff of Sydney, Bourke and other towns into the bush as free labourers or strike breakers. After this there were men who could be termed hoboes travelling the country. It was these men who introduced a way of getting a man's trousers from under his head by fixing a needle on the end of a stick, and while one jabbed the needle into his foot the other grabbed his pants as he sprang up from sleep to see what had bitten him. These men were known as 'Whiteley King' men and 'white wings' and discarded tincan billies, which most of these men carried, were called 'Whiteley King billies'. Mr. Whiteley King was, I think, secretary of the Pastoralists' Union.

Murders became frequent in the bush and it was common to see notices of rewards for conviction or identification stuck on trees in several bush districts of New South Wales. This class of traveller stole from everybody, killed the squatters' sheep wholesale and became a perfect curse.

Thomas Willis could have written 'pages more of the hardships which these men have to face in wet and dry seasons, with no chance of obtaining a decent meal', but hoped he had made it clear that the honest swagman should not be confused with the layabout hobo—'It is well to remember that this army of men is being increased every day by single and married men through no fault of their own.'

Stringybark and greenhide

Along with the humble kerosene tin, stringybark and green-hide were considered the 'complete bushman's trinity'. 'Kero' tins could be reworked into all manner of useful items, from food utensils to the walls of a bush hut and many things in between. Stringybark, the fibrous covering of the stringybark tree, could be plaited into surprisingly strong and useful lengths of cordage. Whatever needed tying-up could be secured with this bush adaptation. Greenhide was the raw skin of cows, so-called because it had not yet undergone the tanning process necessary to turn it into finished leather. Crude though it was, greenhide could be cut into strips and twisted into ropes used in other forms for a variety of needs.

By the 1860s, stringybark and greenhide were so widely used that they were celebrated in song by the goldfields ball-adist, 'George Chanson' (George Loyau):

I sing of a commodity, it's one that will not fail yer,
I mean the common oddity, the mainstay of Australia;
Gold it is a precious thing, for commerce it increases,
But stringy bark and green hide, can beat it all to pieces.

Stringy bark and green hide, that will never fail yer!
Stringy bark and green hide, the mainstay of Australia.

If you travel on the road, and chance to stick in Bargo,
To avoid a bad capsize [*sic*], you must unload your cargo;
For to pull a dray about, I do not see the force on,
Take a bit of green hide, and hook another horse on.

Stringy bark and green hide, that will never fail yer!
Stringy bark and green hide, the mainstay of Australia.

If you chance to take a dray, and break your leader's traces,
Get a bit of green hide, to mend the broken places.
Green hide is a useful thing all that you require;
But stringy bark's another thing when you want a fire.

Stringy bark and green hide, that will never fail yer!
Stringy bark and green hide, the mainstay of Australia.

If you want to build a hut, to keep out wind and weather,
Stringy bark will make it snug, and keep it well together;
Green hide, if it's used by you, will make it all the stronger,
For if you tie it with green hide, its sure to last the longer.

Stringy bark and green hide, that will never fail yer!
Stringy bark and green hide, the mainstay of Australia.

New chums to this golden land, never dream of failure,
Whilst you've got such useful things as these in fair Australia;
For stringy bark and green hide will never, never fail you,
Stringy bark and green hide is the mainstay of Australia.

Stringy bark and green hide, that will never fail yer!
Stringy bark and green hide, the mainstay of Australia.

Drover 'Kurini' Jim Mathers rounding up horses in the outback,
Northern Territory (undated).

9

Mysteries

Her song is silence; Unto her
Its mystery clings.
Silence is the interpreter
Of deeper things.

'An Australian Symphony', George Essex Evans, 1906

The Devil's Pool

The clear waters of Babinda Boulders, south of Cairns in Queensland, tumble through large rocks then drop 15 metres to a churning pool below, concealing dangerous flows and tunnels. In local Aboriginal tradition, the boulders are significant and feared. In 2005, elder Annie Wonga told the legend of doomed love that explains why.

After marrying a tribal elder, the young girl Oolana fell in love with Dyga, a young man from a visiting Aboriginal group. The lovers ran away and were found at Babinda, the place where water flows across the rocks. As the couple were torn apart never to see each other again, the despairing Oolana jumped into the pool. As she drowned, there was a great

disturbance and the waters threw up rocks. It is said that sometimes Oolana might call a wandering man to her in the hope
that he is her lost Dyga. Consequently, the pool is considered
an evil place.

The deep waterhole at Babinda Boulders was already
known as the 'Devil's Pool' in the 1920s, its evil reputation
probably learned from this story. At this time, the place was
generally shunned by Aboriginal people but its natural beauty
was already attracting tourists.

The first recorded drowning was in 1933, then an eight-
year-old boy drowned there in 1940. By 2008 at least another
seventeen deaths had been counted at the same place, causing
great concern in the community. According to local legend,
all those who have died were visitors, never local people. The
locals swim there quite safely.

On one occasion around 2005, a visitor described as
'a hippie' apparently tried to kick a bronze memorial plaque
for a previous fatality. The long-haired man slipped, fell and
drowned in the same hole as the earlier victim. Not surprisingly,
by 2005 local police and emergency teams were becoming frus-
trated at having to risk their own lives to retrieve the bodies
of unwary tourists from Devil's Pool. In one case, that took
almost six weeks.

Aboriginal people feel that these fatalities are a consequence of visitors failing to respect the significance of the site.
One incident involved a group of white people dressing up as
Aborigines and acting out the Oolana and Dyga legend at the
site. This was felt to be deeply disrespectful of both the legend
and the location.

The legend and the reality of the Devil's Pool run side by side.
The Babinda community is united in its concern for the place,
their place. Both the legend of Oolana and Dyga and the stories
surrounding the fatal history of the spot involve outsiders and
the consequences for those who come to Babinda Boulders and
fail to respect either, or both, its spiritual meanings or its very
real dangers.

Tall tales

In August 2016 a large mystery cat was spotted and photographed in West Gippsland. The report and picture were not made public until April 2017 and even then, the man who saw the 'alien big cat', or 'ABCs' as these creatures are often known, wished to remain anonymous. Others are not so reticent and there have been dozens of sightings reported around Victoria and elsewhere in the country. When evidence has been presented, such as photographs or even plaster casts of footprints, experts have declared these to be inconclusive or simply large but standard bush animals.

Mysterious big cats—usually likened to tigers, pumas or panthers—have been reported around Australia, going back decades, or even further. There are now so many of these creatures that any bush region worth its salt is not in the hunt without one. The explanatory folklore surrounding local big cat traditions often involves animals escaping from a passing circus, or sometimes a mascot fleeing from a World War II United States military facility. Wherever they have come from, there is no shortage of outsized phantom cats roaming wherever there is a reasonably substantial stretch of bush, mountains or valleys.

And it's not only big cats, alien or otherwise, who might be roaming the bush. What about 'Melon Man'?

Thought to be a misunderstanding of 'Malaan man', an unexplained creature seen around the Atherton Tableland area in the 1960s and 70s, this anomaly was said to have a pig's head but a man's body. As people drove home from the Saturday night dance, the monster would run alongside their car, looking in at the occupants through the windows. Stories about a hairy gorilla-like creature had been circulating in the area since at least the 1930s, though there doesn't seem to be much of a connection between the pig-headed apparition and the gorilla-man, a variation of the 'Yowie', about which there are many stories throughout the eastern states.

Stories of hairy, ape-like beasts roaming the bush were old hat when Sydney Jephcott, owner of Creewah Station near Bombala, New South Wales, 'discovered the tracks of an apparently immense animal' in 1912. Sydney excitedly ordered a supply of plaster of Paris to make some impressions of the enormous footprints, 45 centimetres long and 20 wide. Around the same time, another man out hunting in the same area reported an encounter with 'an immense object resembling a man'. He approached the creature but it picked up a stick, growled at him and vanished into the thick scrub. A smart move, given the propensity of hunters to shoot.

The Yowie, in one form or another, has become well-known in recent years, mainly through the work of cryptozoologists. The topic is controversial, with some claiming that the Yowie is a 1970s invention derived from American interest in their own 'Bigfoot' and similar fabulous beasts. Whether that is so or not, there have been accounts of hairy, man-like creatures seen in the bush from the early years of European settlement and many Aboriginal traditions include similar figures, often known as 'yahoos', though also bearing a variety of Aboriginal names.

Henry Lawson built one of his short stories around his childhood recollections of bush hairy men:

As far back as I can remember, the yarn of the Hairy Man was told in the Blue Mountain district of New South Wales. It scared children coming home by bush tracks from school and boys out late after lost cows; and even grown bushmen, when going along a lonely track after sunset, would hold their backs hollow and whistle a tune when they suddenly heard a thud, thud of a kangaroo leaping off through the scrub. Other districts also had spooks and bogies—the escaped tiger; the ghost of the convict who had been done to death and buried in his irons; ghosts of men who had hanged themselves; the ghost of the hawker's wife whose husband had murdered her with a tomahawk in the lonely camp by the track; the ghost of the murdered bushman whose mate quietly stepped behind him as he sat reflecting over a pipe and broken in the back of his head with an axe, and afterwards burned the body between two logs; ghosts of victims whose murders had been avenged and of undiscovered murders that had been done right enough—all sorts and conditions of ghosts, none of them cheerful, most of them grimly original and characteristic of the weirdly, melancholy and aggressively lonely Australian bush. But the Hairy Man was permanent, and his country spread from the eastern slopes of the Great Dividing Range right out to the ends of the western spurs. He had been heard of and seen and described so often and by so many reliable liars, that most people agreed that there must be something. The most popular and enduring theory was that he was a gorilla, or an ourang-outang [sic] which had escaped from a menagerie long ago. He was also said to be a new kind of kangaroo, or the last of a species of Australian animals which hadn't been discovered yet. Anyway, in some places, he was regarded as a danger to children coming home from school, as were wild bullocks, snakes, and an occasional bushman in the D.T.'s. So now and then, when the yarn had a revival, search parties were organized, and went out with guns to find the Hairy Man, and to settle him and the question one way or the other. But they never found him.

In Lawson's story, the hairy man is described as, 'About as tall as a man and twice as broad, arms nearly as long as himself, big wide mouth with grinning teeth—and covered all over with red hair.'

Like most rugged areas of the country, the Blue Mountains have long been a favourite location for hairy man/yahoo/Yowie/whatever yarns. A recent television series, *Cleverman*, has made excellent dramatic use of the story, further fuelling the legends.

Small tales

In September 2003, archaeologists were digging in a cave at Liang Bua on the Indonesian island of Flores. The archaeologists were around 6 metres below the cave floor when they removed some soil to reveal a child's skull. A couple of days later the scientists returned to their find with other experts to examine the skull. It was not a child but a full-sized adult.

Further excavations followed, more skeletal remains were discovered, other experts consulted and the results published in scientific journals. The remains were of a dwarf species of early humans and were named *Homo floresiensis*—popularly dubbed 'Hobbits' after J.R.R. Tolkien's famous books. Not everyone was convinced about this unprecedented discovery of ancient human occupation in this part of the world. It was suggested that the bones were those of a group of malformed humans, a freakish anomaly in the long story of human evolution. An extensive scientific controversy ensued. But as more and more scientists reviewed the evidence, the identification of a previously unknown human species was more widely accepted.

The 'Hobbits' probably stood a little over a metre tall and weighed around 20–40 kilograms. They made stone tools and hunted pygmy elephants, Komodo dragons, rats, birds and bats, and probably had learned the use of fire. Their brains were significantly smaller than those of modern humans and they were thought to show more features in common with earlier rather than with modern humans. Whether they were a previously unknown form of human or a different species altogether, they appeared to have occupied Flores for more than half a million years. Further discoveries have since been made on the island, provoking further debate about the origins and meaning of these remains.

One hotly contested aspect of the Hobbit story revolves around the exact dates of their existence. If they were on Flores and perhaps other islands at the time other groups migrated southwards, did they live alongside those groups? If so, for how long? Or perhaps the Hobbits fell prey to larger, stronger and smarter newcomers and faded into oblivion? No one knows for sure, though some research published in 2016 suggests that the Hobbits vanished almost 40,000 years earlier than pre-viously thought. If so, it is unlikely they would have had much, if any, contact with modern humans. And yet, the locals on Flores often report sightings of small human-like beings in their forests. Research continues, along with healthy scientific controversy.

Not surprisingly, in a land as mysterious as ours, there is also a strong tradition of little people in Australia. The rainfor-est around Tully in Queensland is said to harbour a population of 1-metre tall Aborigines. First reported in 1942 by a local farmer, the small people were seen again during scrub clearing in the 1960s. Some people have linked them with another Tully tradition, flying saucers, first reported in the mid-1960s and much embroidered since.

But stories from other parts of the country also tell of small beings still living in remote bush locations. The Ngadjon (also Ngadjonji) people of northern Queensland speak of the *Janjarri*, who are said to be covered in gingery hair. They frequent trees and live mainly on insects. They fear dogs and have a distinctive odour. Reliable witnesses have occasionally caught a glimpse of these beings, but they remain mostly unseen and unknown. In the Kimberley region of Western Australia, the Aboriginal people are familiar with the *Rai*, local little people who carry out mischievous tricks, much like those attributed to small beings, including fairies, in other parts of the world. Further south the Noongar people tell of the *bulyit*, a small hairy devil who comes out after sunset and abducts children.

One strong theme of little people legends involves a battle between them and tall people. The tall group is victorious and wipes out their smaller enemies. If these traditions represented reality, that might explain the reluctance of small people to reveal themselves.

While this is all speculation, there are folk traditions of diminutive beings known around the world. Although these are frequently of a supernatural character—the best-known example would be the Irish leprechaun—the stories are extremely widespread. Small beings are found in African lore, in Celtic legend, in Native American story, in Japan and throughout Europe. So why shouldn't Australia have its own tradition of small folk?

Who stole Waltzing Matilda?

His name was Thomas Wood.

Who?

Dr Thomas Wood, musician, composer, author and traveller, was once a well-known figure in Australian cities, bush and outback. He came here first from England as a mobile music examiner in 1930 and later published a bestselling book about his Australian adventures titled *Cobbers*, which made him a minor celebrity in that period.

Wood was well-connected in society but also had 'the common touch' and interacted with people of all social backgrounds as he travelled through the country assessing the musical skills of Australia. One of his interests was searching for Australian folksongs. In August 1930, he arrived at Winton, Queensland. In conversation with the publican of the North Gregory Hotel, Mr Shanahan, Thomas mentioned 'Waltzing Matilda', a song he thought had 'the right sort of smack' to be a popular folksong. Did Shanahan know it?

'Did he know it? Did he not! It was written in this very town,' was Shanahan's reply. The publican excitedly told the equally excited Wood how 'Banjo' Paterson and Christina Macpherson had together composed the song back in 1895 and the locals had been singing it ever since.

'And a thundering good song it is,' enthused Wood. 'Good enough to be the unofficial national anthem of Australia.'

Wood wrote of the incident: 'I was so pleased with this discovery, and he was so pleased, and we were both so pleased with "Waltzing Matilda" that we said we must make a day of it. We did, not alcoholically, but topographically.' Shanahan then drove the visitor all over the district where he met many 'wonderful people'. The rest of the day was filled with local sightseeing and we hear little more about 'Waltzing Matilda' in *Cobbers*, though Wood would write again, contradictorily, on several occasions about this event.

The version that Mr Shanahan gave to Thomas Wood in the North Gregory Hotel was not the local Queensland favourite, but one that had been adapted in 1903 as an advertising jingle for the Billy Tea company. Changes were made to the original lyrics and promotional copies of the words and music were given away with packets of Billy Tea. This became the most widely known version of the song at this time. It was this version that Thomas Wood stole.

As his subsequent accounts in *Cobbers* and elsewhere make clear, Wood was entranced with the song and his avowedly chance discovery of it. Although he habitually claimed never to have heard the song before encountering Mr Shanahan, it is clear from his diary and other references that he was well aware of 'Waltzing Matilda' before he reached Australia and so before he reached Winton. As early as June 1930 he is quoted in *The Queenslander* newspaper saying: 'Of the folksongs that I have heard which I imagine express Australian individuality, none has impressed me so much as "Waltzing Matilda".' And before then, we know that a young Australian passenger aboard his ship, Rowland Morris, had sung the song one night during a sing-song and Wood also wrote in his diary that he fully intended to acquire a version during his stay Down Under. And he did, with ongoing consequences.

Shortly after collecting it from Mr Shanahan, Wood arranged his new find for piano in his distinctive four-square style, and published it in his travel book *Cobbers*. This came out in 1934 and was an instant bestseller in Australia and in Britain. Unfortunately, Wood and his publishers neglected to clear the small matter of copyright with the owners of that piece of intellectual property, the Australian music publishers Allan and Company. Legal proceedings were instituted, beginning a long and winding trail of correspondence in the files of publishers and lawyers in Britain, the United States and Australia.

While the legal wrangling wound on, Thomas Wood's arrangement of the song, not then the iconic national song it has since become, was taken up by the famed Australian singer, Peter Dawson. He recorded a couple of versions. The first was released in 1938. It was a hit, establishing that particular version of 'Waltzing Matilda' as the unofficial national anthem. The second, complete with a kookaburra call introduction, was released during World War II in 1942, further cementing the widespread popularity of the song.

The minimalist story of a suicidal swagman, a sheep, the squatter and three trooper policemen was created by the poet 'Banjo' Paterson and Christina Macpherson, who adapted the music near Winton in 1895. It is known in various versions, but they all tell an unmistakeable tale of the bush as it was perceived at the end of the nineteenth century. Australians continue to sing the song as a national musical brand and it is known, and played, throughout the world whenever there is a need to herald Australia.

Lasseter's undertaker

'Playing crib and drinking rum are the best things in life and you can do 'em together.' The man who made this statement, Bob Buck, was one of the great characters and bushmen of Australia.

Born in Adelaide in 1881, Robert Buck learned the ways of the bush from his pioneering uncles in the Northern Territory, Joseph and Allan Breaden. He was a drover, saddler and station manager who was renowned for his generosity to travellers and was well-liked by Aboriginal people. In the 1930s, Bob began working for inland expeditions and surveys preparing supplies, airfields and rescue arrangements.

The ill-fated Central Australian Gold Expedition went in search of Harold Lasseter's fabled gold reef in 1930. Lasseter claimed to have stumbled on the reef many years before, some-where in the rugged Petermann Ranges, straddling the border of the Northern Territory and Western Australia in Central Australia. In the economic disaster of the Great Depression of the 1930s, he found some investors willing to take a punt that the intensely convincing Lasseter might just be telling the truth. The company was formed, funds invested and prep-arations made to get Lasseter back to where he said the reef could be found.

It was a disaster from the outset, with Lasseter becoming secretive and paranoid about the location of the reef, squab-bling between the expedition members, and attaining a level of incompetence reminiscent of the Burke and Wills disaster of the previous century. Eventually, Lasseter took off into the desert with only one other expedition member, Paul Johns, and a few camels. Johns later returned, claiming there was a quarrel and Lasseter drew a gun but Johns managed to disarm him. He left the gold-seeker with two camels and provisions for a couple of months. Lasseter headed into country known only to the Pitjantjatjara and was never heard from again. Bob Buck was called in to find him.

It took Buck and two Aboriginal companions weeks to find a trace of Lasseter's trail. They followed it to the small cave where he had died alone after two and-a-half months in the desert. His diary told the grim story of his slow death by starvation and exposure, despite occasional assistance from local Aboriginal people. There was no information about the location of the fatal trove. Buck gathered what effects were left and they buried Lasseter's bones.

The rescuers were in danger of perishing themselves for much of the journey back to Alice Springs but eventually arrived with the expected but grim news. Then the trouble really began and we have been hearing about it ever since.

Did Buck find some indication of the fabled gold's location that he kept to himself? He was to lead another expedition into the Petermann Ranges only a few months later. This

trek was called off but only added to the rumours and speculations fuelled by members of the original expedition in articles
and books.

Was it really Lasseter that Buck buried? He was himself
reluctant to be definite, suggesting the possibility that the
skeleton might have been that of an Aborigine. Apart from the
diary and effects, he had no way of knowing. This uncertainty
produced a rumour that Lasseter was not dead at all. He was
still alive when Buck got there and was helped by the bushman
to escape to America where he became a Mormon pastor.

Buck's notorious sense of humour and propensity for telling
tall tales only added fuel to an already volatile mix. Once,
on being challenged about Lasseter's survival, he allegedly
responded by throwing a set of dentures onto the table, saying,
'They're Lasseter's.'

In 1936, Buck guided the Foy expedition into the desert.
The intention of this group was, reportedly, to shoot documentary film footage, though they passed through what was
then already known as 'Lasseter country'. Along the way they
encountered more than three hundred Aboriginal people 'who
showed no hostility' and camped near Lasseter's last home.
The expedition leader was taken to the gravesite by Buck and
'the mound was found intact, just as Buck had left it some
years previously'.

A few years later, the famous bushman was interviewed
during a visit to Melbourne and gave his considered opinion
on the Lasseter saga:

> Lasseter never found a reef of gold in Central Australia . . . As a
> matter of fact, Lasseter never visited the sand-hill country until
> I took his body there for burial. The story of Lasseter's reef is
> only a myth. Lasseter imagined the existence of a reef in Central
> Australia after he had read a copy of a novel, printed in 1912.
> The novel described a tribe of aborigines who carried spears with
> heads of solid gold. I have been all over the so-called Lasseter
> country and there is not a trace of gold there.

Described as 'short, grey-haired, with keen brown eyes and a sweeping grey moustache', Buck was ever the joker and called his 1295-square kilometre cattle station near Alice Springs 'a small allotment' and said he could 'stand on the back doorstep and throw the dish-water over the whole station'.

Bob Buck died in 1960, shortly after his favourite pub burned down. The local newspaper failed to coax a life story out of the wily bushman: 'I don't think I have long enough left to tell you it all. When they bury me I hope no Territory liar stops away, otherwise I'll be lonely.'

Lost gold

Lasseter's Reef is Australia's and one of the world's most famous lost gold deposits. But there are many real goldmines, now lost in the bush, that once tempted prospectors to seek their fortunes.

The alpine regions of eastern Victoria are said to be peppered with old goldmines. Researchers have found old miners' huts still full of cooking and eating utensils that tell tales of the hard lives fossickers endured in search of the precious metal. The remains of the Razorback Mine, dating from the late nineteenth century, can still be seen above the snowline. Another hardship location was the 'Black Hole' on the eastern branch of the Ovens River, so-called because the sun rarely shone and miners were unable to dry their wet clothes and bedding. Somewhere west of Avoca is the 'Lost Chinaman's Mine', an elusive spot for which modern fossickers are still searching.

As well as mines where people worked honestly to win their wealth—if they were lucky—there are many tales of the ill-gotten hordes hidden by bushrangers. The booty from Frank Gardiner's Eugowra Rocks gold escort robbery of 1862 was rumoured to be hidden somewhere in the Weddin Mountains and still attracts hopeful hunters from time to time. Somewhere north of Dunedoo, in New South Wales, at a place now known as 'The Gap' lie the proceeds of a gold robbery at Gulgong during the 1870s. With the troopers closing in and his horse tiring, one of the numerous local bushrangers opted to 'plant' the two heavy bags. According to legend, he never returned to collect them.

The New England bushranger known as 'Thunderbolt' (Fred Ward) was an efficient robber and modest liver. Much of the loot he lifted was never found and the hunt is still on. Favoured locations are Thunderbolt's Rock near Uralla and Thunderbolt's Cave near Tenterfield.

During the late 1830s and 1840s a gang led by 'Jew Boy' Edward Davis operated around Dungog, Wollombi and Maitland and probably further north. They robbed many people and were thought to have buried the loot. As a local recollected hearing in his childhood during the 1890s: 'Every old resident of the Dungog district knows the local tradition that the treasure of the bushrangers still lies hidden somewhere about Pilcher's Mountain.'

An Irish bushranger named John Tennant was active in what is now the Australian Capital Territory in the 1820s and allegedly stashed his booty on Mount Tennentin Namadji National Park. The hopeful are still looking, including those who follow the digital pastime of 'geocaching'.

Victoria has its share of these legends. 'Captain Melville' (probably Francis McCallum) was busy as leader of the Mount Macedon gang in the 1850s. His swag is thought to be somewhere between Melbourne and Beechworth, possibly in his hideout at Melville Caves. A bushranger named Buttrey robbed the gold coach in the Beechworth area during the goldrushes and before he was caught he managed to hide his haul, reputedly somewhere in the Woolshed Valley.

These are many other legends of this kind known wherever gold has been mined and stolen. The geology, geography and history of this country are all ideally suited to produce such yarns. They are the Australian end of a large body of lost treasures, mines, hordes and the like said to be hidden in many parts of the world. Rarely are any of these located. But every now and then, someone with a metal detector turns up an ancient treasure trove or professional underwater hunters find a long-lost wreck stuffed with goodies. When a story turns out to be true, it inflames what seems to be a perpetual human desire to fantasise about hidden treasures and, for some, to go and hunt for them. Why? Well, why not, you just might get lucky!

The forgotten bushranger

'The people round know me right well—they call me Johnny Troy.' The trouble was that no one did know a bushranger hero named 'Johnny Troy', not in this country, at least. So, who was he, if he ever existed?

There were several incidental mentions of Troy and his deeds in historical documents and folklore. He featured briefly in a poem titled 'The Convict's Tour to Hell', probably composed by 'Frank the Poet' (Francis McNamara), in or before 1839. The poem is a celebration of convicts and bushrangers, including the famous Jack Donohoe, shot dead in 1830. Troy is mentioned in the same breath as the now much better-known Donohoe. The poem is a fantasy of a convict, Frank himself, visiting hell, where he finds all the despised overseers and jailers writhing in eternal agony. When the devil hears that Frank was a convict in life, he immediately says that he has come to the wrong place. Convicts should all go to heaven. When Frank reaches the Pearly Gates, he confronts St Peter who asks:

> Where's your certificate
> Or if you have not one to show
> Pray who in Heaven do you know?

Frank answers:

> Well I know Brave Donohue, Young Troy and Jenkins too
> And many others whom floggers mangled
> And lastly were by Jack Ketch strangled.

Frank is allowed straight into heaven where he is made 'a welcome guest', along with his old convict mates.

But that was about all anyone knew of this Irish bushranger until the 1950s, when American folksong collectors began to hear a 'Johnny Troy' ballad—mainly among lumberjacks. It seems that while Johnny Troy's vigorous song had faded away in Australia, it had been well received by the Americans, who often sang it together with a couple of other Australian bushranger ballads, 'Jack Donohoe' and 'The Wild Colonial Boy'. It is likely that these songs reached America during the California goldrushes, which explains how they got there. But there was still no news of the lost bushranger in Australia. Until some solid research by the late Stephan Williams turned up the whole true history of Johnny Troy.

John Troy, aged eighteen, was transported for burglary and felony from Dublin aboard the ship *Asia* in 1825. He was a weaver by trade and drew a seven-year sentence. Soon after arriving here, he was found guilty of robbery and served two years on the *Phoenix* 'hulk', or prison ship. After completing this sentence, Troy's record was one of continual 'bolting' from iron gangs and involvement in mutinies aboard convict ships, details of which appear in his ballad. He served time at Moreton Bay, in Brisbane, and after being returned to Sydney in 1831 escaped again and took to bushranging. After a busy period of robbing travellers in company with other escaped convicts, Troy was betrayed and recaptured in 1832.

He was tried with three others for highway robbery. The court heard from numerous witnesses and policemen, and eventually the judge 'summed up at considerable length', sending the jury to consider their verdict at 7 p.m. No doubt anxious to be off home or to the pub, the jury came back a few minutes later with a guilty verdict for three of the defendants. John Troy, Tom Smith and Michael Anderson were, unusually, sentenced to hang immediately. The judge was clearly not in a good mood as the legislation for capital punishment clearly provided for a three-day break before execution.

In the event, there was a respite of a week but on 18 August 1832, Troy and Smith (Anderson was reprieved) were led out to be hanged in Sydney Gaol. 'Great crowds assembled to view the awful termination of their lives.' Troy accepted his sentence saying, 'He had committed many offences, and deserved to suffer death.' He preferred death to a lifetime in a penal settlement. He also claimed, in proper outlaw hero style, that Smith was innocent. After some words from the clergy present, the executioners fiddled with the ropes 'in their usual bungling manner'. The condemned men, both carrying red handkerchiefs, were finally put out of their misery and 'after some convulsive struggling, were ushered into eternity'.

And Johnny Troy did, however undeservedly, achieve an immortality of sorts. Hanged criminals were usually thrown into cheap coffins and carted off for burial in the 'Public Nuisance' cart used to collect dead animals from the streets. But in this case the bodies of Troy and Smith were given into the care of a cousin of Troy's. There was an Irish wake around the bodies that night and subscription taken up for good quality coffins. Next day, the coffins were taken out and laid in front of the house of the bushrangers' betrayer, a man named Donohoe (not Jack Donohoe). The red handkerchief Troy had been holding at his death was thrown ominously at the traitor's door. The police had to break up the crowd, which gave 'three groans' for Donohoe, and a long procession followed the dead men to their final burying place.

Troy was a convict hero. The ballad that celebrated his real and imagined activities is much like those romanticising other bushranger heroes, real and mythic. Troy is born in Dublin, 'brought up by honest parents', but is transported to New South Wales after robbing a widow. He escapes and with three companions takes to the bush—'Four of the bravest heroes who ever handled gun.' Robbing on the highway, they come across an old man and demand his gold watch and money—on pain of having his brains blown out. The man pleads that he has none of these and also has a wife and family 'daily to provide'. On hearing this, Troy refuses to rob the man, gets back on his horse and throws the man 50 pounds 'to help you on your way'. The song concludes in proper Robin Hood style with the verse:

> The poor I'll serve both night and day,
> The rich I will annoy;
> The people round know me right well;
> They call me Johnny Troy.

In another American version, the story includes Troy's death 'on his scaffold high' as 'a brave young hero'.

Why Troy was forgotten in the place where he committed his crimes and died for them is a mystery. Perhaps there were enough bushranger ballads and legends around to satisfy the demand. People are still singing many of these in Australia, where they are a strong element of folk tradition. Johnny Troy lives on only in America, though he is in good company, or bad, there. The tradition of the outlaw hero that runs from Robin Hood includes American badmen as well as our bushrangers. Jesse James and Billy the Kid, among many others, are celebrated in the same folkloric style, and just as controversially, as Ben Hall, Frank Gardiner and Ned Kelly.

The Master Bushman legend

Who was the 'Master Bushman'? Was he real, or a journalist's concoction of a number of bush types? We'll never know but, fact or fiction, it's a hell of a yarn that illustrates the ideal bushman image. According to Francis Keen, a northern New South Wales journalist who specialised in bush mysteries:

> The Master Bushman was Australian born, and a splendid type of physical man. Six feet in height, straight-limbed and supple. He had a kingly brow and a noble glance—a magnificent glance which ranged over the plains and the valleys and up to and

over the mountain tops towards where we are taught dwells the Creator who gave him his wonderful accomplishments. He had an imperial presence which compelled homage from those around him.

And that was just for starters. The Master Bushman was a leader of men and loved the land 'and the rattle of a hobble-chain was more to him than the finest Beethoven Symphony'. His life was characterised by outstanding feats. One of these was 'to tell the time to the minute any hour of the day or night in any place without the aid of a timepiece'.

At the age of twenty-five, this hero was living on a station near a centre of 2000-or-so people when he received an anonymous letter from a townsman. The Master Bushman went to town and stayed there for two days, examining every face he came across: 'The second night he walked into the vestibule of a reading-room and placed his hand upon the shoulder of the writer of the letter.'

Five years later he found work at another station where he was not known. Seven local wags made sure the new chum was mounted on the most vicious horse available and sat back to watch the fun. But the stranger was a master of horses and in fifteen minutes of bareback riding had broken-in the outlaw. He returned to the station, eyes blazing and in search of revenge. He saddled the now-pacified horse and, one by one, caught each of the seven pranksters, tying them up to the saddle for half-an-hour's enforced buckjumping. The experience 'made them grave-faced men for the rest of their days'.

The Master Bushman was also a fine singer who could sing a song for every day of the year. He could ride brumbies bareback and was generous to those less fortunate than himself and 'many a time after a long day's toil he had saddled up and ridden a score of miles through darkness and storm to the bedside of a sick woman or child'.

At only fifty years of age, he died as he had lived, 'alone and friendless'. In the end, 'The Master of all came one cold winter and took him to that land from whence no traveller returns. Years of droving and roughing it in the saddle in all kinds of weather, from the storm-swept gulf country to the slopes of the East Coast Ranges had had its effect upon his constitution, and he passed away at a comparatively early age.' The Master Bushman's funeral was attended by men who came 'hundreds and hundreds of miles by rail and saddle to learn particulars of his last hours, and they stood by his grave—men who could neither read nor write—they stood by his grave with their hats in their hands—and wept like children'.

The sentinels of Myrrhee

Overlanders from New South Wales squatted on the area known as Myrrhee in the 1830s. They were followed by several waves of settlers who displaced the original inhabitants and established small farming communities. But even the early occupiers had no idea about the stones and how they got there. And no one does today.

Myrrhee is about 40 kilometres south of Wangaratta, part of northeastern Victoria's Kelly Country and near the famed wine area of Milawa. Locals have long known about the six, some say seven, mysterious stone stacks. They are nestled at the top of a rocky outcrop in Toombullup State Forest looking out across the countryside below like silent sentinels. They were recently rediscovered and photographed for the first time by John Brown of the Brown Brothers Winery. Some of the cairns consist of very large rocks balanced one atop the other, needing many hands to carry out the work. The area in which they stand is inaccessible to any lifting equipment.

Stone arrangements of one kind or another, large and small, are found across Australia. They vary from rings and linear patterns, to the concentric circles that make up Aboriginal ceremonial sites, known as 'Bora' rings. Most of these structures were made by indigenous people and may have been a form of calendar or have a ceremonial function, possibly both.

Wherever they are found, from the immense arrangements on Western Australia's Burrup Peninsula, to what remains of an enormous stone circle at Mullumbimby, New South Wales, they are enigmatic evidence of the duration of human beings in Australia. There are many interpretations of their significance, none final.

Speculations about the origins and meanings of the Myrrhee stone structures are as varied as they are elsewhere in the country. They include Aboriginal people, the explorers Hume and Hovell, or perhaps nineteenth-century Chinese tobacco and peanut farmers. A similarity with 'prayer stones' found in Europe has led to a suggestion that they are related to Buddhism. They might even be a hoax, if a very elaborate one. None of these explanations can be verified and in the absence of any other evidence, speculation continues about the mysterious standing stones of Myrrhee.

Ancient stone arrangements of many kinds exist around the world. Stonehenge in England is perhaps the best-known, prompting comparisons like 'Australia's Stonehenge' whenever a sizeable arrangement is discovered in this country. As researchers have pointed out, this is not an accurate description. Not because Stonehenge is older but because the Australian structures are almost certainly more ancient than those in Europe and, possibly, anywhere else.

At Hanging Rock

On Saint Valentine's Day, 1900, a group of schoolgirls are taken on a day trip to Hanging Rock in Victoria. They arrive at noon, whereupon their watches all mysteriously stop. Edith, Irma, Marion and Miranda climb up into the rock, followed by their mathematics teacher, Greta McCraw. Miranda's special friend, Sara, has to stay behind at the school because she is being disciplined by the headmistress. As the girls climb further into the formation, Irma, Marion and Miranda disappear, leaving Edith to stumble back to the picnic in panic and unable to remember what did or did not happen to her companions. In the meantime, Miss McCraw has also gone missing on the rock.

A search is made immediately, but with no success, followed by several more searches by the local community. Everyone fears the worst for the girls and even the eventual discovery of a confused and dehydrated Irma by a young Englishman conducting his own search sheds no light on the riddle. Concerned parents begin to withdraw their children from the already struggling school and the teaching and pastoral staff leave. One later dies in a hotel fire. Sara also disappears and commits suicide and the headmistress, unable to cope with the destruction of her school and livelihood, throws herself from the rock.

The novel titled *Picnic at Hanging Rock* by Joan Lindsay presents this as a true story. In the later film, also framed as fuzzy fact, a number of elements are changed and some of the sexually charged implications of the novel amplified. The atmosphere created is memorable, mystifying and disturbing, with the riddle of the disappearances unresolved, as in the original book. Few people who have viewed the film ever forget it and many people believe the story to be based on actual events.

But the story of what happened at Hanging Rock that Valentine's Day is a work of writerly imagination, first published in 1967 and, eight years later, made into the movie hit directed by Peter Weir. Since then, tourists regularly visit Hanging Rock and yell out 'Miranda' in emulation of the desperate search for the ethereally beautiful main character and her companions. There is an elaborate display of the tale and its various tellings at the visitor centre.

What is it about this odd tale that draws people in, more than fifty years after the event allegedly occurred?

There has always been a hint that the story is based on real events at the rock. Those living in the area during the 1940s, twenty years or more before Lindsay published her novel, recall local rumours about a missing girl at Hanging Rock, probably murdered. These local traditions may be the basis of Lindsay's imaginative work, though the lack of historical documentation of any relevant incidents in the area has been confirmed by searches of local newspapers and police records. Why then do we continue to believe?

Hanging Rock itself is certainly an eerie place. Thrusting up from the middle of a plain near Mount Macedon, its solitary splendour is ominous and brooding. It has strong spiritual associations for the Wurundjeri people. Compasses and watches often fail in its vicinity, giving Joan Lindsay's artful confabulation of time and place some apparent scientific credibility.

Like all myths, the Hanging Rock story satisfies a communal need to believe that transcends the absence of facts. Although the preferred Australian way is ostensibly down-to-earth and practical with a distrust of anything intangible or transcendent, there is a profound uncertainty beneath this veneer. The vast, unknown nature of the country and its environment and of the spiritual traditions of its first inhabitants echoes through phrases like 'the dead heart'. The enigmas of still-missing explorers, vanished castaways and bleaching bones beside dry, isolated tracks continue to puzzle us. As Henry Lawson and others observed, there is something about the bush and outback that lies beyond rational explanation and comprehension. The work of creative artists such as Sidney Nolan, Arthur Boyd, Patrick White and many others reaches towards this mystique.

The 'mystery' of the picnic at Hanging Rock story with its themes of darkness amidst sunshine and innocence, repressed desire and the unknowable is a powerful projection of our shared, unacknowledged discomforts. Although the story and its mythology originated long before the invention of the internet, it is well-suited to a growing propensity to believe in nonsense, 'memes' and 'fake news' that has become such a pronounced feature of modern life.

The enigmatic picnic at Hanging Rock is a fiction that has burst the boundaries of print and film to become a 'fact' for many people. Like all myths, it is a great story.

The last tiger

Though long gone, the thylacine or Tasmanian tiger still haunts us. Extinct on the mainland and in Papua New Guinea, it was hunted to oblivion in its one remaining haven. The last of these enigmatic animals died of neglect in Hobart's Beaumaris Zoo in 1936. Someone forgot to put the creature back into its enclosure and it perished of exposure. Ever since, people have reported seeing ghostly survivors in the wild and there is a long history of thylacine hunting in Tasmania and beyond. Substantial rewards have been offered for verified sightings or other evidence of the beast's existence. As with other modern 'ABC' (Alien Big Cat) legends, these tales quickly vanish into the air. But the belief remains strong with many and the quest continues.

The thylacine was certainly a striking animal, with black-brown stripes across its back and down its long tail. It was more of a kangaroo than a dog or wolf—as a carnivorous marsupial, its young suckled and were protected in a pouch. Its perceived oddity was reflected in the scientific name given to it; *Thylacinus cynocephalus*, meaning a pouched dog with a wolf-like head. The thylacine stood around 60 centimetres high, grew up to 180 centimetres long and weighed around 30 kilograms as a full adult. Thylacines barked or yelped infrequently and were anything but tiger-like in demeanour, preferring to hide. They sometimes died of fright as soon as they were caught.

Aboriginal traditions on the mainland and in Tasmania provide evidence in rock art and lore of the tiger's once wide distribution around the country. But the advance of European settlement and the exaggerated fear of thylacine attacks on livestock, as well as the possible effects of natural selection and disease, eventually eradicated the animal. The loss of these creatures was foretold as early as the 1850s, when the famous naturalist John Gould predicted: 'When the comparatively small island of Tasmania becomes more densely populated, and its primitive forests are intersected with roads from the eastern to the western coast, the numbers of this singular animal will speedily diminish, extermination will have its full sway, and it will then, like the Wolf in England and Scotland, be recorded as an animal of the past . . .'

Scientists are now planning to resurrect the species. This possibility exists because so many stuffed, desiccated and otherwise preserved thylacine specimens with intact DNA are kept in museums around the world. Around 750 of them, in all. Researchers have recently turned their attention to this 'archive of bodies' created from the European desire for the exotic. Ostensibly, this was proper scientific curiosity. But while this specimen collecting preserved genetic material that might make resurrection of the thylacine possible, the museums in which the bodies are stored are also 'repositories of loss'. They suggest that our ongoing fascination with the thylacine, expressed through the folklore of alleged sightings and the scientific quest for resurrection, are projections of our shared guilt over the extinction of what was a shy and relatively harmless animal.

Australia holds the unenviable world record for mammal extinctions. National Threatened Species Day is held on the anniversary of the sad and lonely death of the last Tasmanian tiger each September 7. Tasmanian tiger skins have become expensive collectors' items.

*Leopold and William De Salis resting in the bush with a man,
horse and sulky, Cuppacumbalong, ACT, circa 1892.*

10

A land without limits

Put a light in every country window,
High speed pumps where now the windmills stand,
Get in and lay the cable so that one day we'll be able
To have electricity all over this wide land.

'Light in Every Country Window', Don Henderson

The World Fair in the desert

It was nothing but desert in 1892. Seven years later Coolgardie was the third-largest town in Western Australia. Shops lined the extraordinarily wide main street, there were seven newspapers, six banks and two stock exchanges, schools, theatres, churches, a synagogue and a mosque for the 'Afghan' cameleers who kept the 5000-or-so inhabitants supplied with goods. And much of their water. Two cemeteries held more than a thousand underground residents, while three breweries and twenty-six hotels slaked the prodigious thirst of the miners. In 1896 the railway arrived and just a few years later 'the mother of the Western Australian goldfields' hosted a World Fair.

237

The first of the grand celebrations of industry and technology that began the World Fair movement was held in Paris
in 1844. Fifty years later they were an international fad and
no self-respecting country or industry could not have one. The
Coolgardie event was officially titled 'The Western Australian
International Mining and Industrial Exhibition'. Nothing like
it had been seen in the west and there would never be anything
quite like it again.

On 21 March 1899, the special train from Perth arrived
carrying 150 VIPs, including the governor and the premier with
their respective families and entourages. They were welcomed
by the mayor and all the dignitaries that Coolgardie boasted,
together with the mayor of Melbourne, an archdeacon and the
vice-consul of Denmark. The triumphal arch of flowers on Bayley
Street had only just been completed in the early hours of the
morning and there were: 'festoons at the end of the street facing
the exhibition, and these, with profuse displays of bunting at the
hotels and other establishments along Bayley Street, comprised
the decorations with which the town had arrayed itself for the
occasion. Interwoven with the arch were the words, "Welcome
to Coolgardie", while similarly hospitable greetings appeared on
the walls of buildings along each side of Bayley Street.'

Anyone who was anyone was there, as well as many who
were not. The speeches, toasts and backslapping were almost
endless. The shortest was made by a colourful entrepreneur
named Jules Joubert, manager of the event. Joubert was an
early example of a global organiser that we have become
familiar with through international sporting networks and
affiliations. He had parlayed an earlier involvement with the
World Fair movement into a position of control and influence.
Not surprisingly, he was happy. He claimed to have 'managed
fifty exhibitions, and the present one was therefore his jubilee'.
Joubert extravagantly declared that, 'He would have liked to
have stopped the sun for a fortnight, for then they would have
had one of the best exhibitions ever seen in Australasia.'

All who atttended were in good spirits, especially when the

official opening of the Grand Exhibition Building finally took place. There were more speeches, of course. Premier Forrest was overflowing with praise, emphasising that the government was in full support of the event and 'were most anxious that the Exhibition should do all its promoters desired it should do'. With a hint of self-promotion, he added: 'There had been a great many sceptics and unbelievers, and people who threw cold water on the project, and if it had not been for the people of Coolgardie—supported, he thought, by himself and he might say the Government—this Exhibition would not have been in the position it was now.'

And there was more, rather a lot. But the topic that most affected every miner and business-owner in the goldfields finally came:

> There was one thing he missed, which he had hoped to see, and that was a river of water coming into the town—(cheers)—a river he had promised he would do his best to bring. And they were bringing it. People might say what they liked, they might be sceptical or disbelievers, but he could tell them that the great water scheme was raising itself up like the Temple of Jerusalem was raised silently. (Cheers.) There was no great sound of hammers going on. These hammers were, however, being applied, and in a very short time, like that magnificent edifice, this great water scheme would rear itself up, and fresh water would flow into the town. (Cheers.)

A strike of wharfies at Fremantle meant that loads of exhibits being wagoned from Perth were still wending their way towards the glittering event. Despite this, the show went on with balls, orchestras and entertainments of all kinds—'Dancing was indulged in till after midnight.' More than 5000 people attended on the first day and more than 60,000 were estimated to have visited by the time the exhibition ended almost three and a half months later. The event was pronounced a great success, particularly in the circumstances, as the press pointed out:

It may be safely asserted that no event of this nature has been attempted under more discouraging circumstances than those which have attended the present undertaking in this remote portion of the Australian continent, where eight years ago there was not a vestige of civilisation, and when the aboriginal, like Robinson Crusoe, was monarch of all he surveyed, but which through the discovery of gold has become a great mining centre and a hive of industry. It was undoubtedly a bold undertaking to induce the manufacturers of the old world to unite in displaying their wares and products to the population of these fields. Coolgardie being in the heart of a wilderness, and at a distance of nearly 400 miles from the sea coast, presented almost an insurmountable difficulty in this respect alone.

The city in the bush was on its way to even greater things!

But it was not to be. Rich as Coolgardie's lodes of gold might be, they were outdone by the even richer and more abundant ores of Kalgoorlie and Boulder, not much further down the track, now known as the 'Super Pit'. Combined with the slump in gold prices at this period, Coolgardie began a slow decline. A School of Mines was opened in 1902 but closed a year later, supplanted by Kalgoorlie's own school. In the 1930s the Grand Exhibition Building burned down, by which time the town was in terminal decline. Not quite a ghost town, Coolgardie today has about 900 people living there, but its glory days have long faded and its mainstay, like many bush towns, is tourism.

End of the line

There was only one reason why Birdum was there at all. The reason was the North Australia Railway (NAR), also known as the Palmerston to Pine Creek Railway.

Intended to link Darwin with Adelaide, the construction of the narrow-gauge railway began in the 1880s. Thousands of Indian, Singhalese and Chinese labourers got the line built to Pine Creek and the railway was officially opened in 1889.

It was extended to Katherine in 1917 and finally to Birdum, more than 500 kilometres south of Darwin, in 1929. But there it stayed. Despite promises and projects by governments and private enterprise, the railway extended no further south than Birdum, with its one pub and scattering of railway workers' cottages.

A train known locally as 'Leaping Lena' (also as 'the Spirit of Protest') took three days to reach Birdum from the capital. There was an official timetable, though this seems to have been more symbolic than actual. 'Train Day' was the highlight of the week, bringing the mail along with visitors from Darwin. It was the best time for a 'wongy', Territory slang for a yarning session. Birdum was considered the best place for these gossip exchanges because there was nothing else to do. The train was itself the object of more than few yarns:

> There were dozens of stories about this train. One, of how the engine-driver had been prevailed upon by a bottle of whisky to drive through the usual stopping place, Pine Creek, to 40 miles on, where the passengers had arranged a party, was told me at a camp on the Finke River. What was said by the passengers left behind at Pine Creek was never revealed. But as the train was a day late arriving at Birdum, even the engine-driver seems to have found the party worth any consequences.

Local identities apparently included 'Footboard Bob', known for his delight in riding on the footboards of other people's cars, and the 'Great Eater' who could clear out the stores of three hotels and consider that just an entrée.

Fear of Japanese invasion during World War II gave the settlement its finest moments. Civilians who were evacuated from Darwin after the Japanese bombing raids in 1942 were trained to Birdum and from there went by road to the safety of Alice Springs. 'Leaping Lena' found a new role as a hospital train. The United States Army built a hospital at Birdum and the Royal Australian Air Force established a telecommunications

unit as part of the wartime defence arrangement. RAAF personnel stationed there knew the local hotel as 'the pub with no
beer' and worked in a corrugated iron-clad structure without
window glass. Instead, hessian sacking was hung above the
open window apertures and lower to keep out the dust storms
and tumbleweed whenever necessary, which was often.

The station had various tasks. Communications between
allied aeroplanes, or 'listening watches', were important for
knowing if raids had been successful. They also received and
transmitted coded information for the South-West Pacific area,
updating weather reports and other communications every
three hours, nonstop.

But all this activity signalled the beginning of decline. The
next station up the line, Larrimah, was adjacent to a road
vital for transportation, while Birdum was not. Trains now
stopped at Larrimah, leaving Birdum to wither away. The pub,
with or without beer, moved to Larrimah and it was only a
matter of time before the settlement further south closed down.
It happened in 1976 when the line was closed and most of the
houses and railway buildings dismantled.

So quickly did the desert reclaim what was left of the town
that when heritage fieldworkers visited forty or so years later,
they had to burn off the vegetation covering it so they could
walk over the area and document it. The only structure left
was the overhead tank used to water the locomotives. The
rest was concrete floor slabs and 'scatters of artefacts on and
in the ground, including numerous 44-gallon fuel drums and
carbide drums; a few upright posts and some stumps; derelict
fencing; several pits which may have been earth closets or
refuse pits'. Investigators also noted the survival of many
inverted bottles pushed into the ground to form paths and
garden edgings, and a complete floor to what was probably a
bakery attached to the pub. Although the report did not say so,
we can be pretty sure they were mostly beer bottles.

The heritage report concludes with a sober official assess-
ment of the ghost town at the end of the line:

Birdum is rapidly being destroyed by the elements, vegetation growth and intermittent fires due to wet season burn off, remnant artefacts are being trampled by livestock. Human interference is also taking its toll, the pillage of remnants by surrounding station personnel, the few tourists that make it down to Birdum unsupervised in the dry season take souvenirs, and some local residents of Larrimah also take items for display in their businesses or personal use.

Ice and fire

> Put a light in every country window,
> High speed pumps where now the windmills stand,
> Get in and lay the cable so that one day we'll be able
> To have electricity all over this wide land.

The chorus of Don Henderson's song, celebrating the completion of the Snowy Mountains Hydro-Electric Scheme, reflected the bright anticipation of mains electricity in many parts of the Victorian and New South Wales bush. Construction of 'the Snowy' neared completion in the early 1970s after more than twenty years of drilling, blasting and damming. 'The Snowy will be finished before long,' the song promised, and then 'the ice and the fire that's coming down the wire' would make the old-fashioned Coolgardie Safe and wood stove nothing but 'relics of the past'.

The Snowy River Scheme delivered on its promise, providing cheap, relatively clean electricity and irrigation for agriculture, and creating a viable rural economy in the region which continues today in towns like Thredbo and Perisher.

As well as an engineering feat, the building of 'the Snowy' was a social and cultural experience that brought many migrants from a still war-ravaged Europe. Large numbers of men, mostly without their families, migrated to Australia to work on the vast scheme. They came from all over—Italy, France, Germany, Spain, Croatia, the Netherlands, Norway,

Yugoslavia, Poland, Russia, Greece, Britain, America and elsewhere in the world—eventually making up around 70 per cent of the Snowy workforce. In this melting pot of migrant and local labour, a distinctive culture evolved, similar in many ways to that of the earlier 'navvies' who built Britain's canals and railways. Camps and a few towns were established and the sleepy farming village of Cooma quickly became a regional centre, complete with health and other facilities and an unprecedented nightlife as workers let off steam after an arduous week.

By most accounts, the great mix of nationalities labouring on the gigantic plan did so free of trouble and workers on the scheme developed a fierce pride in their accomplishment, easily the most significant infrastructure project in Australian history. Siobhán McHugh wrote a prize-winning oral history of the Snowy River Scheme, first published in 1989. She interviewed about two hundred workers, each one proud of their part in building what was widely considered an impossible vision. Three thousand ex-workers attended a reunion in 2009, where the 121 employees who died on the project were remembered.

The project had environmental consequences, drowning valleys and the town of old Jindabyne for its dams and killing the Snowy River. But the official completion of the scheme was enthusiastically celebrated as an outstanding example of nation building and the country took pride in the accomplishment for a few years. Then we somehow just forgot about 'the Snowy'. It was done, running and contributing to the energy needs of the eastern states as a taken-for-granted element of the energy infrastructure. We remembered it again in 2006 when a proposal by the joint owners—Victoria, New South Wales and the federal government—to privatise the facility was widely attacked and had to be abandoned.

Then we forgot about it once more until the federal government suddenly announced in the midst of the 2017 energy crisis that the scheme would be extended. Most of the country was taken by surprise: 'the Snowy'—of course, we have it already!

Selling the bush

A great many products have depended on a real or suggested bush connection to appeal to buyers. The commercial exploitation of the bush takes various forms. One of the most basic is to market products derived from the bush itself. Eucalyptus oil is an old favourite, as is goanna salve. Sandalwood is still in demand for its fragrance and ti-tree oil as a remedy or balm for many ailments.

Even if your product has no direct connection to the environment, there is always the possibility of suggesting one, either through a brand name or a logo. There is a lengthy list of products that depend on bush-related names, including Billy Tea, together with its swagman and kangaroo logo, and Rosella tomato sauce. Pioneer jelly crystals were said to 'set in any weather'.

Makers of leather preservers often favoured the bush theme, including Emu shoe polish and Jacko shoe shine, which featured a kookaburra in its advertising, trading on the term 'laughing jackass' once often used as a name for the bird. The best-known kookaburra branding is probably the 'Early Kooka' range of gas stoves introduced by the Metters company in the 1930s. Other shoe products included Roo boot polish, Koala boot polish, Emu boot polish and, not very attractively you'd think, Bunyip boot polish.

If your product was not especially related to the bush, you could still leverage the romance in your marketing. The most famous example is probably the parrot logo of Arnott's biscuits. From small origins in the 1860s, Arnott's grew to be the major biscuiteer of the country, with an enviable national image to match. Many of the company's biscuit varieties have become associated with Australian identity, including Milk Arrowroot, Jatz and Sao crackers, Monte Carlo, and the list goes on. The most popular current line is probably the Tim Tam chocolate biscuit.

Arnott's also used to produce a more solid version of the

Milk Arrowroot biscuit aimed at the outdoors market and known as 'Bush Biscuits'. The Iced VoVo, invented by Arnott's in 1906, has entered popular culture and featured in Kevin Rudd's election speech in 2007, causing a sales spike of the sweet icing biscuits laced with raspberry jam and sprinkled with desiccated cocoanut.

Bush brands also include the famed Akubra hats, the Driza-Bone raincoat popularised by singer John Farnham, and the leather and clothing products of bushman R.M. Williams. Born into a pioneer South Australian family in 1908, Reginald Murray Williams went on the track at the age of thirteen. He lived a typical bushman's life of wandering, working with stock, including camels, and farming. Leatherworking skills were still in demand in this era and Williams was taught by a man known as 'Dollar Mick'. He began selling his saddles and developed a unique one-piece riding boot that was soon in high demand. From this, Williams went on to make a fortune and to win many awards and honours. R.M. Williams died in 2003 but his name is now a well-known Australian and international clothing brand.

Few bush animals have not been pressed into the service of commerce, including dingoes, lyrebirds, magpies, cockatoos, possums and platypuses. Native plants have also been profitably plundered in marketing, notably gum trees, waratahs and wattle.

'Boomerang Brandy' and 'Boomerang Tyres' were two of the less objectionable brands drawing on Aboriginal culture, which included the 'Abo' brand and 'Niggerboy Licorice', actually produced by an American company that also operated in Australia.

The bush continues to play a major role in the marketing of ecological or green products, including health foods, beauty preparations, body scrubs, soaps and a host of 'natural' offerings, made from 'native bush flowers' and 'bush honey'. There is even an 'Australian Bush Flower Essences Love System'. You can only wonder what Reg Williams might have made of that.

The Iron Trail

There were strikes over ham and eggs for the workers, political fights over the cost—more than seven million pounds—and a shortage of steel needed to fight the Great War. It was remarkable that the long-mooted Trans-Australian Railway was begun at all. It was even more remarkable that it was completed in the midst of a major conflict in which thousands of Australians were killed and maimed.

It was not war, but the line was a dangerous workplace. Dan O'Shea worked with the lift gang from Golden Ridge. He was 'killed on the line', run over by a locomotive 25 kilometres on the west Augusta railway. At least another twenty died in work-related incidents and probably another twenty-five died of typhoid in 1912 and 1915.

After years of construction across the unforgiving wastes between Kalgoorlie and South Australia, the first train to run on the 'Iron Trail' as it was sometimes known, left Port Augusta for Kalgoorlie in October 1917. It arrived a little less than 43 hours later. For the first time there was a major land transport link between Australia's east and west coasts—'From sea to sea', as Sydney's *Daily Telegraph* enthused.

The link was difficult, with multiple changes of railway gauge across the nearly 1700 kilometres, forcing frequent changes of train. The 'Battle of the Gauges' was fought out for months in the political arenas of federal and state politics:

> The final determination was the adoption of the 'standard gauge' of 4 ft. 8 1/2 in., as distinct from the gauges of South Australia, West Australia, and Victoria. The attached list will show the width of the railways upon which travellers between Fremantle and Brisbane will ride in making the overland trip:—
> Fremantle to Kalgoorlie, 3 ft. 6 in.
> Kalgoorlie to Port Augusta, 4 ft. 8 in
> Port Augusta to Terowie, 3 ft 6 in
> Terowie to Albury (N.S.W.), 5 ft. 3 in.

Albury to Wallangarra. 4 ft. 8 ½ in.
To Brisbane, 3 ft. 6 in.

But it worked. Now passengers and freight could travel east to west and west to east across the Nullarbor Plain, fulfilling a national vision.

The completion of the project was widely seen as a triumph for Sir John Forrest, Western Australia's first premier and now Commonwealth treasurer. But it was a truly national achievement that Forrest saluted, even while patting himself on the back, like any good politician:

> I rejoice to see this day. I have longed to see it, and am glad. For 25 years I have strenuously and incessantly labored to connect the railway systems of Eastern and Western Australia, and to-day that great work . . . is accomplished, it is indeed a day of rejoicing for all who have assisted in promoting and bringing into existence such a great national and beneficent undertaking. Western Australia, comprising one-third of the continent, hitherto isolated and practically unknown, is from to-day in reality a part of the Australian Federation. From to-day east and west arc indissolubly joined together by bands of steel, and the result must be increased prosperity and happiness for the Australian people. The improved means of communication will, I believe, create a broader and nobler national life, and the closer union will, I feel sure, mean a wider sympathy with our kinsmen in the old land and with the British people throughout the world. I am indeed grateful, and rejoice that this inspiring prospect, this great triumph for civilisation, has come in my day.

Congratulations came from London, much trumpeted at that time of imperial loyalty. Forrest, in his capacity as treasurer, was also quick to link the grand achievement with the federal government's appeal for 20 million pounds to fight the war—'The Liberty Loan', as it was called—at 4.5 per cent interest, tax free and guaranteed by the Commonwealth.

The railway, soon known as 'the Trans', was also widely applauded by politicians and the press throughout Australia. Controversy continued after the railway began operating. People complained about the fares and there was ongoing criticism of the different gauges, an early indication of what would become the usual failure of the states to agree on much. The railway continues today, now connected to the long-promised Adelaide–Darwin line completed in 2004.

Waters of life

Interest in drawing water from underground or artesian sources began in the 1830s and gradually grew over the following twenty years. By the 1850s it was speculated that there was some sort of underground water supply in the eastern colonies. Governments began voting funds to explore the possibility. An early attempt was made in the Murray Basin in 1859 but it was not until the 1870s that the first successful bores were put down near Bourke and not until the late 1880s that the practicality of using this water source was confirmed.

And then the race was on. Everyone wanted an artesian bore. One place in particular put their artesian water resource to very good use.

It is often claimed that the southern Queensland town of Thargomindah was the first town in Australia and the third in the world to get electric street lights, in 1893 after London and Paris. It turns out that this is not correct. The first city in the southern hemisphere to have electric street lights was Tamworth in New South Wales, where they began generating electricity from coal in 1888.

But Thargomindah can still boast of being the first town in Australia to generate hydro-electricity. The settlement was established in the 1860s on the Bulloo River, more than 1000 kilometres west of Brisbane, and developed quickly as the district pastoral industry grew. The town enjoyed access to the Great Artesian Basin flows and after several years of drilling, local entrepreneurs opened up a pressurised hot spring that produced enough heated high-pressure water to turn a turbine and generate electricity. The street lights in the very small community—current population about 200—were lit by this method until 1951.

The bores at Bourke, Thargomindah and elsewhere revealed the existence of a vast body of subterranean water gurgling through aquifers that cover more than 20 per cent of Australia's landmass. The Great Artesian Basin lies beneath more than 1.7 million square kilometres of Queensland, New South Wales, the Northern Territory and South Australia, and is one of the world's largest underground reservoirs of fresh water.

Unfortunately, the practice with artesian bores, once running, was to leave them that way. Vast amounts of ancient water were wasted through spillage and evaporation. The damage to the resource was recognised in the early twentieth century, as water volume and pressure decreased. But it was many decades before serious measures were taken to deal with the problem. Since 1999 the federal government has provided funds for capping and piping artesian bores in the hope that the basin will eventually recharge itself from falling rains.

This hope has been challenged by some scientists who disagree with the traditional view that the Great Artesian Basin is formed by rain falling in northern Australia and then flowing south through aquifers. They claim that the water is from sources trapped in deep rock formations millions of years ago. If this is correct, the Great Artesian Basin will never recharge. Controversy continues.

While it does, the physical structures that pump artesian as well as sub-artesian water from bores to thirsty stock and settlements are disappearing. The characteristic windmills that dot the outback are Australian icons, found not only in the Great Artesian area but also wherever underground water sources exist, which is pretty much across the whole continent. The windmills are being replaced by cheaper electric pumps and parts for the older windmills are no longer in regular manufacture. As well as evocative symbols of the conquest of nature—not always with desirable environmental consequences—these giants of the outback are also becoming part of a fading pioneer heritage.

How the outback began

'The Land Question' was a vexed issue in the 1860s. As well as the politics and investment involved, the difficulties of farming and pastoral development were as numerous then as they are today. In late 1868, drought afflicted many areas of New South Wales and a Mr H. Rourke of the Barwon country provided his observations on the state of the 'interior'. Rourke's account gives a good idea of the difficulties faced by all who sought to make a living in the bush. Despite these, as he points out, improvements and progress of various kinds continued. Rourke's letter also contains one of the earliest uses of the term 'outback' to mean somewhere beyond the limits of settlement:

Dungalear, Barwon River, Nov. 12, 1868.

Dear Sir,—According to promise, I send a few lines to give you an idea of what has come under my observation since I left Maitland on the 27th September last. I came by road direct, as my horses were in good condition, and found the roads in excellent order, more particularly the macadamised portion of them. Great improvements have been made in erecting bridges over many bad portions of the road, especially the bridges over the Mooki at Breeza, and Cox's Creek. From Maitland to Liverpool Plains grass was exceedingly scarce; on Liverpool Plains to Gunnedah there was some feed; Gunnedah to Narrabri there was none; from Narrabri to Wee Waa the grass was good; thence to Walgett, there was not as much as would fill a tobacco pipe. Had my horses not been in good condition I could never have reached here, being obliged to feed them with corn out of nose bags three times a day; we had to put them in stock yards at night, as it would be a waste of time to hobble them out. The rate I travelled at was forty to sixty miles a day.

The day after my arrival I took a ride over the run to examine the condition of the stock, and found considerable loss in cattle getting bogged: they have to travel from ten to fifteen miles back for feed, and when they come to the water are so exhausted as to be quite unable to get out of the mud, and perish there. I notice the greatest loss is among the breeding cattle, more particularly when the calves are not weaned; both cow and calf perish, as they cannot reach out to where the feed is. We are now weaning all the calves we can lay hold of, and find the wells very useful. Over 150 are watered at one well, and we find them no trouble, as they will not leave the troughs. There are also great losses among the bulls; they seem to have nearly all died on the different stations in this locality. When the drought breaks up there will be a good demand for this description of stock, also for store cattle.

Rourke went on to describe the improvements he noted along the way:

It is astonishing, the great energy and enterprise existing among the Crown tenants in the Liverpool Plains, Warrego, and Riverina districts; they are carrying out works of great magnitude in fencing, making reservoirs, and sinking wells. The latter do not seem to answer so well; a large number of them dry up, and the loss in sinking is great, nearly 50 per cent turn out salt. The money expended in the above districts in improvements the last few years must be immense; if such had not been the case the greater portion of the interior must have been abandoned ere this. You may think it fabulous when I tell you that for 200 miles of the frontage of the Barwon and Namoi a stock horse cannot subsist. Hay and corn are kept on all the stations, and paid for at exorbitant prices. Since we shifted the sheep out-back there are few losses by deaths; the labour and expense of drawing water is very great.

The word and the idea of 'outback' was well enough established by this time for Rourke to use it without explanation, knowing his readers would comprehend it. Another newspaper report from the same year confirms the general use of the word: 'A rumour has reached Hay of the skeleton of a man having been found somewhere outback from Booligal. It is supposed that it must have belonged to a young man most respectably connected, who has been missing for some time.'

By the 1880s even Nyngan, in central New South Wales, was considered by those 'further out' to be nowhere near the outback:

> Large numbers of fat cattle and sheep are continually passing here en route to the city market. Within the last month at least 20 lots have crossed, all in splendid condition, notwithstanding the great heat and length of travel, some of them having already come nearly a thousand miles; but the railway terminus is close at hand. Fancy Nyngan only 140 miles from here! Outbackers may well say that our town is a suburb of Sydney.

Bush learning

The writer and bushman Edward Sorenson provided us with a wonderful description of country childhood learning, as it was around the middle of the nineteenth century and for a long time after:

> It is surprising how soon these children learn the bush, what clever little heads they have for working out the problems of their timbered world. I have met them, boys and girls, riding along mountain spurs, miles away from home, looking for cattle. And if you ask them at any time in what direction home lies, no matter how they have turned and twisted during the day, they will at once point to it like a compass. Fences do not stop them from going as straight as the crow flies either; they strap down the wires, with a stick across for the horse to see, and lead or ride

him over. Rail fences give a little trouble; but when a loose top rail is found, they jump their cuddies over the bottom one. They can describe a beast minutely, even to a single white spot at the tip of its tail, or a tiny black streak on its off-side horn. They can recognise a beast or a horse at sight, though they may not have seen it for a couple of years or more; and they have a wonderful memory for brands and earmarks. Though they may be otherwise illiterate, they will squat on the road, and with a stick faultlessly portray the brands and earmarks of every station and selection for miles around them.

I was one day travelling towards Bourke with a mob of Queensland cattle when a boy rode up and asked me where they were from. I named a squattage south of the border. He grinned.

'You can't stuff me with that,' he said. 'Them's Queensland brands.'

'How do you know a Queensland brand from a New South Wales brand?' I asked him.

'Why,' he said, 'a Queensland brand has letters an' a number; New South Wales brands ain't got no number.'

Another day I was trying to catch up to a man who was riding a day in front of me, and asked a boy at a wayside hut if he had seen him pass. He didn't remember him according to my descriptions; but he had seen a person go by wearing a straw hat and riding a brown horse branded H.P., with a star on its forehead, off fetlock white, and carrying its tail a little aside as though it had been broken, and it had cast its near fore-shoe. This was correct in every particular; yet that boy had never seen the horse before in his life, and had just leaned lazily on a rail as it was ridden past him.

Sorenson was also well aware of how difficult it was for the children to get an education, even when it was available at a bush school:

In regard to ordinary school tasks they are poor scholars, principally through lack of opportunity. The bush school is often a small, isolated building standing among the trees, with no fence around it and no house in sight of it. But little tracks, winding through the bush in many directions, show where the children come from. Some of them walk four or five miles to school, starting away at daylight on winter mornings, and returning in the twilight or after dark. When grass is white with frost or wet with dew, when rains have left pools and sheets of surface water along the track and set the creeks and gullies running, the bush kiddies carry their boots in their hands or over their shoulders to keep them dry, putting them on when they reach the school. In the dry interior regions, besides the usual dinner-bags and books, they carry bottles and water-bags. They get over rivers in flat-bottomed punts, and any creek that is too deep to ford is crossed on the trunk of a tree that has been felled across from bank to bank; they pass through mobs of half-wild cattle, and at times through miles of burnt and burning grass; but they very seldom come to any harm. Some drive to and fro in light traps; others ride—at times three and four on a horse—and have races, jumping contests over logs, humiliating busters, and all sorts of adventures along the road. Many a coat is peeled off on the school track, too, and many a punched nose goes bleeding to the waterhole. Frequently half a dozen are seen running through the bush, the big ones in front, the little ones, flushed and panting, in the rear. They have been playing on the road, or have started late, and are making up for it. Some have to run part of the way home, so as to be in time to put the calves up or to change their clothes and carry an armful of wood or a bucket of water for the morning; and if they live on a farm they have to join the parents after tea in the barn, husking corn. Preparing for examination under these circumstances is pretty stiff work for Bushman Junior.

Looking for paradise

Australia has a forgotten history of utopian communities. Established mostly in rural areas, these attempts to find social, religious or other forms of heaven on earth did not usually survive for long, riven by personality clashes, differing philosophies and, in many cases, a puzzling ignorance of the realities of the land.

The first of these optimistic groups settled in Victoria. The Herrnhut ('Lord's Watch') German commune was founded in 1852 and established at Penshurst in 1853. Its ugly but charismatic leader, Johann Friedrich Krumnow, preached a mixed bag of religious and social ideas spiced up with communism. His ideal way of life was a commune in which everyone followed what was believed to be the shared life of Jesus Christ and the Apostles. Krumnow did not recognise the authority of the state, preferring to deal directly with God. The commune did well for many years but after conflict, defections, diminishing finances and Krumnow's death, it was dissolved by 1897.

Queensland had a brief but colourful experience with a Finnish utopia during the 1890s. Its inevitably charismatic leader was Matti Kurikka, a man who combined the Finnish mythological cycle known as the 'Kalevala', with Marxism. Accompanied by more than seventy followers, Kurikka travelled from Finland to Chillagoe in 1899. The plan was for everyone to live in common, work for wages and pool their earnings to buy land for their bush paradise.

But the Finns had no knowledge of the harsh conditions they would experience, nor much idea of farming, by which they intended to live. Things quickly fell apart as conflict with the locals, the exploitation of their labour in cutting sleepers for the Chillagoe railway and the hardships of living in tents undermined the dreams of the communards. Their leader allegedly preyed on some of the women in the group, further heightening tensions. Like the Biblical Moses, Kurikka and many of his followers then struck out for Cape York Peninsula to find paradise in the wilderness. Amazingly, it seems that none died in this hopeless trek. They were rescued just in time. But it was the end of the madness, at least in Australia. The idealistic Kurikka and some still-faithful followers then moved to British Columbia where they established a similar and marginally more successful community.

Kurikka's parting words expressed his frustration at the treatment he and his followers received:

> I have been here now eight months. What did I find here? Disappointments only disappointments! All the prospects of possibility for the immigrants to gain money in a short time and get their own land which the Government of Queensland had represented in their pamphlets, have vanished as soap-bubbles. All my essays to open the eyes of the Government to comprehend the great advantage to this indebted country of the bending of the large Finnish emigration from America to Queensland, got lost. My task for the 'Huguenots' of Finland was impossible to realise in that way.
>
> Alright, did I think, I will try the other, although harder way. I will become an ordinary worker, become a good member of the Labour [sic] party, win in that way an influence in the party, and begin then anew the realisation of my great idea. But, after the experience I got in Brisbane, in some other places, and at last by the Chillagoe railway, I have already given up this programme, too.
>
> Meanwhile I collect some experiences of a worker. I learnt to know that the labourers in Queensland—there are of course, exceptions—are too drunk, too vulgar, and too hateful against all foreigners that are sober, friendly, and honest as the Finns, to think that they could become equals with them striving for the same holy ideals.

The disappointed idealist concluded his farewell letter with a parting shot: 'My friendly hope is only that the people of Queensland as soon as possible will rise to the same level of civilisation as the other cultured peoples of the world.'

There were a good many of these experiments during the 1890s as the governments of every colony, except Western Australia, provided subsidies in hope of providing a living for the unemployed and their families. In Victoria, a Village

Settlement scheme produced seventy-eight communities, most
of which soon fell apart. Around the same time about seven
hundred Christian followers of ministers Horace Tucker
and Charles Strong began to live and farm communally at
seven locations, including Horsham, Red Hill and Jindivick.
Attempting to live by steam-powered irrigation and farming
techniques, the groups were underfunded and poorly managed.
They all collapsed in poverty by 1895.

In Tasmania, a commune was set up at Southport in 1894
with twenty families. It barely lasted a year. Thirteen communal
settlements were planted in South Australia from 1894, attracting almost 2000 people. These communities did well for a while
but the usual conflicts led to most of them dissolving by 1902,
although the upper Murray Lyrup Village Association continues today as a form of irrigation co-operative, a more familiar
form of collaboration in rural Australia. In New South Wales,
the same fad for communes produced the towns of Bega, Pitt
Town and Wilberforce. They were all dissolved after three or
four years, though the towns survived.

A commune known as 'New Jerusalem' was encouraged
by the West Australian government at Wickepin in 1902. It
was the continuation of an earlier settlement of the 'Church of
the Firstborn' in Victoria and was led by another charismatic
combiner of religious, social and political ideas known colloquially as 'The Messiah of Nunawading'. An escaped convict,
his adopted name was James Cowley Morgan Fisher and he
thought of himself and his followers as 'Christian Jews'. His
philosophy included polygamy—on his part, at least—and
patriarchy, with himself as undisputed religious dictator. This
operation did well, using modern farm machinery, building
a village with a school and convincing the government to
provide a rail link to Wickepin. But when Fisher died in 1913,
the enterprise soon reverted to the individualism usually found
in regional Australia.

There were other attempts to create viable livelihoods based
on communal principles, but most followed the same pattern

of hope, optimism, internal dissension and collapse. Paradise is hard to find. Yet, people continue to see the bush as the place to find it. Nimbin is probably the best-known modern example. A product of the 1960s and 70s 'hippy' movement, it has long-ceased to be a commune. Many similar initiatives were set up in Queensland from the 1970s and a number have continued to the present.

By song and star

The 'wond'rous glory of the everlasting stars' was how 'Banjo' Paterson famously described the night sky beyond the city lights in 'Clancy of the Overflow'. Many explorers and settlers were equally impressed with the clear expanse of stars that dome the bush night, often using them to guide them through unfamiliar country.

But long before the coming of roads, railways and airways, Australia had a vast overland transportation and communication system. Over perhaps more than 70,000 years, Aborigines evolved ways to walk across the country, guided by song, story and patterns of the stars. These were sometimes known as 'dreaming tracks' and were taught to generation after generation so travellers would know how to reach important ceremonial sites and, just as importantly, how to return home. These traditional ways are associated with creation stories, the land and sources of water. One of the longest and most important is the 'Seven Sisters', a multi-layered story trail that crosses the continent from west to east.

The Seven Sisters songline is really a complex interweaving of many variations of a creation story known to Aboriginal groups across Australia. In the National Museum of Australia's exhibition 'Songlines: Tracking the Seven Sisters', a group of these stories from the Martu, Ngaanyatjarra and Anangu Pitjantjatjara Yankunytjatjara (APY) traditions of the Central and Western Deserts can be seen in an immersive audio-visual display. The evil sorcerer Wati Nyiru (or Yurla in some versions) chases the seven sisters across the land, sky and water with lustful intentions. The sisters elude his shape-shifting guises and as they flee create the rocks, trees and waterholes, eventually finding eternal safety as the seven stars that make up the Pleiades in the constellation of Orion.

The existence of this and the vast number of other such routes throughout the continent has only gradually become known outside Aboriginal culture, but their mystery and antiquity so intrigued an English writer that he was drawn to visit Australia and write a book that gave the tracks a name that has become popular. His name was Bruce Chatwin and the book was called *The Songlines*, first published in 1987.

Chatwin died in 1989 but much of his adult life was spent in pursuit of what he called 'nomadism', the idea that the proper state of humanity was to be more or less continually on the move rather than settled down in one place. He certainly lived up to his ideas and roamed the world ceaselessly, writing highly regarded books about his experiences in South America and elsewhere. When he reached Australia he travelled the country in search of evidence to support his theory. The book he eventually produced was a thinly disguised fiction based on where he went, what he did and what he saw. It is effectively an extremely readable manifesto of nomadism by a fine writer who was able to draw readers into his cunningly wrought confabulations.

In Chatwin's rendition of the dreaming tracks, he implied that Aboriginal people were able to navigate by the melody as well as the words of the songs they sang as they went. The rise and fall of the tune matched the rise and fall of the landscape, while the lyrics told of the sacred stories attached to each section of the journey. So they literally sang themselves across the country and back again. This extraordinary navigational technique Chatwin called 'songlines'. At the time, there was scepticism. While it was known that Aboriginal people were able to use their songs and stories like a memory map to get them from place to place, the notion that the melodies actually replicated the physical landscape was thought to be a writer's poetic extravagance. But in the years since Chatwin published his book, the possibility that the songlines do include this navigational device, together with some even more profound techniques, has gained broader acceptance.

During those years, a greater understanding of how Aboriginal people used the night sky has also contributed to the appeal of the songlines idea. While the star patterns are not used as in Western forms of celestial navigation, their positions and relationships at different times of the year have been shown to reliably indicate the direction of travel and the location of important waypoints. Knowledge of these patterns and of the traditional stories associated with them, together with the songs transmitted for millennia by oral tradition, gives Aboriginal people the ability to move with confidence through the land.

The songlines were also trade routes and channels for passing information between different groups in different parts of the country. Stories as well as goods passed along these ways, forming the extraordinary coherence of indigenous mythology and spirituality across the continent, that, at the same time, is also specific to local groups. The substantial memory power needed to store this information in story, song and art was aided by memory objects, such as wooden bowls and stone *tjuringas*—spiritual objects decorated with markings that could be used as a mnemonic.

The nomadic English writer may have been a dreamer, but his instinctive understanding of indigenous creativity gave us a way to understand some of the complexities of what many consider to be the world's oldest living culture. The songlines and star maps of ancient Australia are still helping us navigate the land. Many of the early-settler pioneer tracks and droving trails follow Aboriginal footsteps. Even some major roads align with the star patterns. The reason, of course, is that songlines, star maps and frontier settlement all depend on knowing the location of the same vital commodity—water.

Notes

Chapter 1: Bush ways

Across the Blue Mountains

Elizabeth Hawkins (with introduction by H. Selkirk), 'Journey from Sydney to Bathurst in 1822', *Journal and Proceedings (Royal Australian Historical Society)*, Vol. 9, Part 4, 1923, pp. 177–97. Descendants: Nepean Times, 4 June 1910, p. 7.

Death: 'Hawkins, Thomas Fitzherbert (1781–1837)', *Australian Dictionary of Biography*, National Centre of Biography, Australian National University, http://adb.anu.edu.au/biography/hawkins-thomas-fitzherbert-2169/text2727, published first in hardcopy 1966, accessed 13 November 2017.

On foot to Appin

James Backhouse, *A Narrative of a Visit to the Australian Colonies*, Hamilton, Adams, London, 1843, pp. 421–22.

Bush generosity

Walter Spencer Stanhope Tyrwhitt, *The New Chum in the Australian Bush*, Vincent, Oxford, 1888, pp. 81–82.

Bush song: *The Queenslander*, 29 September 1894, p. 596. 'Supplied by E Blaxland, Rawbelle'.

Whoppers!

Jugiong: From '—Exchange' in the *Bathurst Daily Argus*, 1 July 1909, p. 3.

Bullock teams: A version set at Cooper's Creek in Ron Edwards, *The Australian Yarn*, Rigby, Adelaide, 1977, pp. 216–18.

Dreadful tale: *The North Queensland Register,* 27 May 1939, p. 60.

Jackaroo: *The Narromine News and Trangie Advocate*, 14 June 1929, p. 3, by Bill Bowyang.

Talking bush
Goodge: *The Clipper*, 5 August 1899, p. 8 (also published two years earlier).

Revenge: There are many versions of this chestnut, see Bill Wannan, *Come In, Spinner: A Treasury of Popular Australian Humour*, Currey, O'Neill, Melbourne 1976, p. 149.

Bush names
Jesse Thompson, 'Humpty Doo: Origins of town's name continues to elude historians', at http://www.abc.net.au/news/2018-02-08/humpty-doo-name-mystery-history/9400266, accessed February 2018.

Hypocoristics: *Australian Style*, December 2004, p. 1.

Jack/Ned: Edward Sorenson, *Life in the Australian Backblocks*, Whitcomb & Tombs, London, 1911 at http://gutenberg.net.au/ebooks13/1305751h.html#s22, accessed October 2017.

The boy with the pony
One-pound note: *The Sydney Morning Herald*, 20 April 1932, p. 12.

Children's ball: *The Sydney Morning Herald*, 9 May 1932, p. 10.

Letter: *The Sydney Morning Herald*, 11 June 1932, p. 18.

Stephanie Owen Reeder, *Lennie the Legend: Solo to Sydney by Pony*, National Library of Australia, Canberra, 2015.

Solo equestrian: The Long Riders Guild, http://www.thelongridersguild.com/Records.htm, accessed October 2017.

The man from furthest out
Paterson and Lawson's contributions were published in *The Bulletin* between July and October, 1892.

A.B. Paterson, 'Banjo Paterson Tells His Own Story', *The Sydney Morning Herald*, 4 February–4 March 1939.

Chapter 2: Bush folk

Burgoo Bill
The Bendigo Independent, 22 October 1918, p. 6, by Duncan Campbell.

Bundaburra Jack
Bundaburra Jack: *Truth*, 7 October 1900, p. 4.

Publican: *The Land*, 15 October 1937, p. 2 and an earlier recollection of the tale in *The Narromine News and Trangie Advocate*, 14 June 1929, p. 3 and another version with an extra sting in the tale in *The Land*, 3 October 1947, p. 20.

Grog: *The Wyalong Star and Temora and Barmedman Advertiser*,
    21 January 1902, p. 2.
Pretensions: *Freeman's Journal*, 22 April 1899, p. 21; *Molong Argus*,
    28 December 1906, p. 13.
Certain town: *Nepean Times*, 5 April 1902, p. 8. Variation of the same
    yarn in *The Bathurst Daily Argus*, 26 January 1909, p. 2, *Smith's
    Weekly*, 28 June 1919, p. 19. That one and others at *The Dubbo
    Liberal and Macquarie Advocate*, 1 July 1911, p. 4.
Jack observes: *The Forbes Advocate*, 1 October 1915, p. 2.
Rum: *The Forbes Advocate*, 26 January 1917, p. 2.
Death: *Mudgee Guardian and North-Western Representative*,
    18 January 1909, p. 2.
Funeral: Folklorist Rob Willis collected and researched some of the
    stories of Bundaburra Jack, used here with permission.
1923: *Northern Star* (Lismore), 18 August 1923, p. 6.
Antics: *The Land*, 12 November 1937, p. 2.
Smith's Weekly: The Land, 14 October 1949, p. 31.

Bob, the railway dog
Southern Argus, 22 August 1895, p. 3; 'Koolie', at https://en.
    wikipedia.org/wiki/Koolie, accessed August 2017.
Particular: *The Advertiser* (Adelaide), 5 February 1935, p. 11.
American design: State Library of South Australia.
The Spectator, 24 August 1895, p. 16.
Bob's Legend: *The Advertiser* (Adelaide), 17 August 1895, p. 6,
    accessed August 2017. See also Olwyn M. Parker, *The Railway
    Dog: The True Story of an Outback Dog*, Brolga Publishing,
    Melbourne 2010.
The Spectator, 19 October 1895, p. 17.

Bill Bowyang
The Australian Worker, 14 November 1918, p. 10.
David Barker: And later Charles Barrett.
On the track: *Bowen Independent*, 24 February 1920, p. 4.
Vennard: *The Richmond River Herald and Northern Districts
    Advertiser*, 5 September 1919, p. 6.

Jack-the-Rager
Edward Sorenson, *Life in the Australian Backblocks*, Whitcomb &
    Tombs, London, 1911 at http://gutenberg.net.au/ebooks13/
    1305751h.html#s22, accessed October 2017.

Don't mess with Jess!
Discharged: *The Cumberland Argus and Fruitgrowers Advocate*,
    15 February 1919, p. 12.
Long Bay: *The Cumberland Argus and Fruitgrowers Advocate*,
    16 August 1913, p. 6.

The Cumberland Argus and Fruitgrowers Advocate, 23 February 1918, p. 12.

Success: https://broadly.vice.com/en_us/article/nejbjw/the-lady-bushranger-remembering-australias-forgotten-female-outlaw, quoting Pat Studdy-Clift, author of one of several books on Jessie Hickman, accessed November 2017.

Fined: *The Cumberland Argus and Fruitgrowers Advocate,* 29 March 1919, p. 5.

Bush: *Evening News* (Sydney), 29 October 1928, p. 8.

Escape: Elizabeth Jessie (Hunt) Hickman at https://www.wikitree.com/wiki/Hunt-6626#, accessed December 2017.

Little known: Pat Studdy-Clift, *The Lady Bushranger*, Hesperian Press, Perth, 1996 and Di Moore, *Out of the Mists: The Hidden History of Elizabeth Jessie Hickman*, Balboa Press, Bloomington Indiana, 2014. Moore is Jessie's granddaughter. 'The Lady Bushranger' (film project) at http://www.theladybushranger.com, accessed November 2017.

Lord of the bush

Anthony Hordern: https://collection.maas.museum/object/126875, accessed July 2017.

Chiffonier: http://www.ubuyonline.com.au/furniture.6.html, accessed July 2017.

Sotheby's: http://trove.nla.gov.au/work/23775434?selectedversion=NBD9862651, accessed July 2017.

Obituary at http://www.smh.com.au/comment/obituaries/lord-mcalpine-of-west-green-conservative-fundraier-cleaned-out-by-broome-20140124-31dm1.html, accessed July 2017.

Chapter 3: Plagues and perishes

Bloody flies!

For a useful scientific debunking of fly myths see http://www.news.com.au/lifestyle/why-do-flies-bug-us-so-much-the-csiro-helps-dispel-urban-myths/news-story/86ba341ec20ac0ca62dc0c3e9c833c92, accessed July 2017.

Walter Spencer Stanhope Tyrwhitt, *The New Chum in the Australian Bush*, Vincent, Oxford, 1888, p. 37. Tyrwhitt studied history at Oxford and was an artist of landscapes and architectural subjects, particularly in the Middle East. He exhibited at the Royal Academy between 1913 and 1921 and died at Oxford, England in 1932. His colonial adventure is an excellent read.

Australian Dung Beetle project, at https://en.m.wikipedia.org/wiki/Australian_Dung_Beetle_Project, accessed July 2017.

Last of the nomads

W.J. Peasley, *The Last of the Nomads*, Fremantle Arts Centre Press, Fremantle, 1983 and numerous later editions.

A new chum is bushed

Walter Spencer Stanhope Tyrwhitt, *The New Chum in the Australian Bush*, Vincent, Oxford, 1888, pp. 67ff.

The emu wars

War games: *The Sydney Morning Herald*, 9 November 1932, p. 14.
The Sunday Herald (Sydney), 5 July 1953, p. 13.

Black days

Henry Kingsley, *The Recollections of Geoffry Hamlyn*, Macmillan and Co. Cambridge and London, 1859, at http://setis.library.usyd.edu.au/ozlit/pdf/p00046.pdf, accessed February 2018.
Don Watson, *The Bush*, Penguin Group (Australia), Melbourne, 2016, (first published 2014), p. 13.

Perishes

Smith's Weekly, 6 September 1919, p. 17.
Mount Browne: *The Maitland Mercury and Hunter River General Advertiser*, 31 March 1881, p. 6.
http://www.smh.com.au/news/national/outback-tourist-rescued-twice-in-a-week/2006/09/13/1157826982171.html, accessed February 2018.
Lucy Marks, 'Larapinta Trail: American hiker dies after taking wrong turn in 42C heat', http://www.abc.net.au/news/2018-01-11/larapinta-trail-american-tourist-dies-after-taking-wrong-turn/9319512, accessed January 2018.
Alaskan: https://www.theguardian.com/world/1999/aug/24/7, accessed February 2018, though this source states that the man was lost for 40 days.
Sarah Mashman, 'How Five Aboriginal Women Survived Five Days in the Outback Using the Stories of the Land', at http://www.abc.net.au/news/2017-05-01/how-oral-tradition-helped-five-aboriginal-women-survive/8480060, accessed October 2017.

The grave nomads

At www.outbackgraves.org, accessed December 2017.
Palmer: *Centralian Advocate*, 5 July 1947, p. 3.
Emma Siossian, 'Community group identifies 1,500 unmarked graves in project to ensure lives are not forgotten', at http://www.abc.net.au/news/2018-02-08/community-group-identifies-1500-unmarked-graves-nsw/9404278, accessed February 2018.
Outback Communities Authority Annual Report 2011–12, http://oca.sa.gov.au/burialregister, accessed October 2017.

The 'Fergies' and the flood

Jamie Duncan, 'How farmers with tractors fought Murray River floods to save entire town', *Herald Sun*, 12 May 2016 at http://www.heraldsun.com.au/news/victoria/how-farmers-with-tractors-fought-murray-river-floods-to-save-entire-town/news-story/85ed91dc56a54178f7933ad9fe927b33, accessed June 2017, and http://visitwentworth.com.au/1956-wentworth-floods/, accessed August 2017.

Aimee Volkofsky, 'Twenty Ferguson tractors trek 2,300 kilometres following Burke and Wills' footsteps' at http://www.abc.net.au/news/2017-08-22/tractor-trek-traces-burke-and-wills-journey/8828316, accessed January 2018.

Chapter 4: Pastimes and pleasures

The Legend of the lost library

From Spencer's diary, quoted by Robin Hardiman, 'The Lost Library of Borroloola, at http://www.artplan.com.au/bnp/BNP10text/26.htm, accessed July 2017.

Ernestine Hill, 'Town Dies, Books Live', *The Sun* (Sydney), 25 June 1933, p. 6.

Webster's: http://www.aussietowns.com.au/town/borroloola-nt, accessed July 2017.

Bill Harney wrote many books and articles about his outback life, see Jennifer J. Kennedy, 'Harney, William Edward (Bill) (1895–1962)', *Australian Dictionary of Biography*, National Centre of Biography, Australian National University, http://adb.anu.edu.au/biography/harney-william-edward-bill-10428/text18485, published first in hardcopy 1996, accessed December 2017.

The flying Viola girls

Millie: *Barrier Miner*, 19 July 1890, p. 3.

No show: *Gippsland Times*, 13 February 1891, p. 3.

Goulburn Evening Penny Post, 4 July 1893, p. 2.

The Australian Star, 22 April 1895, p. 6.

The Daily Northern Argus, 14 May 1895, p. 2.

Niagara: *Indianapolis News*, 10 December 1895, p. 1.

Ruby: *The San Francisco Call*, 3 April 1897, p. 13.

George Blaikie, *Scandals of Australia's Strange Past*, Rigby, Adelaide, 963, pp. 156ff.

Grog

Tightrope: Bill Wannan, *Folklore of the Australian Pub*, Macmillan, South Melbourne, 1972, pp. 56–58.

Smith's Weekly, 6 September 1919, p. 17, from 'J H'.

Killing a kangaroo

A.W. Stirling, *The Never Never Land: A Ride in North Queensland*, Sampson, Lowe, Marston, Searle and Rivington, London, 1884, pp. 45–46.

Painting the land

'Utopia', at http://www.diggins.com.au/artwork/aboriginal-main/utopia/, accessed October 2017.

John Curtin Gallery, Curtin University at http://johncurtingallery.curtin.edu.au/carrolup/, accessed October 2017.

Anna Haebich and Chris Malcolm, 'The Return of the Carrolup Drawings', *Griffith Review* 47, 2015, pp. 97–104.

Buckjumpers

Edward Sorenson, *Life in the Australian Backblocks*, Whitcomb & Tombs, London, 1911 at http://gutenberg.net.au/ebooks13/1305751h.html#s22, accessed October 2017.

The tea and scone ladies

CWA: *The West Australian*, 26 April 1941, p. 5.

Boggabilla: http://www.abc.net.au/radionational/programs/sundayextra/a-history-of-cwa-aboriginal-branches/6880434, accessed February 2018.

Resistance: Jennifer Jones, *Country Women and the Colour Bar: Grassroots Activism and the Country Women's Association*, Aboriginal Studies Press, Canberra, 2015.

Eliza Laschon, 'WA Country Women's Association to protest for the first time in its history over education cuts' at http://www.abc.net.au/news/2018-02-12/cwa-protests-state-government-education-funding-cuts/9422218, accessed February 2018.

http://www.geelongadvertiser.com.au/news/geelong/how-to-make-the-perfect-scone-according-to-the-country-womens-association/news story/a0180b76e18bf60ac0273ee9c7a3fc4e, accessed November 2017.

I mean to get a wife!

The Queenslander, 3 November 1894, p. 836. The song was also printed in 'Banjo' Paterson's collection of *Old Bush Songs*, where he explained that: 'A paddymelon is a small but speedy marsupial, a sort of poor relation of the great kangaroo family. An offsider is a bullock driver's assistant, one who walks on the offside of the team and flogs the bullocks when the occasion arises. The word afterwards came to mean an assistant of any kind.'

Chapter 5: Wrongdoing

We'll take the whole damn country

A version appears in print in *Australian Town and Country Journal*, 12 December 1906, p. 26.

'How Gilbert Died', *The Australian Worker*, 16 May 1923, p. 13.
A.B. Paterson, first published 1894.

The death of Ben Hall
Truth, 30 April 1911, p. 11.
Forbes: John Manifold (ed), *The Penguin Book of Australian
    Ballads*, Penguin, Ringwood Vic., 1964, pp. 60–61 published a
    more polished version of this poem, with a tune, collected from
    Mrs Ewell of Bathurst.

Hang him like a dog
The Brisbane Courier, 19 November 1872, p. 3. Unless otherwise
    noted, all quotations from this source.
Glenn A. Davies, 'The Grand Panjandrum: The 1872 Suspension
    of Gold Commissioner W.S.E.M. Charters', *Journal of the
    Royal Historical Society of Queensland*, Vol. 15, Issue 3, 1993,
    pp. 130–44.
In custody: *The Queenslander*, 9 November 1872, p. 3.
Never faced court: 'Australian Trevethan Family', at http://www.
    trevethan.net/Australia.htm, accessed July 2017.

All in the family
Francis Augustus Hare, *The Last of the Bushrangers: An Account of
    the Capture of the Kelly Gang*, 4th edn, Hurst & Blackett, London,
    1895, pp. 203–04.
Hearing: Public Record Office Victoria, VPRS 4966 P0 unit 1
    Item 4-1.

The Namoi horror
The Advertiser (Adelaide), 23 December 1908, p. 6.
Bank book: *The Argus*, 26 December 1908, p. 10.
The Border Morning Mail and Riverina Times, 25 June 1910, p. 3.

Murder by the book
Hanged: See Terry Walker, *Murder on the Rabbit-Proof Fence*,
    Hesperian Press, Carlisle, 1993 for a detailed look at the case
    which has also been the subject of several film and television
    productions.
Stephen Knight, 'Upfield, Arthur William (1890–1964)', *Australian
    Dictionary of Biography*, National Centre of Biography, Australian
    National University, http://adb.anu.edu.au/biography/upfield-
    arthur-william-8900/text15635, published first in hardcopy 1990,
    accessed 19 July 2017.

Murderer's bore
Booze: *The Courier-Mail*, 8 January 1941, p. 3.
Cracked skull: *Barrier Miner*, 9 January 1941, p. 1.

https://kilcowerastation.wordpress.com/2011/09/29/cougars-toyboys-and-murderers'-bore/, accessed December 2017.

A dingo's got my baby
Raymond: *Singleton Argus*, 14 February 1925, p. 6.
Party jokes: The examples given here, as well as other related materials, are documented in Graham Seal, 'Azaria Chamberlain and the Media Charivari', *Australian Folklore* 1, March 1987.
National Museum: http://www.nma.gov.au/collections/highlights/azaria-chamberlains-dress, accessed November 2017.

Chapter 6: Where the dead men lie

Unhallowed graves
Cecil Hadgraft, 'Boake, Barcroft Henry (1866–1892)', *Australian Dictionary of Biography*, National Centre of Biography, Australian National University, http://adb.anu.edu.au/biography/boake-barcroft-henry-3018/text4421, published first in hardcopy 1969, accessed April 2018.
Stephens: *The Brisbane Courier*, 2 October 1897, p. 8.
Suicide: Cecil Hadgraft, 'Boake, Barcroft Henry (1866–1892)', *Australian Dictionary of Biography*, National Centre of Biography, Australian National University, http://adb.anu.edu.au/biography/boake-barcroft-henry-3018/text4421, published first in hardcopy 1969, accessed 19 July 2017. 'Where the Dead Men Lie' was first published in *The Bulletin* in December 1891.

A lady explorer
Creaghe, Emily Caroline and Monteath, Peter, *The Diary of Emily Caroline Creaghe: Explorer*, Corkwood Press, North Adelaide, S.A, 2004; Winsome J.M. Maff, 'Barnett, Emily Caroline (1860–1944)', *Australian Dictionary of Biography*, National Centre of Biography, Australian National University, http://adb.anu.edu.au/biography/barnett-emily-caroline-9439/text16595, published first in hardcopy 1993, accessed August 2017.

The lost boy
Joseph Furphy (writing as Tom Collins), *Such Is Life: Being Certain Extracts from the Diary of Tom Collins*, Bulletin Newspaper Company, Sydney, 1903, though written in the 1890s.

The great heat of '96
Too hot: *Evening Journal* (Adelaide), 17 February 1896, p. 2.
Death rolls: *Barrier Miner*, 14 January 1896, p. 2.
Bulli: *The Illawarra Mercury*, 20 January 1896, p. 4.
Keogh: *The Argus*, 22 January 1896, p. 5.
Cunnamulla: *The Queenslander*, 1 February 1896, p. 232.

Suffering: *Wellington Times and Agricultural Mining Gazette*,
25 January 1896, p. 3.
Controversy: Neville Nicholls and Sophie Lewis, 'Factcheck: Was the
1896 Heatwave Wiped from the Record?', *The Conversation*,
6 November 2014 at https://theconversation.com/factcheck-
was-the-1896-heatwave-wiped-from-the-record-33742, accessed
November 2017.

The union buries its dead

First published in *The Bulletin* in 1893 and subsequently in Henry
Lawson, *While the Billy Boils*, Angus & Robertson, Sydney, 1896.

The Never Never

Superintendent: *The Darling Downs Gazette and General Advertiser*,
10 October 1861, p. 3.
A.W. Stirling, *The Never Never Land: A Ride in North Queensland*,
Sampson, Lowe, Marston, Searle and Rivington, London, 1884, p. vi.
Henry Lawson, *Joe Wilson and His Mates*, Blackwood, Edinburgh,
1901, pp. 351 ff.
How to get to the outback: Quoted in Bill Wannan, *The Australian:
Yarns, Ballads, Legends, Traditions of the Australian People*,
Australasian Book Society, Melbourne, 1954, p. 2.

The stockman's last bed

Composed by W. Shield but based on a much older ballad.
http://www.sl.nsw.gov.au/collection-items/stockmans-last-bed-parody-
popular-song-last-whistle-written-two-daughters-colonel, accessed
July 2017, punctuation amended. See also Graeme Skinner
(University of Sydney), 'Maria and Bessie Gray and The Stockman's
Last Bed (1846)', Australharmony (an online resource towards the
history of music and musicians in colonial and early Federation
Australia): http://sydney.edu.au/paradisec/australharmony/gray-
maria-and-bessie-and-the-stockmans-last-bed.php; accessed
19 July 2017.
Final verse: 'An Old Explorer', *The Queenslanders' New Colonial
Camp Fire Song Book*, F. Cunninghame, Sydney, 1865.
Australian Town and Country Journal, 14 October 1893, p. 17.
John Thompson, 'An Australian Folk Song A Day' at http://
ozfolksongaday.blogspot.com.au/2011/02/stockmans-last-bed.html,
accessed July 2017.

Chapter 7: Hard yakka

The overlanders

The Overlanders at http://www.samemory.sa.gov.au/site/page.
cfm?u=1322, accessed July 2017.

Ballad: *Australian Tradition*, No. 19, March, 1960. Among many other versions, an early one in *The Queenslanders' New Colonial Camp Fire Song Book*, F. Cunninghame, Sydney, 1865.

Trouble on the diggings

George Dunderdale, *The Book of the Bush*, Ward, Lock & Co., London, 1870(?) at http://www.gutenberg.org/files/16349/16349-h/16349-h.htm#ch-07, accessed July 2017.

The blades that felled the bush

http://bushcraftoz.com/forums/showthread.php?3120-The-History-of-the-Axe-and-Related-Tools-in-Australia/page2, accessed August 2017.

McLaren: *Boy's Life*, February 1929, p. 68 at https://www.bladeforums.com/threads/peter-mclaren-americas-champion-chopper-from-australia.834782/, accessed August 2017.

Detroit Free Press, 31 May 1947, p. 5.

Champion: An Australian title.

Death: *Gympie Times*, 26 March 2015 at https://www.gympietimes.com.au/news/vic-summers-96-a-champion-lost/2587042/, accessed February 2018.

McGinniss: *The Coffs Harbour Advocate*, 21 May 2012, https://www.coffscoastadvocate.com.au/news/woodchop-legend-competes-age-93/1387503/, accessed August 2017.

Irishwoman: *The Sunday Herald* (Sydney), 6 April 1952, p. 5.

Bush cooks

Cooking: Edward Sorenson, *Life in the Australian Backblocks*, Whitcomb & Tombs, London, 1911 at http://gutenberg.net.au/ebooks13/1305751h.html#s22, accessed October 2017.

'The Station Cook', collected by Dr Percy Jones and sung to the tune of 'The Lachlan Tigers', Douglas Stewart and Nancy Keesing (eds), *Old Bush Songs and Rhymes of Colonial Times*, Angus & Robertson, Sydney, 1957, p. 260.

Edward Sorenson, *Life in the Australian Backblocks*, Whitcomb & Tombs, London, 1911 at http://gutenberg.net.au/ebooks13/1305751h.html#s22, accessed October 2017.

Shearers' cook: *The Scone Advocate*, Friday 21 July 1933, p. 4.

Ploughing time

The Argus, 19 April 1880, p. 6.

Blackbirds

Discrimination: Clem Lack, '1100 Kanakas in Queensland: A South Sea Legacy', *Sunday Mail* (Brisbane), 13 February 1938, p. 33.

Estimates of the exact number vary, but over 60,000 is the most frequently cited.

'The Kanaka Labour Traffic', *The Argus*, 22 December 1892, p. 5.

'The Cane Cutter's Lament', Australian Folk Songs at http://folkstream. com/020.html, accessed November 2017.

Interview by Rob Willis, not yet publicly available.

Acknowledgement: Australian South Sea Islander Association at http:// www.assipj.com.au/, accessed November 2017.

The boundary rider

1840s: John Pickard, *Illustrated Glossary of Australian Rural Fence Terms*, 2009 p. 30 at http://www.environment.nsw.gov.au/resources/ heritagebranch/heritage/IllustratedglossaryofAustralianruralfence terms2009.pdf, accessed November 2017.

Hard life: *Illustrated Australian News*, 30 September 1885.

Smith's Weekly, 6 September 1919, p. 17.

John Pickard, p. 25, quoting Lamond, H.G. (1955b) 'Fencing Aids II' in *Cummins & Campbell's Monthly Magazine*, May 1955, p. 5.

Taylah Smith, 'Rebuilding the Dingo Fence in outback Australia', at http://www.abc.net.au/heywire/heywire-winner-2018-taylah-smith-mintaro-sa/9138846, accessed February 2018.

Chapter 8: Stringybark and greenhide

I was by no means an exception

Winifred Moore, 'The Heart-Warming Story of a Pioneer Home-Maker', *The Courier-Mail*, 30 June 1951, p. 2.

Making do: Beverley Kingston, 'Rawson, Wilhelmina Frances (Mina) (1851–1933)', *Australian Dictionary of Biography*, National Centre of Biography, Australian National University, http://adb. anu.edu.au/biography/rawson-wilhelmina-frances-mina-8163/ text14269, published first in hardcopy 1988, accessed July 2017.

Reflections: Mrs Lance Rawson, 'Making the Best of it', *The Queenslander*, 3 April 1920, p. 6.

The gum leaf bands

Gulgong: Written by J.C. Johnson and quoted in Warren Fahey, 'I've Got the Music Right Here in My Pocket: The Role of Songsters in Australian Music', at http://www.warrenfahey.com.au/enter-the-collection/the-collection-m-z/songsters-songbooks/, accessed July 2017.

Roseina: Robin Ryan, 'Cross Cultural Perspectives on Gumleaf Performance Behaviour', in Gerry Bloustien (ed.), *Musical Visions: elected Conference Proceedings from the 6th National Australia/ New Zealand IASPM and Inaugural Arnhem Land Performance Conference, Adelaide, June 1999*, Wakefield Press, Kent Town, pp. 122–24.

Graham Seal and Rob Willis (eds), *Verandah Music: The Roots of Australian Tradition*, Curtin University Books, Fremantle, 2003.

Bush carpentry

The Old Bark Hut: A.B. Paterson (ed.), *Old Bush Songs*: composed and sung in the bushranging, digging and overlanding days, 4th edn, Angus & Robertson, Sydney, 1924. One of many versions.

Camping: Edward Sorenson, *Life in the Australian Backblocks*, Whitcomb & Tombs, London, 1911 at http://gutenberg.net.au/ebooks13/1305751h.html#s22, accessed October 2017.

Henry Lawson, *While the Billy Boils* (First Series), Angus & Robertson, Sydney, 1896.

A lady in the bush

Katherine Kirkland, *Life in the Bush*, published by Kenneth W. Mackenzie, 'Trawalla', Beaufort, Victoria, c. 1995: reprinted from *Chambers's Miscellany of Useful and Entertaining Tracts*, William and Robert Chambers, Edinburgh, Vol. 1, No. 8, printed in 1844, p. 48. See also Barbara Dawson, *In the Eye of the Beholder: What Six Nineteenth-century Women Tell Us About Indigenous Authority and Identity*, ANU Press, Canberra, 2014, pp. 73–98.

Published: *Vegetarian cookery by a Lady; with an introduction explanatory of the principles of vegetarianism by Jas. Simpson*, 6th edn, Fred Pitman, London, pp. 186–(?).

Building the Barcoo Hotel

Captain Tomalin, *Venturesome Tom: A Story of Stirring Adventure by Land and Sea*, Fredrick Tarrant & Co., London, 1908, in Bill Wannan, *Folklore of the Australian Pub*, MacMillan, South Melbourne, 1972, pp. 19–21.

Listenable at http://ozfolksongaday.blogspot.com.au/2011/05/thousand-miles-away.html, accessed August 2017. The song is sometimes titled 'Ten Thousand Miles Away'.

Gum trees and gumsuckers

Changing attitudes: Lucy Kaldor, 'Gum Tree', in Melissa Harper and Richard White (eds), *Symbols of Australia: Uncovering the Stories Behind the Myths*, University of NSW Press/National Museum of Australia, Sydney and Canberra, 2010.

Useful tree: Genelle Weule, 'Eucalypts: 10 things you may not know about an iconic Australian', at http://www.abc.net.au/news/science/2018-01-26/eucalyptus-trees-an-iconic-australian/9330782, accessed February 2018.

Slippery Bob and other delights

Bushman's diet: *Chambers's Edinburgh Journal*, Edinburgh, 1843, p. 174.

Our Special Correspondent (Charles Bean), 'The Barrier Railway', *The Sydney Morning Herald*, 13 June 1908, p. 8.

Concoctions: Helen Pitt, 'Health and medicine' in 'Gold' at https://www.sbs.com.au/gold/story.php?storyid=16, accessed December 2017.

Michael M. Knehans, 'The Archaeology and History of Pharmacy in Victoria', *Australian Historical Archaeology* 23, 2005, pp. 41–46.

The swagman's story

Morning Bulletin (Rockhampton, Qld), 23 February 1931, p. 1.

Stringybark and greenhide

Trinity: *Port Adelaide News*, 2 August 1918, p. 1.

See http://www.abc.net.au/news/2017-07-03/greenhide-rope-making-a-dying-artform/8666434 for the surviving craft of making greenhide rope, used mainly in what is now the sport of bronco branding in which cattle are controlled in the bush by ropes rather than penned in a yard.

George Chanson, 'Stringybark and Greenhide', in *The Sydney Songster*, c. 1866, p. 13, with the note 'A Character Song, as sung by Mr J.S. Brice, at the Theatre Royal, Lambing Flat, Forbes, etc.'. See also Hugh Anderson, *George Loyau: The Man Who Wrote Bush Ballads*, Red Rooster Press, Ascot Vale, 1991.

Chapter 9: Mysteries

The Devil's Pool

Babinda Information Centre at http://www.babindainfocentre.com.au/what-to-see/attractions/babinda-boulders/the-boulders-legend/, accessed April 2018.

Tourists: *Cairns Post*, 22 August 1929, p. 14.

Disrespectful: Message Stick, ABC1 Radio, 27 May 2005 at http://www.abc.net.au/tv/messagestick/stories/s1381165.htm, accessed August 2017.

Tall tales

Laura Armitage, 'Big cat sightings: dozens of people report seeing big cats around Australia', 20 April 2017 at http://www.heraldsun.com.au/leader/outer-east/big-cat-sightings-dozens-of-people-report-seeing-big-cats-around-australia/news-story/0cbf6d0e90e69e2f6a78b7bfa38a49fe, accessed April 2018.

Malaan man: Ron Edwards, *The Australian Yarn*, Rigby, Adelaide, 1977, p. 211.

Gorrilla: http://ozcrypto.net/home/index.php?option=com_content&view=article&id=58:1950s-qld-millaa-millaa&catid=1:yowiereports&Itemid=7, August 2017.

Immense object: 'A Bush Mystery', *The Maitland Weekly Mercury*, 19 October 1912, p. 6.

Yahoos: Robert Holden and Nicholas Holden, *Bunyips: Australia's Folklore of Fear,* National Library of Australia, Canberra, 2001; Graham Seal, *Great Australian Stories*, Allen & Unwin, Sydney 2009, pp. 65–80.

'The Hairy Man', *Humorous Stories of Henry Lawson*, Sydney, Angus & Robertson, 1982, (1907), pp. 64–72.

Small tales

Alice Roberts, 'Ancestors of Flores Hobbits may have been pioneers of first 'human' migration out of Africa', *The Conversation,* 24 April 2017 at https://theconversation.com/ancestors-of-flores-hobbits-may-have-been-pioneers-of-first-human-migration-out-of-africa-76560, accessed December 2017.

Contested aspect: Debbie Argue, 'The Struggle to Understand the Hobbit', *Cosmos*, 27 September 2017 at https://theconversation.com/ancestors-of-flores-hobbits-may-have-been-pioneers-of-first-human-migration-out-of-africa-76560, accessed December 2017.

Nicholas Rothwell, 'In Search of the Indigenous Little People of Northern Australia', *The Weekend Australian*, 3 May 2014 at http://www.theaustralian.com.au/arts/review/in-search-of-the-indigenous-little-people-of-northern-australia/news-story/4b6a79f0661a7ed0c55ae00e29fb119a, accessed July 2017.

Who stole Waltzing Matilda?

Thomas Wood, *Cobbers*, Oxford University Press/Humphrey Milford, London, 1934; Richard Magoffin, *Waltzing Matilda: The Story behind the Legend*, ABC Enterprises for the Australian Broadcasting Corporation, Sydney, 1987. Author's unpublished research. As Wood confesses in the introduction to *Cobbers*, the exact chronology of his Australian wanderings and the events he describes is not accurate.

Lasseter's undertaker

Gravesite: *The Courier-Mail*, 7 July 1936, p. 14.

Interview: *The Argus*, 23 September, 1979, p. 7.

Small allotment: *The Canberra Times*, 7 October 1939, p. 3.

Obituary in *The Centralian Advocate*, 12 August 1960 at http://oa.anu.edu.au/obituary/buck-robert-henry-bob-1621, accessed August 2017.

Lost gold

Ovens River: http://www.abc.net.au/local/stories/2006/05/05/1631688.htm, accessed October 2017.

The Gap: Roy Cameron, 'Mudgee History: Buried Gold, Part 1', *Mudgee Guardian*, 19 May 2017 at http://www.mudgeeguardian.com.au/story/4664134/mudgee-history-gold-in-them-hills/, accessed October 2017.

Thunderbolt: *Truth* (Sydney), 18 January 1953, p. 12.
Dungog: *Windsor and Richmond Gazette*, 17 April 1925, p. 2.
John Tennant: David R. Reid, 'The Terror of Argyle's Treasure' at
http://www.davesact.com/2011/07/terror-of-argyles-treasure.html,
accessed October 2017.
Still looking: *The Canberra Times*, 17 March 2012 at http://www.
canberratimes.com.au/act-news/tennants-treasure-20120315-
1v8u5.html, accessed October 2017.
https://www.geocaching.com/geocache/GC6093Y_bushranger-
booty?guid=500a640e-9a85-4da5-a0cc-5aa0cd64eb02, accessed
October 2017.
Buttney: ABC Radio Local, http://www.abc.net.au/local/stories/2013/
09/04/3841126.htm?site=goulbu, accessed October 2017.

The forgotten bushranger

Kenneth W. Porter, 'Johnny Troy: A "Lost" Australian Bushranger
Ballad' in the United States, *Meanjin Quarterly*, Vol. 24,
No. 2, 1965, pp. 227–38 at http://search.informit.com.au/
documentSummary;dn=965759253841134;res=IELLC,
accessed August 2017 and Kenneth Goldstein, notes to LP
'Songs of a New York Lumberjack', Folkways Records, 1958,
by Ellen Stekert.
Stephan Williams, *Johnny Troy*, Popinjay Publications, Canberra,
2001 (revised from original 1993 edition). It is fitting that Stephan
Williams resurrected this story of the vanishing bushranger as he
was himself an unsung hero of Australian folk history, mainly
through his impeccably researched series of self-publications issued
under his Popinjay imprint.
Hanged: Stephan Williams, from the *Sydney Gazette*, 21 August 1832.
Folk tradition: Graham Seal, *Outlaw Heroes in Myth and History*,
Anthem Press, London, 2011.

The Master Bushman legend

Francis Keen, 'Mysteries of the Australian Bush', *The World's News*,
6 January 1912, p. 19. Francis Keen was a northern New South
Wales journalist who specialised in bush mysteries. He sought to
publish his collected writings in 1914 but was unsuccessful. He
died at Narrabri in 1919 (NSW Births, Deaths and Marriages,
Registration Number: 2825). See also *The North Western Courier*,
4 February 1914, p. 3.

The sentinels of Myrrhee

Personal communication, Douglas Brockfield, August 2017.
Hamish Fitzsimmons, 'The World's Oldest Observatory? How
Aboriginal astronomy provides clues to ancient life', at

http://www.abc.net.au/news/2016-10-12/aboriginal-astronomy-
provides-clues-to-ancient-life/7925024, accessed January 2018,
regarding archaeological studies at Wurdi Youang near Little River
in Victoria.

At Hanging Rock

Joan Lindsay, *Picnic at Hanging Rock*, F.W. Cheshire, Melbourne,
1967. When first published, the original concluding chapter was
omitted, increasing the enigma of the story. That chapter was later
published.

Lindsay got the date of (Saint) Valentine's Day 1900 wrong, an error
that has only served to increase the chronological uncertainty of
the story, aided by Lindsay's own preference for having no clocks
in her home.

Local rumours: Conversation with folksinger Phyl Lobl (nee
Vinnicombe), who grew up mainly in Newham, close to Hanging
Rock, 2 January 2017.

Discomfort: On Saint Valentine's Day, 2017, the fiftieth anniversary
of the novel's publication, a protest was held at Hanging Rock to
draw attention to the exploitation of the story for tourism and the
consequent loss of the indigenous significance of the area, see the
'Miranda Must Go' campaign at http://www.mirandamustgo.info,
February 2018.

The last tiger

See the International Thylacine Specimen Database at http://www.
naturalworlds.org/thylacine/mrp/itsd/itsd_1.htm, accessed May
2018.

Quest continues: There is an extensive literature on the long history
of posthumous thylacine hunting. See Col Bailey, *Lure of the
Thylacine: True Stories and Legendary Tales of the Tasmanian
Tiger*, Echo Publishing, South Melbourne 2016, for some examples
of sightings, as well as innumerable online sites, including the
Wikipedia entry, which provides a reasonable and referenced
overview.

Striking animal: Parks and Wildlife Service Tasmania at http://www.
parks.tas.gov.au/?base=4765, accessed April 2018.

Gould: Quoted in Robert Paddle, *The Last Tasmanian Tiger: The
History and Extinction of the Thylacine*, Cambridge University
Press, Cambridge, 2000, p. 223.

Extinctions: Penny Edmonds and Hannah Stark, 'On the trail of the
London thylacines', *The Conversation* at https://theconversation.
com/friday-essay-on-the-trail-of-the-london-thylacines-91473,
accessed April 2018.

Chapter 10: A land without limits

The World Fair in the desert

The cameleers also came from various regions of India and what is
now Pakistan; 'Afghan' was a colloquial term.

Quotations from *The West Australian,* 22 March 1899, p. 5; see
also Lynne Stevenson, 'The Coolgardie International Exhibition,
1899' in Lenore Layman and Tom Stannage (eds), *Celebrations in
Western Australia*, Studies in Western Australian History, No. 10,
April 1989, pp. 100–06.

End of the line

Local identities: Catherine Duncan, 'Up the Birdum Road', *The Sun*
(NSW), 4 January 1942, p. 2.

9 Wireless Telegraph Station, Birdum, NT at http://www.ozatwar.com/
raaf/9wt.htm, accessed August 2017.

Heritage report: Register of the National Estate ID 102990, Place
File No. 7/04/013/0001 at http://www.environment.gov.au/cgibin/
ahdb/search.pl?mode=place_detail;place_id=102990, accessed
August 2017.

Ice and fire

'Light in Every Country Window' was composed in 1960, see The
Don Henderson project at http://donhenderson.com.au/index.html,
accessed February 2018.

Siobhán McHugh, *The Snowy: The People Behind the Power*,
Heinemann, Melbourne, 1989.

Consequences: http://www.abc.net.au/news/2014-12-19/50th-
anniversary-of-opening-of-new-jindabyne-township/5975138,
accessed January 2018.

The Iron Trail

O'Shea: *The Daily News* (Perth), 2 May 1917, p. 6.

Deaths: 'The Trans-Australian Railway: Nomination for Award as a
National Engineering Landmark', Institute of Engineers, Australia
at https://www.slideshare.net/AussieSteamTrains/trans-australian-
railway, accessed October 2017.

Gauges: *Kalgoorlie Miner*, 24 October 1917, p. 8.

Completion: *Chronicle* (Adelaide), 20 October 1917, p. 32.

Waters of life

1859: *The Age*, 16 December 1859, p. 5. See also Michael Cathcart,
*The Water Dreamers: The Remarkable History of Our Dry
Continent*, Text, Melbourne, 2009, p. 166ff.

Great Artesian Basin Protection Group at http://www.gabpg.org.au/
great-artesian-basin, accessed October 2017.

How the outback began

Rourke letter: *The Maitland Mercury and Hunter River General
Advertiser*, 21 November 1868, p. 6.
Hay: *The Sydney Morning Herald*, 28 December 1868, p. 2.
Nyngan: *The Sydney Mail and New South Wales Advertiser*, 15
December 1883, p. 1126.

Bush learning

Edward Sorenson, *Life in the Australian Backblocks*, Whitcomb &
Tombs, London, 1911 at http://gutenberg.net.au/ebooks13/
1305751h.html#s22, accessed October 2017.

Looking for paradise

Victorian Heritage Database Report 'Herrnhut Utopian Commune',
2006 at http://vhd.heritagecouncil.vic.gov.au/places/14358/
download-report, accessed October 2017.
Kurikka: *The Worker*, 28 July 1900, p. 2 and *Maryborough Chronicle,
Wide Bay and Burnett Advertiser*, 27 July 1900, p. 3.
Wickepin: Bill Metcalf and Guy Featherstone, 'A Messiah for
the West: J.C.M. Fisher and the Church of the Firstborn in
Western Australia', *Journal of Australian Colonial History*
2006, at https://research-repository.griffith.edu.au/bitstream/
handle/10072/13812/39617.pdf?sequence=1, accessed October
2017.
Bill Metcalf, 'The Encyclopedia of Australian Utopian Communalism',
Arena Journal 2008 at https://research-repository.griffith.edu.
au/bitstream/handle/10072/26302/52785_2.pdf?sequence=1,
accessed October 2017; David Levenson and Karen Christensen
(eds), *Encyclopedia of Community: From the Village to the Virtual
World*, Vol. 1, Sage, New York, 2003 pp. 705ff.

By song and star

'Songlines: Tracking the Seven Sisters' at http://www.nma.gov.au/
exhibitions/songlines, accessed September 2017.
Robert S. Fuller, Michelle Trudgett, Ray P. Norris and Michael G.
Anderson, 'Star Maps and Travelling to Ceremonies: The Euahlayi
People and Their Use of the Night Sky', *Journal of Astronomical
History and Heritage*, Vol. 17, Issue 2, 2014, pp. 149–60 at
http://www.narit.or.th/en/files/2014JAHHvol17/2014JAHH
vol17no2Complete.pdf, accessed September 2017; Aaron Corn,
'Dr Joe Gumbula, the Ancestral Chorus, and how we value
Indigenous Knowledges', *The Conversation*, 29 September 2017

at https://theconversation.com/friday-essay-dr-joe-gumbula-the-ancestral-chorus-and-how-we-value-indigenous-knowledges-84438, accessed October 2017.

Lynne Kelly, 'This Ancient Memory Technique Builds a Palace of Memory', *Aeon* at https://aeon.co/ideas/this-ancient-mnemonic-technique-builds-a-palace-of-memory, accessed September 2017; also Lynne Kelly, *The Memory Code*, Allen & Unwin, Sydney, 2016.

Oldest culture: Anna-Sapfo Malaspinas, Michael C. Westaway et al, 'A genomic history of Aboriginal Australia', *Nature,* Vol. 538, pp. 207–14 (13 October 2016) doi:10.1038/nature18299.

Acknowledgements

Maureen Seal, Kylie Pollard-Seal, Rob Willis, Olya Willis, Mark Gregory, Douglas Brockfield, Elizabeth Weiss and staff at Allen & Unwin.

Photo Credits

Page xii 'Logger in his camp putting the billy on, Victoria, circa 1900.' Courtesy of the State Library of Victoria, ID H33027/18c.

Page 8 'Nine-year-old farm boy Lennie Gwyther with his beloved pony, "Ginger Mick", on his 1000-kilometre journey from his home in Leongatha, Victoria, to Sydney for the opening of the Harbour Bridge in 1932.' Courtesy of the Leongatha and District Historical Society and the Gwyther Family.

Page 34 'Bob, the Railway Dog, South Australia, 1892', one of a group of photographs from the MS Fisher papers. Photograph by George Hiscock. Courtesy of the State Library of South Australia, ID PRG 117/5/1.

Page 34 'Railway crew congregated around a locomotive with Bob, the Railway Dog perched on top of the driver's car, Port Augusta railway yard, South Australia, 1887.' Photographer unknown. Courtesy of the State Library of South Australia, ID B-6422.

Page 60 'Men working to get a submerged vehicle out of the overflowing Mitchell River using a Spanish windlass, Mitchell River, Queensland, circa 1920–30.' Courtesy of the State Library of Queensland.

285

Page 86 'Influential anthropologists Baldwin Spencer
(front right) and Frank Gillen (front left) on their 1901
expedition in the Northern Territory with (back from left)
Purunda (Warwick), Mounted Constable Harry Chance
and Erlikilyika (Jim Kite).' Photographer unknown.
Courtesy of the Museum of Victoria, ID XP14528.

Page 108 'Photo by Arthur Upfield of camel turn-out at
government Camel Station, Western Australia, circa
1930.' Courtesy of the National Library of Australia,
Bib ID 2278250.

Page 134 'Australia's "bard of the bush", Henry Lawson,
in Sydney, 1915.' Courtesy of the State Library of
Queensland.

Page 158 'Champion tree-feller and axeman Vic Summers,
Gympie.' Courtesy of the State Library of NSW,
ID IE3349973.

Page 184 'Wilhelmina and Winifred Rawson with their
goats at The Hollow, Queensland, 1880.' Photographer
unknown. Courtesy of the State Library of Queensland,
ID raw00135 / DTL system number 224884.

Page 210 'Drover 'Kurini' Jim Mathers rounding up horses in
the outback, Northern Territory (undated).' Original title
'Drover', from the B.C. Mettam Collection, photographer
unknown. Courtesy of the Northern Territory Library,
ID PH0429/0171 or hdl10070/27313.

Page 236 'Leopold and William De Salis resting in the bush
with a man, horse and sulky, Cuppacumbalong, ACT,
circa 1892.' Courtesy of the National Library of Australia,
ID 44501949.